# Mystery
at the
# Church

# BOOKS BY CLARE CHASE

# Mystery
## at the
# Church

## CLARE CHASE

*bookouture*

Published by Bookouture in 2021

An imprint of Storyfire Ltd.
Carmelite House
50 Victoria Embankment
London EC4Y 0DZ

www.bookouture.com

ISBN: 978-1-80019-530-1
eBook ISBN: 978-1-80019-529-5

*For Emma and Hannah*

# PROLOGUE

Rufus Beaumont, the youngest member of the Beaumont acting dynasty, had played his final scene. The actor turned television director lay in the vestry of All Souls Church. He looked peaceful. All the laughter and bravado had left him. The feelings he'd buried, the compromises he'd made, the bad decisions, the lies he'd told himself. All gone.

The stuffy room smelled of dust and alcohol: the spirits he'd been drinking all evening, as well as what his killer had given him just before he died. All around him was quiet order – empty bookshelves, curtains faded by decades of sun, hangers in a wardrobe which had once held the vicar's ceremonial vestments.

No one used the church for services these days. It was hired out to film crews, and the murderer had staged something worthy of a prime-time drama.

A rush of adrenaline swept over them as they cast aside the cushion they'd used to smother the man. Taking off their gloves, they felt a sense of invulnerability.

The deep breath they took was full of satisfaction and relief. The scales of justice had balanced again.

# CHAPTER ONE

*One Day Earlier*

As an obituary writer, Eve Mallow was passionate about telling people's life stories. Interviewing a deceased person's contacts presented a fascinating puzzle. She loved extracting strands of truth from their biased views. But Eve was practical, and freelance journalism was an uncertain career. She usually had a part-time job alongside her writing to ensure a steady income. For almost two years now, she'd been moonlighting at Monty's teashop, in her adopted home of Saxford St Peter. Viv, her friend and Monty's owner, had persuaded her to join the business as soon as she'd moved from London to Suffolk. Viv's baking was sublime, but chaos was her friend. She said Eve's 'weird obsessive organisational skills' were essential to keep her on the straight and narrow.

But, for two days only, Eve was adding a third role to her employment mix. She'd leaped at the chance to work as a television extra. She wanted to see the actors and production team up close, to find out how they interacted and see them off guard. What kind of temperament did you need to take direction, repeat scenes over and over, and slip into a character's shoes? How did you make it seem real?

There were downsides: Eve was currently standing in hot August sunshine, dressed all in black, from her high-heeled shoes to her veiled pillbox hat. She, Viv and a multitude of villagers were to form the congregation in a dramatic funeral scene. The dark clothes absorbed the heat, and Eve tried to think of ice cubes. Someone had told her that brought relief, but as she'd suspected, they were wrong. Still, there was the shade of the church's interior to look forward to. She might get away with slipping off her high heels and resting her feet on the cool stone floor...

The filming was for a TV mini-series, *Last of the Lindens*, a project from the successful producer/director partnership Quinn and Beaumont. Saxford's villagers had a special interest in the supporting actress, Dot Hampshire. Her aunt was a local, the doyenne of the flower club. Dot had starred in Quinn and Beaumont's previous production, *The Pedestal*, to a rapturous reception from the critics. Her photograph had been splashed across the Sunday colour supplements for weeks when she won a BAFTA for Best Actress.

Of course, her aunt had given the villagers *all* the background. Eve could repeat, word for word, what some of the reviewers had said, thanks to the woman's regular repetition of the quotes... Dot had a much quieter fan in Toby Falconer, who ran the local pub with his brother and sister-in-law. Eve gathered he and Dot had struck up a friendship a few years back, when Dot had visited her aunt, though nothing lasting had come of it, according to the local rumour mill. Toby had looked wistful when Eve mentioned taking part in the filming. They couldn't close the pub, so he wasn't amongst the crowds, sweating in a dark suit.

Right now, Eve was standing in a line of villagers, waiting to be 'checked'. The production team had already sorted out their costumes and make-up in the dedicated location trailers. This was a last once-over before a final run-through, and then filming would start.

Down the line, Eve could see the vicar being scrutinised by an elegant-looking woman with red-gold hair, perfect make-up and high cheekbones. Eve could tell from his look of fierce concentration that he was trying not to laugh. She couldn't get used to the sight of him dressed up as a lay person.

But the weirdness of seeing him without his white collar was nothing compared to seeing Viv, standing next to her, with brown hair. Since Eve had known her she'd had it shocking pink, sea green, daffodil yellow and more besides, but never like this.

Viv spotted the direction of her gaze. 'I'm dying it cerise again the minute filming's over. I still can't believe they insisted on something dull. My hair's pretty much hidden under my hat in any case.'

But Eve could see the production team's point. The cerise had been self-advertising.

The intense heat turned her thoughts to cakes. On top of acting, the assistant director had commissioned her and Viv to provide refreshments for the extras, cast and crew. It was meant to be a sweetener, to make up for the long hours and low pay, though most people hadn't needed any encouragement.

The bakes were in cool boxes in the back of Viv's van, but Eve doubted they'd be at fridge temperature by the time they were needed. And how would they fare once they were laid out in the sun?

'You're thinking about the cakes, aren't you?' Viv gave her a sidelong glance. 'Has anyone ever told you that you worry too much?'

'Worrying and being prepared are much the same thing. At least we didn't opt for the chocolate and espresso cakes.'

Viv crossed her arms. It wasn't the first time they'd squabbled over what to serve. 'All right, you win. They would have been a disaster in this heat. But I didn't know it would be so intense when I suggested them.'

'I looked at the weather forecast. I must explain it to you sometime.'

Viv stuck out her tongue, just as the glamorous costume supervisor, Brooke, arrived to spot-check her.

'So sorry.' Her friend instantly became sombre. 'Do go ahead.'

As the woman gave Viv a once-over, Eve looked again at their surroundings. The site the production team had hired was known as Watcher's Wood, and All Souls, a deconsecrated church, sat at its centre. It was south of Saxford, and Eve had walked there before. She'd always wished she could go inside the church. She loved its ancient flint walls and its quirks, which included a squat tower and a lopsided late-medieval porch. The building looked as though it had hunkered down in the clearing it occupied, ready to dig in for the long haul.

A local landowner had sealed its fate as a place of worship by moving the location of the nearest hamlet south two centuries earlier, and by the 1840s the church had closed. But it dated back to Saxon times, and had endured for countless generations.

Rehearsals had finally allowed Eve to see inside. The place felt peaceful. Most of the walls were whitewashed but there were ancient wall paintings too, and brasses which dated back to the 1400s.

The sun smacked down on the church in its clearing, but it was surrounded by thick, lush trees. The towering oaks, beeches and sycamores were interspersed with silver birches and hawthorns. In the mottled sunlight, Eve could see white admiral butterflies, gliding from branches to the woodland floor with a couple of easy wingbeats.

'It's such a beautiful place,' she said to the costume supervisor, who'd just reached her. She was struck by its feeling of separate stillness, but she was partly making conversation too. There was something awkward about staring straight ahead as a total stranger peered at you from odd angles and fiddled with your hat.

'Gorgeous, isn't it?' Brooke agreed. Her intent, assessing look didn't relax as she spoke, leaving Eve faintly anxious. 'Rufus was dead against it, but I can't imagine why. I gather he didn't have a better suggestion, so in the end the producer pulled rank.'

The producer, Isla Quinn, had worked with Rufus Beaumont for years. The costume supervisor's words surprised Eve. She found the site entrancing, and perfect for the scene they were filming.

At last, Eve was given the seal of approval, which left her free to watch her neighbours again.

Moira, Saxford's village storekeeper, had managed to collar Rufus. He was handsome with reddish hair, and shared a family likeness with his world-famous actor brother. Eve was familiar with the Beaumonts by reputation. Rufus's parents had excelled in acting and directing, winning Oscars for both. Then Rufus's elder brother and sister had followed in their footsteps. Eve had known less about Rufus himself, but she'd done her research before turning up to her first rehearsal. He'd given up acting early in his career, by his mid-twenties, but his work as a television director had earned him awards too. He was only in his late thirties now, but at the top of his game. Yet Eve sensed there was a prejudice in the entertainment industry, a feeling that those who made their names in television didn't quite compare with creatives who made it on the big screen. Perhaps that hadn't affected Rufus though. Eve felt there was a slight haughtiness about him that his older brother lacked: a mouth that might slip into a sneer.

'…very sorry to bother you,' Moira was saying, gazing up into Rufus's eyes. 'It's just that I wanted to ask about my approach to my part, as I'll be sitting in the second to front row.' Her cheeks were flushed, her dyed auburn hair gleaming under her black fascinator.

Eve knew it was the assistant director who was in charge of extras. She felt a twinge of anxiety about Rufus's response, but he smiled generously and appeared earnest as he replied. Moira watched him with rapt attention.

'Do you think she's hoping for a BAFTA, just like Dot?' Viv muttered.

Eve shot her a warning look and watched Moira nod solemnly at something Rufus had said. A moment later she was beaming with pleasure. Eve caught the words: 'What it is to have a good director!'

'Have you told her that you'll be filmed on your own tomorrow?' Viv asked, with an evil glint in her eye. 'She's not going to like it!'

'I won't be on my own. There's Gus.' Rufus wanted a shot of a dog walker, appearing through the trees in a red polka-dot dress. She and her dachshund were going to oblige. Eve felt rather nervous about it. With Gus, you never could tell. If he took a dislike to one of the camera crew it would all be very awkward.

Viv shook her head. 'You'll be the only human in shot. A starring role. You must have noticed there's a battle going on for queen of the extras.'

Rufus put a light hand on the storekeeper's shoulder, shepherding her towards the assistant director. 'I'll leave you in my colleague's capable hands.'

He'd clearly hit the right note, giving his attention briefly then moving effortlessly on. The storekeeper was all smiles as she turned to the assistant director, and he was ready for her. Eve could tell he anticipated all situations, just like she did. He was always at the producer's side just when she had a question, and he'd been very specific about quantities when he'd ordered their cakes. There was a quiet, organised energy about him.

After a word with Moira, he looked up and caught Brooke the costume supervisor's eye as she reached the final extra. She nodded and gave him a thumbs up. The assistant director pushed his almost-black hair off his forehead, his dark eyes alert.

'Ladies and gents, we'll file into the church in just a moment. You all know the scene well by now.'

They'd run through it without the main actors, and had had a talk about it too. It featured Saskia Thomas, a new young actress Quinn and Beaumont had picked to play the lead. She was the last of the Lindens, and had been driven away by her parents' ward, played by Dot. Saskia was to burst through the church door during her father's funeral, to an emotional reunion with her mother, and a livid reaction from Dot, whose inheritance depended on Saskia's continued estrangement from her family.

'Please remember your allocated places and stick to them,' the assistant director finished as the producer joined him, speaking softly as he nodded and showed her his clipboard, which sparked further discussion.

The queue of villagers snaked round to file through the church-yard, bringing Moira within feet of a fellow member of Saxford's amateur dramatics club, who'd been allocated a place near the back.

The storekeeper leaned towards the woman eagerly. 'Play with your part, that's my advice, my dear. You've got plenty of flexibility, being further from the action.'

As they entered the church via its great arched doorway, Viv bit her cheek and Eve tried not to catch her eye. Laughing at this stage might get them thrown out. The assistant director had to deal with the practicalities of the filming and every hour must cost a fortune. Inside, his focus seemed absolute as he watched them take their places, but his eyes were bright too. Eve could tell he was as excited about the scene as any of them.

People took a minute to quieten down. It was all so far outside their experience. The camera crew was set up and ready, the chief operator exchanging quiet words with his team, adjusting equipment, altering angles. Eve glimpsed the producer again: tall, glamorous and imperious with her wavy blonde hair and expensive-looking hammered silver jewellery. She'd moved to watch proceedings from the door of the vestry. Eve had researched her, just as she had Rufus. Apparently it was her style to rule over her productions with an iron grip, never delegating. She'd wondered if it might annoy Rufus, but he had the air of someone who was running the show too. Maybe she trusted him enough to give him free rein, even though she was breathing down his neck. She must value him, given their long partnership.

At that moment, the main actors took their places and more murmuring ensued. Dot Hampshire's aunt nudged her neighbour and pointed at her niece.

The assistant director held up a hand and the congregation hushed. 'We'll run through the scene with a stand-in playing Saskia's part. Quiet please.'

So Saskia wasn't even doing the run-through. They must want her fresh for the actual take. Eve had heard Rufus wanted to film the scene once only. She felt her stomach knot, despite being tucked away several rows from the front. It increased the pressure.

In the tense quiet, Eve heard footsteps behind her. From where she sat, four rows back, she craned round automatically to see the church door had opened. Craning was what they'd been told to do, so that was good. After that they were meant to show their shock at seeing the long-lost Linden daughter, then exchange glances with their neighbours, followed by surreptitious curiosity at Dot Hampshire's reaction. Eve found herself caught up in the proceedings. She really did feel curious. Especially when she saw Dot Hampshire's face. She believed in her shock and fury. The mother was convincing too, her disbelief followed by joy made Eve's eyes prick with emotion.

'All right,' Rufus Beaumont said. 'Thank you, everyone.' He strolled slowly over to where Dot Hampshire was sitting and eyed her, his arms folded. 'Dolly, darling, I want to do this in one take. I believe I might have mentioned it. Saskia will be primed and ready and you should be too. It's not as though you don't have the experience. It's called acting…'

Eve felt a blush come to her face. She'd been convinced Dot had done an excellent job, but of course, Rufus had years of experience. Maybe he'd picked up on small details she wouldn't notice. But it was still a shock to hear him sound so belittling in front of an audience. Eve had been right about the sneer. It was also the only time she'd heard anyone refer to Dot Hampshire as Dolly. Eve was pretty sure it wasn't a name she chose to go by. Was Rufus using it simply to irk her? A pet name to make her seem less serious in other people's eyes?

She exchanged glances with Viv, who mimed an exaggerated snooty face, which made Eve feel a little better. All the same, she hoped Rufus hadn't noticed.

The producer stepped forward from behind a bank of equipment, her eyes on the director. He shot her an irritated look which she returned.

Murmuring broke out in the congregation as Saskia's stand-in exited the church again and the crew pottered about, fiddling with bits of equipment.

They ran through the scene two more times before Eve heard a car draw up. Rufus was trotting lightly down the nave before the engine cut out. He exited through the church's main door, but moments later, he was back. As he returned to his position behind the cameras his warning look was on Dot Hampshire.

Eve saw the actress's cheeks flush and the producer's shoulders rise and fall in what looked like suppressed annoyance. Eve wasn't sure if it was with Rufus or Dot.

The assistant director looked poised, up on his toes, ready for whatever happened next. There must be a lot riding on his shoulders.

'Saskia's ready.' Rufus sounded like a father, talking about a favourite child. 'Stand by. Action!'

And for the fourth time that day, Eve heard the church door open, and found herself craning round and not having to act her curiosity. She saw a young woman pause tentatively in the doorway before walking up the aisle. As she got nearer, Eve took in her striking blue eyes, high cheekbones, long dark hair and sensitive mouth.

It felt as though the entire congregation was holding its breath as they all glanced at their neighbours, then turned their gaze on

Dot Hampshire and the woman acting Saskia's mother. The organ music played on.

After Rufus's criticism of Dot, Eve focused almost exclusively on her face. The anger in her eyes would have been frightening if she hadn't been acting. Surely that had to be a perfect performance?

There was a pause at the end of the scene before Rufus shouted, 'Cut!' He was beaming, his eyes shining with emotion. 'Excellent. Excellent, everyone!' He gave an extravagant wave of his hand. 'Even you, Dolly.' But his gaze was wintery when it fell on her.

# CHAPTER TWO

As soon as Rufus let them go, Eve and Viv went to change back into their normal clothes, ready to dish out Monty's wares. They fetched the cakes from the van, which was parked with its rear doors facing a large open space at the centre of a camp ringed with trailers: accommodation for the actors and crew. The filming in Suffolk had already taken several weeks and was due to continue for another month. They were using a manor house on the Watcher's Wood site as well as the church, surrounding parkland and woods.

All around, people were strolling into the clearing, flexing shoulders, and stretching, their expressions relaxed. There was a general easing of tension, though Dot Hampshire still looked tetchy, her face lined with irritation. She was rubbing the back of her neck.

And the lead, Saskia Thomas, looked done in, Eve noticed. Her long hair had fallen forward and she had one hand up over her eyes as though she wanted to hide her expression.

Eve had seen bereaved interviewees adopt the same pose to hide their feelings. Her mind was on the actress as she extracted a tray of orange and raspberry cupcakes from the cool boxes in the van. As she turned cautiously (there were so many people milling about), she saw Rufus walk to a patch of grass beyond the trailers. He bent to pick a poppy. A moment later he'd given it to Saskia, who held it close to her chest. She still looked rather glazed. Maybe it was reaction to her performance – it had been short, but powerful and full of emotion.

The director patted her on the shoulder, but the pat became a caress. She was a lot younger than him, but Eve was starting to question her assumption that his attitude was fatherly.

Between two trailers, she caught sight of Dot Hampshire miming puking, seemingly in response to the pair. By her side, Brooke, the costume supervisor who'd checked Eve's appearance, laughed.

'Getting an eyeful of the off-set drama, I see.' Viv was standing next to Eve, carrying a tray of honey and apricot cakes. 'Not that I'm complaining. I might not have noticed if I hadn't followed your gaze. Isn't he a bit old for her?'

'I don't imagine that would stop him.' Eve's ex-husband had left her for a younger woman, though not as young as Saskia, admittedly. Eve's replacement had dumped him since then. The thought always gave Eve a warm glow.

She began to do the rounds with her cakes, dipping in and out of conversations as she went. She couldn't resist offering Monty's wares to Rufus and Saskia as a priority. She was curious to get a closer look at them.

'Thank you.' The lead actress's voice was low and husky. 'But I don't really feel like eating.'

'As your director, I think you should. I'll keep one by for you.' Rufus took two of Eve's cupcakes and thanked her. 'They look stupendous. We're lucky to have you and your friend to boost our energy at the end of a long day.'

His smile was so warm, Eve felt herself glow automatically. She'd baked the raspberry and orange cakes herself. Viv had been training her up since she'd started at Monty's and the results were beginning to show. But as she turned to leave the pair, she caught sight of Dot and the memory of Rufus's cold-eyed stare came back to her. She wouldn't want to be out of favour with him.

Eve had been round most of the gathered cast and crew with her tray when she spotted Saxford's storekeeper bustling back into the clearing ahead of her. Eve guessed Moira might have returned from a trip to the bathroom, but couldn't imagine what had happened to her en route. She was red in the face, her eyes popping.

Rufus Beaumont and Saskia Thomas appeared half a second later, hard on her heels. The director looked a little flushed himself. He was walking quickly.

'Oh dear me, I *am* sorry!' Moira said, turning when she realised they were on her tail. 'I didn't mean to interrupt you.' Her glance from one of them to the other said it all.

Eve guessed Rufus had followed Moira back into the clearing in the hope of quelling her gossip. In fact, he'd sprung her into an apology, which made it easy to guess what he and Saskia Thomas had been up to.

There was a collective intake of breath, followed by complete silence, which made Eve think their relationship was a revelation to the entire cast and crew. The producer's look was sour.

Fleetingly, Eve remembered Rufus was married. She'd read about him and his wife's 'dream partnership' in a women's glossy magazine. They were both phenomenally successful; Cassie Beaumont was a well-known interior designer.

It was only a moment before Rufus laughed. 'Nonsense, there's no need to apologise. It wasn't private. Just natural exuberance after a filming triumph!'

Dot swallowed the last of her cake and walked straight over to Rufus. 'Oh yes. We actor types are so flamboyant, aren't we? Let's celebrate that glorious scene in the standard way. Totally normal. Nothing to see here.' Then she reached up and gave the director a smacking kiss on the lips, before spinning round and stalking off between the trailers.

'Well, I never did!' Dot's aunt said, shaking her head. The posse of am-dram and flower club members around her had their mouths open.

Eve's cheeks felt hot as she did another fly-past with her orange and raspberry cakes. It was as though everyone was holding their breath. Eve didn't much like the tension but it was too early to escape. Besides, her screwed-up stomach muscles aside, she was curious. Dot had every right to be angry with Rufus for being unprofessional, but did the antagonism between them go deeper than that? Was there any chance Dot had once been his lover? A relationship gone sour might explain the way he'd overlooked her for the lead role in *Last of the Lindens*. Eve felt her adrenaline kick in. It didn't say much for his professionalism if he abused his position and allowed his affairs to influence casting.

'We did too many cakes,' Viv said as Eve returned to the refreshments table half an hour later. 'I'm sure they'd happily stand here eating and drinking for at least another hour. Do you think we can leave today's platters and bring more tomorrow?'

'Sounds like a plan.' Eve went to ask permission to leave, but she was only halfway towards the dark-eyed assistant director when Rufus made his way into the centre of the clearing. He looked light-hearted, his eyes sparkling.

'Who have I got to thank for these?' He laughed and held up a bunch of purple hooded flowers. 'Did any of you put them in my trailer? I'd like the chance to say thank you. There's no need to be shy.'

'Maybe one of the villagers got star struck,' Viv whispered. 'He's quite a looker, even if he is a philandering, first-class sh—' But then she saw Eve's face. 'What is it?'

'Those flowers. They're beautiful, but not the safest bouquet to have in your possession.'

Her friend frowned. 'I don't recognise them.'

'Wolfsbane. Also known as queen of poisons.'

*

Five minutes after Rufus had shown the assembled crowds the flowers, Eve was in his trailer, explaining wolfsbane's properties.

The director shook his head. 'So I'd have to eat them or get the poison in my bloodstream to do serious damage?' He laughed. 'That's a relief. I thought for a moment I was history. It's a bit ironic, someone picking a whole bunch of something so deadly. I can see why they chose them though. They're very striking.'

There was no denying the purple was beautiful, but an article Eve had read made her deeply wary of them. They'd been used in multiple murders, and caused the accidental death of a couple of gardeners too, by all accounts. Eve would have chucked them in the bin without delay, striking or not.

'Don't worry. I'll get rid of them.' Rufus's blue eyes were on hers. He must have guessed what she was thinking. 'Maybe after everyone's gone home so I don't cause offence, and I'll wash my hands carefully afterwards. I'm very grateful to you for telling me.' Eve warmed to his tone.

'Thanks. I wasn't meaning to make a fuss.' She'd spent too much time writing the obituaries of murder victims, that was her trouble. It had made her jump at shadows.

'Not at all.' He smiled.

But as he replied, Eve noticed something, down on the floor of the living room in Rufus's trailer. A piece of white paper, half under the table. Kicked there, maybe? Still slightly rolled, as though it had been wrapped around something. And a little damp in one place.

She could just see the printed words on it, mostly hidden, thanks to the curl of the paper.

Before she acknowledged to herself what she was doing she'd picked it up. In that microsecond she knew she was handling something private and moved to hand it straight to Rufus, but as she did so, the printed words were revealed.

*Poison for the poisonous.*

Rufus must have seen it in the same moment she had. And knew that she'd seen it too.

'I'm sorry.'

His face was still and for a second he looked at her, all the friendly warmth gone from his expression. The change was so pronounced that it shook her.

Eve tried to imagine how she'd feel if someone sent her poisonous flowers with a threatening note. Scared. Shocked. Confused. She'd wonder who was responsible and what she could have done to inspire such an act.

But Rufus looked none of those things. He looked livid. Livid with her. She was sure his primary emotion was anger that she'd seen the message. Maybe he knew who'd written it, and was worried Eve might guess his private business. But in an instant she changed her mind. Because confusion was the second emotion to show in his face. And his look in her direction was still unfriendly. Challenging almost. She was seeing him in a position of weakness. Instinct told her *that's* what he couldn't tolerate. The flowers were evidence that he was hated.

Eve swallowed. 'Do you think it's worth mentioning to the police?'

The slight sneer was back, his upper lip twitching. 'Over a ridiculous prank? I certainly don't.'

Eve had the immediate desire to get out of his trailer. There was nothing else she could do anyway, but her chest felt tight with tension as she rose to leave.

A short while later, Viv drove Eve back into Saxford, the van's windows down, the warm breeze ruffling their hair. Viv cast her a sidelong glance.

'You know Moira and her crew all think you gave Rufus the flowers now? They were hyperventilating when you went into his trailer.'

Eve groaned and Viv shrugged annoyingly. 'You knew it would be like this when you swapped London for village life.'

Eve had only lived in cities before moving to Suffolk: Seattle until she was eighteen, with her British dad and American mom, then the UK's capital, where she'd studied, married and raised a family. Her beloved adult twins were still in the city.

'Ugh. It's true, I did. In fairness, it cuts both ways. Observing my fellow Saxfordites up close is fascinating. And Ian's still lurking in London.' The idea of putting some distance between her and her ex had appealed. After Ian walked out, he'd paid Eve regular visits to 'check she was okay'. He'd perfected a noble, concerned-ex-husband face that drove her up the wall.

'And of course, I'm in Saxford,' Viv said. 'I'm surprised that wasn't first on your list of advantages.'

'Hmm.'

'So why are you so uptight?'

Eve explained about the note that had come with Rufus Beaumont's flowers and Viv let out a sigh.

'Wow. So it was malice after all. Do you think someone wanted to harm him?'

Eve frowned. 'Not today. They'd have chosen a more certain method. The sender might just be playing games, but I'm not so sure. It's possible the note's a warning. Rufus is friendly on the surface – charming and apparently thoughtful. But there's a whole load of anger simmering just beneath that veneer. Pride. Defensiveness. And we know he's got entanglements. There's his affair with Saskia, and the dynamic between him and Dot Hampshire. And the atmosphere turned toxic when I saw the note that came with the flowers. It was like I'd flicked a switch. Who knows how dysfunctional his relationships have become? I can believe there's someone out there with a serious grudge.'

Viv looked at her more closely, making Eve grip the dashboard as the van jolted on a rut in Old Yard Lane and veered towards a whitewashed cottage. 'Blimey, you really have got the wind up, haven't you?'

'My alarm was down to your driving, but yes, I have a little. I'm going to keep an eye on proceedings tomorrow.'

# CHAPTER THREE

The following day, Eve discovered that Viv had been right: Moira wasn't pleased that Eve was to be filmed in glorious isolation, with only Gus to upstage her. The storekeeper bustled up to her as Eve came out of the costume trailer.

'When did you say this was decided, Eve? I *thought* you were some time with Rufus yesterday.'

Eve took a deep breath. 'Drew Fawcett asked me about it when we were here for the final run-through last week.' The assistant director had taken her to one side. He probably realised there'd be competition for the part if he announced it more broadly. 'I came back with Gus to practise on my own, but I didn't mention it in case they changed their minds.'

She felt strange in the stiff cotton polka-dot dress, but it fitted her like a glove and she'd certainly show up in red and white against the intense greenery of the woods.

The costume supervisor checked her over then took her to Rufus's personal assistant, Margot, who'd been looking after Gus while she got ready. The PA was busy making a massive fuss of him. Eve was hit with mixed emotions. Anyone who loved her dachshund on sight got her vote. But oh boy was he overexcited. It wasn't ideal.

'Here we are!' Margot stood up, smart in her summer suit, with her cropped silver hair, gleaming lipstick and pearl earrings. 'He's been as good as gold, haven't you?'

Gus leaped up, his tongue hanging out, and Eve put her shoulders back as the assistant director called her into the woods.

Drew Fawcett ran his gaze over the crew. She sensed he knew exactly what each of them was doing and what needed to happen next. Who would have thought it would take so many people to film one short scene? Drew's dark eyes were on Gus, who was still a bit jittery.

Eve glanced down at him. 'Calm down now, buddy, okay?' The words resulted in a little extra bounce. Drew was probably wondering why he'd thought she was a reliable bet for the part. Eve's stomach tensed as Rufus caught her eye, but he seemed to have shelved his anger from the day before, his professional mask back on. He smiled and nodded quickly.

'Standby! Action!'

By some miracle, Gus pulled himself together. Maybe all the attention meant he knew something special was expected. He trotted along the exact route they were supposed to follow, albeit with a slightly self-conscious air, his head held high. Eve was sure Moira would tell her friends he'd overacted.

'And cut!' Rufus was beaming, despite Eve's minor contribution. 'That was perfect. Very well done.'

As Eve walked back towards the crowds of extras, she was struck by the charming face he was presenting once again. It seemed he'd buried the incident in his trailer. His ability to shut out unpleasantness could be dangerous – a genuine threat might go unnoticed, and if he couldn't take criticism it must make him hard to work with, too.

A minute later, Eve found his PA again, laughing about something with the costume supervisor.

The woman turned to face her. 'All finished? I can't wait to spend more time with Gus!'

She'd offered to mind him while Eve and the other villagers took part as extras again, this time in an outdoor buffet scene – the funeral wake.

Gus dashed up to Margot, straining on his leash as though he couldn't wait to swap Eve for someone more exciting.

Eve suppressed a sigh. 'Thanks so much for taking care of him!'

'My pleasure.'

She had to go through costume again and met Viv and the other villagers in the garden of the old manor house where the wake scene was to be recorded.

As filming started, Eve kept a careful eye on the cast, the crew and her neighbours. If she watched closely, she might get a hint as to who had given Rufus Beaumont the wolfsbane.

Eve and Viv had formed a pair, holding their plates of sandwiches and glasses of wine. The food was real, the alcohol not. They'd been advised to eat slowly in case the scene required multiple takes.

Just then, Eve's attention was caught by a man standing just to one side of them, who'd already taken a sizeable bite of the sausage roll on his plate. She'd spotted him the previous day too, though she hadn't seen him in rehearsals. For a crazy moment, she'd wondered if she should say something to someone. What if he had no business being there? But he'd looked harmless enough: young and eager. And unless he was a habitual smart dresser, he must have been through costume. Eve guessed he was in his mid-twenties, with brown hair that flopped forward boyishly over his forehead.

As they watched Rufus lean in earnestly to say something to Saskia, the young man spoke. 'You have to be crazily dedicated if you're going to act for Rufus Beaumont.'

He sounded like someone with inside information.

'He's into method acting,' the man continued. 'Saskia cut herself off from her family for six months before yesterday's shoot. She came straight here after reuniting with them; they only live in Norfolk so it worked all right. It was supposed to help her convey her emotion at seeing her mother again in the drama. Can you imagine going through all that?'

He hadn't lowered his voice much, though Eve didn't think the main actors and crew were listening.

Nonetheless, she replied in an undertone. 'It was a big ask. You're working for Rufus too – not just as an extra, I mean?' It would explain his insights.

The man shook his head and grinned, gripping his wine glass and plate one-handed so he could shake hands. 'Rick Sutton, at your service. Custodian of Watcher's Wood.' He turned to Viv and gave her a mini salute. 'The crew asked if I wanted to join in yesterday.'

That explained it. Rick must have his work cut out. The Watcher's Wood site covered a couple of holiday cottages as well as the woods, parkland, campsite, church and manor house that the TV crew was renting.

'I only took the post on recently,' he added. 'I was thrilled when I got the Quinn and Beaumont booking. What an experience!'

He looked starry-eyed. Eve wondered how much attention he was paying to the other aspects of his job. But of course, the filming must be his chief focus at the moment.

Rick glanced up at the main actors. 'Excuse me. I can feel the word "action!" coming on. I'm just going to see if I can persuade the nice woman with the food to replenish my plate.'

'Cheeky!' Viv said, as he wandered off.

Eve was inclined to agree. He was the face of Watcher's Wood, but he came across as someone who was in it for the food and the showbiz gossip. She reminded herself not to be sour. She was mainly in it for the people-watching, after all.

A couple of minutes later, all eyes were on Rufus. To absolute silence, he said the word Rick Sutton had been anticipating. 'Action!'

Eve wondered if the custodian had achieved his objective, but there was no time to look for him now.

She and Viv peered dutifully at Saskia, Dot and their fellow actors.

'I'm looking forward to our cakes later,' Viv said. 'Food loses its appeal if you can't eat freely.'

Once again, they'd travelled to the site by van and had plenty of fresh offerings.

It was only a minute before Rufus called: 'Cut!' His voice was irritable. 'Kip!'

A big bulky man with close-cropped brown hair stood up tall behind a camera and folded his arms. Rufus drew himself up taller too, in response. Eve was reminded of animals squaring off against each other.

As Rufus opened his mouth, his expression ugly, Isla Quinn stepped forward. She cast the director a quick glance, then switched her cool gaze to the camera operator.

'Your attention was off, Kip. I could see that from over there. You need to focus now.' The producer's voice was firm.

Eve recognised Kip. She'd watched him directing operations inside the church the day before and had the impression he was senior to the others. His stance remained aggressive, but when Isla raised an eyebrow and gave him a long look his shoulders went down. But Eve could see he was still angry. His fists were clenched, knuckles white, as he shook his head.

'We'll go again.' Rufus's voice was weary. 'Standby! Action!'

The temptation to discuss the interruption was strong. Viv opened her mouth but before she could speak, Eve launched back into the part she'd been given. The extras were meant to be gossiping about the reappearance of the long-lost Linden daughter and surreptitiously peering at the family, who were standing closer to the house. Viv put her head on one side and gave Eve a frustrated glare. Over her shoulder, Rick Sutton caught Eve's attention once again, his eyes sparkling. He wasn't following instructions. You couldn't call his staring surreptitious, and she'd swear he was gradually moving closer to the main actors.

In the end, the scene took four takes, and they were allowed to eat their sandwiches for lunch before someone brought on a fresh lot.

'Not sorry that's over,' Viv said as they trooped back to the trailers, ready to get their cakes out. 'Are your antennae quivering again? No love lost between Kip the cameraman and either Rufus or Isla Quinn, I'd say. The look on his face when they criticised him.'

Eve nodded. 'It can't be easy, being shown up in front of such a big group, but I guess the crew must be used to it.'

They went off to change.

Reunited with Gus, who was allowed to run free in the production team's camp, Eve went to and fro with a tray of lemon and lime cakes, finished with a frosted topping. They ought to be refreshing in the heat. Her feet were aching after hours in the black high heels and she wished she could have a cup of tea instead of the lemonade from Moira's store. It was one of her favourite drinks, but being the temperature of bathwater didn't improve it.

The evening stretched ahead of her too: an affair of two halves. Rufus had invited the extras to join him and the team for drinks at the Cross Keys to celebrate the end of their contribution to *Last of the Lindens*. He'd looked keen to play host and Eve was glad he'd suggested it too. It would be one last chance to observe the actors and crew. It must surely be one of them who'd left the flowers for Rufus – she couldn't imagine any of the villagers, who barely knew him, sending him that melodramatic note.

It was her appointment after the pub that filled Eve with dread. She was due at Viv's brother's fiancée's thirtieth birthday party. Polly was twenty years younger than Eve and would no doubt shimmer onto the dance floor with youthful vigour. Eve secretly wished she could stay at home with a good book.

A moment later, she was carrying her platter towards Moira the storekeeper and her posse, which included Dot Hampshire's aunt, Babs Lewis. Eve's mind was still on which outfit to wear that night.

'... thought the mother sounded *very* scripted.' Moira was shaking her head as Eve approached. 'Oh Eve, dear. Now, we all thought you did really quite well during that solo scene, for someone with no experience.' She took a cupcake. 'Thanks ever so much. I'm quite drained after that last take.'

As Eve drifted to one side, Moira turned to Babs Lewis. 'Such a shame Dot didn't get the lead part this time.'

Babs was frowning. 'I can't think what can have gone wrong.'

'Of course,' Moira was saying knowledgeably, as Eve offered her cakes to a nearby group of villagers, 'Isla and Rufus might simply have wanted a new face.'

Eve glimpsed Dot's aunt's furrowed brow. 'But look at all the times whatsit and Ivory used Helena Bonham Carter! And Dot got such excellent reviews after her previous role. I can only imagine she said something to upset Rufus, so he didn't pick her this time.' She shook her head. 'Truth be told, she was a little madam as a child. And if she behaves like she did yesterday, well...'

Eve tried to signal with her eyes that Dot was just behind them, but their minds were on cake and dissecting the woman's shortcomings.

Dot inserted herself into their circle now. 'You were saying?'

Moira put her hand to her cheek. 'I was thinking it was unfair that you hadn't been given the lead. But I suppose sometimes it's just a particular face that's needed for a certain part.'

Dot nodded and fixed Moira with a look. 'Yes, I'm sure you're right. But thank you all *so* much for your support!'

The storekeeper had the grace to blush. 'Perhaps I'll go and powder my nose now, if I'm not required at present.'

'I shouldn't imagine anything urgent will crop up,' Dot Hampshire muttered, as Moira darted off between the trailers.

'I'll just go and get some lemonade, dear,' her aunt said. 'It really is awfully hot. But you know, it would be worth considering what you might have done to upset Rufus. Maybe he'll give you a second chance in his next production if you modify your behaviour.'

Eve ground her teeth on Dot's behalf. Why automatically assume she was at fault? She held her tray up to the actress as she was released from the disintegrating circle of Saxford locals.

'Thank you.' Dot took one and raised an eyebrow. 'I had a nasty feeling filming in Suffolk would have its downsides.'

As the actress walked off, Eve wondered if she could be letting off steam by taunting Rufus with anonymous notes. Eve could imagine her doing it, then laughing her socks off back in her trailer.

Whoever was responsible, maybe they'd carry on and give themselves away ultimately. The staginess of it almost made Eve less worried. If someone genuinely meant Rufus harm, she assumed they'd be plotting quietly, not hamming it up in front of everyone.

Eve turned and saw Rufus had cracked open some fizz. He was beaming and waving aside the thanks of the locals.

'You're all most welcome. I'm indebted to you for taking part.'

Kip Clayton, the camera operator, looked on, his expression sour.

A moment later, Rufus moved out of the clearing, nipping between his trailer and a red BMW, leaving his glass of champagne on the car's bonnet as he passed.

The rest of the crew and actors were milling round at the other end of the clearing now, close to where the champagne was being served by Rufus's PA. Viv had put her tray of cakes down on the table there too. Eve had just decided to follow suit when she noticed Kip was hanging back, waiting on the steps of an open trailer. He was looking to left and right, like a wary animal checking its surroundings.

Eve felt her pulse quicken. He was glancing at Rufus's drink now, then back at the crowd. She turned away but watched him surreptitiously as she carried her cakes towards the table. With one last glance at the crowds clustered round the food and drink, Kip walked swiftly towards the BMW, took up Rufus's glass and spat into it. In a second, he'd dashed it down on the car's bonnet again and disappeared in the same direction as the director.

# CHAPTER FOUR

Eve could see Viv by the drinks table, holding up a glass of champagne. She caught Eve's eye, pointed to it, and beckoned her over.

*There in a minute*, Eve mouthed. She was torn. Seeing Kip spit into Rufus's drink had left her strangely shaken. Her mind had instantly leaped to the poisonous flowers again. But spitting was different: sudden and visceral. And the look in Kip's eye spoke of the hatred behind the act. Maybe she was wrong to feel the melodrama of the note meant the sender wasn't serious. If Kip had delivered the flowers, the drink incident could be a sign that he was losing control of his feelings. Here was a group of people kept in close confinement for months on end. If they made enemies there was no escaping them. Feelings could build as knives turned in wounds, day in, day out.

What if things escalated further and she'd done nothing, despite what she knew? But reporting the camera operator didn't feel right. She didn't understand the background and there was no proof he was responsible for the flowers.

She glanced quickly at the trailer she'd seen him emerge from. He'd left his door wide open. If he was responsible for the wolfsbane, he'd probably picked it wearing gloves. She wouldn't touch the plant without them. And if he'd chosen disposable ones, they might still be in his bin...

Her heart pounded as she mounted his trailer steps. She wasn't the sort of journalist who normally indulged in low tactics, and sneaking onto his property was wrong. But the alternative was to do nothing, or rat on him without knowing the details. Those options felt wrong too. Getting evidence of his involvement with the flowers would help make up her mind.

Eve knocked on the open door as she went in. 'Hello? Just coming to see if you'd like some cake.' *Yeah, right…*

The trailer was empty, of course, and Eve couldn't risk or justify loitering for more than a second. Just the amount of time it would have taken to ascertain Kip was absent. She let her eyes glide over the contents of the small space inside, then focused on his bin.

No gloves.

Eve immediately reversed out of the trailer. Rummaging would be going too far. But although she hadn't seen any gloves, the bin's contents set her thinking.

Gus pottered up to her with questioning eyes as she emerged, blinking in the sunlight, which was still bright in the late afternoon.

'I know what you're thinking, buddy. Low tactics. And trespassing has left me with more questions.' Eve visualised the scene in Kip's trailer as she walked over to the food and drink table, carrying her tray.

The bin had contained a photograph of Saskia Thomas. Someone had crushed it, but Eve had seen clearly enough. Yet on top of that had been signs that Kip had recently entertained a woman. Last night, at a guess. Eve hoped he'd have thrown away the bin's contents if it had been any longer ago. At least they'd used protection. There'd been two empty shot glasses next to his tiny sink, too, and the place smelled of whisky. The final item of interest in the bin was an upmarket paper tissue of the sort you got in a mini pack. It had a beautiful peacock design on it, with intense emerald greens, blues and purples.

She frowned as she put the tray down on the table. She'd waded into Kip's private life on a pretext, but it was impossible to stop her thoughts multiplying now. Could Saskia be in an ongoing relationship with him as well as Rufus? Had she and Kip made up last night after Moira saw the director and the lead actress together? The crumpled photograph was underneath everything else. Maybe he'd screwed it up in his anger but forgiven Saskia later.

Yet he'd been volatile and distracted during filming that day, and spat in Rufus's drink. Of course, he'd likely still be livid, even if they'd made up, but Eve wondered about her reconciliation theory. Kip didn't look like the tender, forgiving type, and Saskia had been drawn and strained that day too. Eve had been utterly convinced by her acting earlier, but maybe her upset had helped with her emotional performance. It all fitted with Rufus's preference for method acting. She could use her real emotions.

'What's that brooding look for?' Viv said loudly. She was already halfway down her champagne.

'Hush! I'll tell you on the way home.' Eve poured herself a thimbleful of the drink. 'And I'll drive.' She raised a hand when Viv opened her mouth. 'Honestly, it's not a problem.' It would be good if all the villagers made it back to Saxford in one piece. Several of them had come on foot and would be walking the route they drove.

Eve watched Saskia Thomas, who was eating a lemon and lime cake. Kip was walking in her direction but when he got level with her, she turned pointedly away.

Brooke, who was refilling her drink next to Eve, followed her gaze and shook her head.

'That situation will run and run. It's bound to cause no end of trouble. What a pain.'

'What happened?'

The costume supervisor tucked a strand of sleek red hair behind one ear. She was as striking as any of the actors. 'Kip and Saskia were in a relationship, but Rufus told them they had to knock it on the head. For the duration of the production, he *said*. So Saskia could focus on her role. Kip wasn't happy, but Saskia wants to make the big time, so she went along with it. That was two months ago now.' She sipped her fizz. 'They'd developed an uneasy truce, but yesterday brought an end to that. Thanks to your friend, Kip knows Rufus has taken his place and they've both got vile tempers when the mood takes them. Rufus can turn from charming to insufferable in an instant. Take it from me.'

But Eve didn't have to. She'd seen it for herself.

# CHAPTER FIVE

Eve and Viv left their cake platters at Watcher's Wood again that evening. Eve wanted time to shower before the pub and Simon's fiancée's party, and it seemed too rude to whisk the trays away when people were still eating.

'I'll nip and get them in the morning,' she said.

Half an hour later, Eve was taking refuge in her seventeenth-century home, Elizabeth's Cottage. The thick walls meant it was pleasantly cool as she pottered about under its low beams, getting ready for the evening ahead. Mixed emotions about the programme of events continued to swirl in her mind: curiosity for the pub trip and a sinking feeling about perfect Polly's party.

She kept the following day in mind as a reward. She'd spend an hour or two in the morning scouring for new obituary subjects in her shady dining room, then pop along to work a shift at Monty's. The balance of quiet and company kept her happy.

A while later, after feeding Gus, showering and changing into a sea-green dress, decorated at the neck with blue sequins, she was ready to tackle the outside world again. She was more dolled-up than usual for the pub, but she wasn't changing again before Polly's party. There were limits.

She bent to give Gus a cuddle.

'I know. You feel you're missing out. But you'd be dog-tired if I took you along.'

He gave her a withering glance.

Eve turned to peer at herself in the mirror by the door, remembering the costume supervisor's critical look. She added some extra mascara from the tube she had in her bag, then let herself out into the warm fragrant evening. On Haunted Lane, a white-throated warbler was darting in and out of the tangle of fruiting blackberries and honeysuckle. The intense heat of the day had abated, and she felt better.

She wondered how Rufus, Saskia and Kip Clayton would behave at the Cross Keys, and whether Dot Hampshire would mellow in the pub's relaxed surroundings. The poisonous flowers played on her mind.

After a moment, she was trying to imagine feeling vicious enough to spit into someone's drink. It was immediate: an impulse. That fitted with her impression of Kip Clayton. It went well with the open sulks he'd displayed when Rufus and Isla Quinn had told him off. She wouldn't be surprised to see Kip punch Rufus on the nose in a fit of temper, but the theatricals were another matter. It was hard to imagine the hulking camera operator deciding to pick flowers as a prop.

When Eve pushed the heavy pub door open, she found the Cross Keys was packed. She felt less guilty about Gus now. There was no way he and the pub schnauzer, Hetty, could have enjoyed their usual rough and tumble with so many people around. Not that it would have stopped them trying.

Ahead of her, Eve could see Jo Falconer, the Cross Keys' cook, who ran the pub with her husband and brother-in-law. She was delivering platefuls of salmon, samphire and new potatoes to a table in the centre of the room. The whole place smelled of delicious food, which made Eve's stomach rumble.

'It's too damned hot,' Jo said, wafting herself with a menu as she neared Eve. 'Still, I'd better get back in there. The entire crew and half the extras have put in orders! I ask you.'

Eve was gladder than ever that she'd left Gus behind. Jo's patience with canine antics was limited, even at the best of times.

Matt Falconer, her husband, roared with laughter. 'Don't let her put you off. You can order too if you want. Though I suppose you'll be eating at the stables?'

Simon, Polly's fiancée and Viv's brother, owned Honeysuckle Cottage, the stable yard and the land around it too.

'That's right.' Eve ordered a white wine spritzer.

'The first one's on us.' Drew Fawcett, the assistant director, had appeared at her side. He must have been looking out for newcomers. His irises were so dark she could barely distinguish his pupils, yet there was a spark in his eyes.

Just beyond him, Toby was serving Dot Hampshire. She was laughing about something and Eve caught the wicked look in her eye. Toby blushed. That and his smile said it all. When he'd spoken to Eve about their old friendship, he'd sounded deferential, as though the likes of him couldn't really call themselves friends of the likes of her, but Eve knew their connection dated to before Dot hit the big time. The actress's look was warm. That might just be down to fond memories, but for a second, Eve felt sentimental. Toby hadn't had much luck with women. It would be nice to see him happy. An actress and a publican might not be a practical combination, but stranger things had happened.

Matt handed Eve her drink and added it to the crew's tab.

'Rufus sends his apologies,' Drew said, as he walked outside with Eve into the pub's sweeping garden. 'He's got one or two things to iron out before tomorrow.'

'Of course.' Eve smiled, but she was already questioning the explanation. He'd been intent on attending earlier. She had the impression he relished showing off his largesse – he'd lapped up the looks of admiration when he'd broken open the champagne, yet he'd abandoned the chance to personally ply the adoring villagers with more free drinks.

Eve found herself a space on the edge of a bench at one of the pub's longest tables. She had a view down to the fields and marshes beyond the Cross Keys' garden. In the distance she could see flocks of wading birds: black-tailed godwits, sandpipers and dunlins feeding on the mudflats while the tide was out.

'What's happened to Saskia?' It was Kip Clayton who'd spoken.

'Didn't feel up to it.' Drew sat at the table. His expression told the camera operator to leave it.

Kip instantly looked bulkier at Drew's response, shoulders raised, bullish head forward. 'Rufus is giving her a pep talk, I suppose.' He had a beer, three quarters empty, at his elbow, with a whisky chaser next to it. He drained the spirit now, his knuckles white on the glass.

Isla Quinn, who was next to Drew, raised a cool eyebrow. 'Not still sulking, are you?' A moment later she laughed in response to a foul look from Kip. Eve could imagine him spitting in *her* drink too. His transparency confirmed what she'd felt earlier. He might brood, but if he got angry his feelings would boil over in plain sight. She doubted he'd creep about subtly hinting at his hatred for Rufus.

Viv must have arrived earlier. She was on the opposite side of the table from Eve, and further down. Eve double-took. True to her word, she'd already dyed her hair cerise. How had she had the time? She caught Eve's eye and gave her a meaningful look, her chin tilted towards Kip, as though Eve might not have noticed the latest tensions. Eve looked away pointedly and counted to ten.

She was surprised by Isla's approach. If the producer wanted to make peace, Eve could think of better ways. But maybe Isla figured being upfront would put Kip off making snide remarks.

She struck Eve as the sort to take no prisoners. She was impressive to look at: her hair streaked blonde in loose waves, elegant bone structure and a statement designer necklace in silver which looked stunning with her plain black sleeveless dress. But her eyes were hard and her bearing said she meant business. It made sense: she had to take full responsibility for each production, getting the commission and overseeing every aspect of the project. Eve was a planner. She'd have no problem with that side of things, but she'd hate the pressure and the need to deal with unforeseen problems. Eve wondered what she'd said to Rufus, once she discovered his affair with their lead actress. It was enough to foul up the way the team worked together. She was probably livid with her partner.

A moment later, Isla had turned to Drew and was having a low conversation with him about the following day's filming. The assistant director pulled out his phone and referred to some notes, nodding at the producer, leaning forward and talking earnestly. A pair of workaholics. Eve recognised something of herself in Drew, who appeared to have a passion and intensity behind his focus. She guessed Isla had a steely resolve behind hers.

Kip Clayton was still grumbling under his breath, and now a small woman with mouse-brown hair spoke hesitantly. Eve recognised her as an actress playing a minor member of the Linden family. 'I think Saskia was upset earlier. And yesterday too. She said she'd get an early night.'

Eve could see the kind of early night Kip was imagining from his expression. Even she had thought instantly of rumpled sheets and the good-looking director.

Isla paused in her conversation with Drew and glanced at the mousy actress. 'Rufus shouldn't pander to her. It's a ridiculous affectation, this reaction to her method acting. It's a career and you have to get on with it. It's something Rufus needs to teach her.'

Her lips were thin. Eve had been right about her anger towards the director. And now she guessed it might have been building up for some time. Even if news of Rufus's affair with Saskia was new, the way he indulged her might not be.

'Rufus mentioned her having bad news.' The mouse-haired woman still sounded hesitant.

'He probably wanted to explain away her histrionics,' Isla replied, 'because he knows I disapprove. That's just like him. Far better to tackle it head-on than let her wallow.' She waved an elegant hand, with a flash of silver rings. 'Just so long as Saskia's better in the morning. The schedule's tight. We can't afford a lame duck.'

*Talk about outspoken…* Maybe her feelings were spilling over, in response to the way the pair were behaving.

On a neighbouring table, near to the pub's back door, Dot Hampshire had gone still. Eve guessed she was listening in. Was she wondering why she hadn't been given the lead when Isla and Rufus already knew her? Eve could barely begin to imagine her fury if Rufus had been swayed by his attraction to Saskia. It seemed as though Dot's career was stalling when it had hardly begun. Once again, the flowers drifted through her mind. She could imagine her wanting to make Rufus sweat. And unlike Kip, Eve could see her opting for mind games. She could be outrageous and direct – witness the ironic kiss she'd given Rufus – but she'd delivered that performance with perfect control, aiming to embarrass with a calculated manoeuvre.

Eve had felt for Dot when Rufus had been so belittling the day before, but she had no idea what she was really like. And why had she decided to accept a lesser part and continue working with him? Her mind turned to Toby Falconer again. She hoped Dot wasn't going to play with his emotions.

Isla finished her drink. 'Well, thank you again, extras!' She smiled down on them all as she stood, taking in multiple tables where locals were perched next to actors and crew. 'You've been wonderful.' She glanced at Drew. 'We must go and check through tomorrow's logistics now.'

He nodded. 'I'm ready. Bye, all. Thanks again.' He got up quickly, despite the long day.

'For Pete's sake, have another drink, Drew!' Kip Clayton spoke as Isla disappeared through the pub, a little ahead of the assistant director. 'You're not paid to slave all night.'

But Drew shook his head. 'I want *Lindens* to work like a dream. I'll save the boozy evenings for when filming's over.' He paused. 'You might consider calling it a night too. Early start tomorrow.'

Kip grunted as Drew walked towards the pub's rear entrance. Eve saw him pause briefly next to Dot. They exchanged a couple of words, but she couldn't catch what was said.

'One-drink loser,' Kip muttered under his breath as Drew exited through the pub. He swigged the last of his pint.

Eve was beginning to wish she wasn't on the same table as him. She hadn't wanted to arrive at Polly's thirtieth too early, but it might be the lesser of two evils. Eve normally arrived on time or ahead of it – she couldn't help herself – but a party was different. Lateness was expected; on time was around half an hour after the start. If she and Viv dashed along before that they'd be the only ones there.

But at that moment, Dot appeared at Kip's side, a gin and tonic still in her hand. 'Come on,' she said to him. 'Let's go and walk off our pent-up rage.' Downing her drink in one, she put it on the table. 'I'm exhausted anyway and it'll only feel worse tomorrow if your head's hammering. Bye, all!'

At last, Kip pushed himself to his feet and stomped after her.

Viv shuffled along the bench so she was opposite Eve. 'Interesting evening so far, huh? You missed Rick Sutton the custodian, by the way, but I took careful note in your absence and I think he behaved oddly. He bought a drink and settled down on a neighbouring table, only to neck it and leave when his neighbour said they'd heard Saskia Thomas wasn't coming.' She shook her head.

'How could you hear what was said if you weren't on their table?'

Viv grinned winningly. 'I got up to stretch my legs. But I was really subtle. Promise! You can thank me by being first on the dance floor at Polly's party. I can't be the only one gyrating!'

# CHAPTER SIX

Eve and Viv walked over to the stables together. Eve had slipped on a pair of pumps she'd had in her bag, so she could cope with the ruts on Old Yard Lane. She held her high heels in her left hand.

Viv gave her a sidelong glance as she teetered along in her sling-backs. 'Is this abhorrent sensible streak something that struck in middle age or have you been this way since you were a child?'

'I'm not having sore feet and wrecked shoes on top of everything else. I've already had to endure Polly going on about her "milestone" birthday for the last month when she's twenty years younger than I am.'

'I can't deny there's more than a pinch of smug about her.' Viv shook her head. 'I so wish you hadn't broken up with Simon. I'd far rather have you as a sister-in-law. You're still intimidating, but in a different way.'

'Yeah, thanks.'

But then Viv's look turned sly. 'Still, I suppose you've got other fish to fry with Suffolk's best-looking gardener.'

Eve felt the heat come to her cheeks and glanced around the deserted lane. 'Shush! You promised not to say anything.'

Viv waved a hand. 'There's no one to hear.'

It was true. Eve could already hear music from the direction of the stables, but she guessed most of the guests would arrive later. They weren't ignorers of social conventions like Viv.

Her friend shook her head. 'I just wish Robin would come along to village events so I can spy on you both. And I can't stop trying to guess what the big mystery is.' She sighed heavily but then held up a hand. 'It's okay. Jim Thackeray said it wasn't your secret to tell.'

Eve and the vicar of Saxford St Peter were the only villagers who knew Robin's full history, and the reason he kept out of the public eye. And only Viv, and Eve's treasured neighbours, Sylvia and Daphne, knew she and the gardener were close.

'Jim's right,' she said, smiling sweetly. 'It isn't.'


It was as Eve had feared. Thanks to Viv's enthusiasm, they were amongst the first people to arrive at the party.

'Nice and early,' Polly said, as though she would have preferred them at least twenty minutes later. She looked phenomenal in a figure-hugging midnight-blue dress, her wavy golden hair cascading over her slender shoulders.

'Didn't want to miss any dancing time!' Viv beamed, unrepentant.

Eve had already replaced her pumps in her bag and donned her high heels again. Now she retrieved her present for Polly, which she'd slid into a front pocket to keep it separate.

'Thank you so much!' Polly said, adding Eve's small box, which contained dangly earrings, to a pile on a side table. Viv's bulkier offering went the same way. She'd have more than she knew what to do with. Eve couldn't help feeling slightly aggrieved.

Simon arrived at that moment and kissed both her and Viv. He was dressed in an open-necked white shirt and dark trousers, conventional where his sister was outlandish, but their openness and enthusiasm were the same.

'Have some fizz!' He was grinning. 'And the food's all on the side there. Except your cake of course. That's to be served at midnight, just before the fireworks.'

Eve maintained her smile as the reality set in.

'A quick bit of pizza, and then, to the dance floor!' Viv said, with a challenging look at Eve.

It took around forty minutes for guests to arrive in serious numbers. At one point before that, Simon spotted Eve looking awkward and got her twisting to 'Shake a Tail Feather' as Viv did an energetic solo. Eve only hoped no one had captured the debacle on camera.

When she left the dance floor for a breather, she found Moira had arrived.

'Goodness, Eve, you looked *very* enthusiastic.' The storekeeper's brow furrowed. 'Where's Polly, I wonder?'

'She's busy adding to her present pile.' Viv had joined them and was laughing, a glass of fizz in her hand now. 'How are things back at the store?'

Moira shook her head. 'Really rather quiet.' She thrived on gossip. 'I shall miss the excitement of our little foray into the acting world.' Then her lips pursed. 'Though I'm sure we'll hear a lot more about proceedings from Babs Lewis.'

Eve imagined Dot Hampshire's aunt hanging around the set, pressuring her niece for updates after each day's filming. Eve didn't envy Dot, though she was sure the actress would give as good as she got. The sight of her kissing Rufus ironically on the lips came back to her. Eve couldn't help but admire her style.

She turned her focus on Moira now. She wouldn't normally encourage her, but she wanted to know exactly what she'd seen over at Watcher's Wood. It would make Eve sound nosy, but only Viv was close enough to hear. The thought of the wolfsbane drove her on; understanding the undercurrents might help. At least no one from the television production was present.

'It must have been embarrassing, accidentally seeing Rufus and Saskia together.' Eve stepped a little further away from the loudspeakers as she spoke, to reduce the need to shout.

The storekeeper put her hand to her cheek. 'Oh yes!' She leaned forward. 'And do you know, I honestly don't believe it was just exuberance.'

'No, really?'

Viv's sarcasm was lost on Moira, who nodded earnestly. 'When I saw them, he had his hands on her shoulders and at first she pulled back quite sharply. But then after a moment they were – well,' she flushed, '*all* over each other! Hands everywhere.'

Eve pondered Moira's words as Viv dragged her back onto the dance floor. The storekeeper must have had a good, extended look at the pair. Saskia's initial reticence might mean it was a new relationship, and she'd only given in to her feelings for the first time yesterday. It would be natural to hold back, given Rufus was married. Or perhaps the affair was ongoing, and Saskia was simply nervous of getting caught. Eve tried to focus as Viv grabbed her hand and swung her round forcefully. Or, of course, Saskia might have held back because she was out of sorts. After all, she'd abandoned the pub trip that evening, and her colleague said she was down. It didn't get Eve much further, but it was interesting.

At nine, the music quietened, and Simon coaxed an (apparently) unwilling Polly to a position near a microphone. Who installed a microphone at a birthday party? It wasn't as though Polly was the sort to embrace karaoke.

'Thank you all for coming along tonight,' Simon gave his fiancée's hand a squeeze, 'to celebrate my intended's thirtieth and no doubt marvel at why she's chosen me for a life partner.'

'Very curious,' Viv whispered, 'when he could have had you!' She glanced at Eve. 'You and he were a picture on the dance floor.'

'Shut up!' Eve felt a blush rise up her neck. Most unhelpful. Her feelings towards Simon were blissfully simple and sisterly now, but the villagers were always hungry for gossip. They might get the wrong impression.

Simon went on to tell a series of amusing anecdotes about his and Polly's formative dates and his marriage proposal. There was plenty of warm laughter. He might be dragging it out a bit, but they were all very fond of Simon. Then Polly took a turn, all blushes and demure smiles… After a few minutes of the gathered crowd clapping and murmuring appreciative responses, she handed back to Simon. Eve was desperate for him to finish. She needed the loo.

'Stick around until midnight and there will be fireworks and cake for all. In the meantime, get stuck in!' he said at last, to Eve's relief. 'Here's to Polly, and a very happy thirtieth!'

'To Polly,' the crowd murmured dutifully, raising their glasses.

A moment later, Simon disappeared inside the house and the music started again.

'Come on!' Viv was plucking at Eve's sleeve.

'I need the loo. I'll be back in two ticks.'

Her friend gave her a severe look.

'Promise.'

Simon's downstairs bathroom had been Pollyfied. There was a box of tissues on a side table next to the basin, along with an upmarket pump-action hand cream and little packets of mint breath-fresheners, as though Eve was a guest at a hotel.

When she exited the room she saw Simon to her right, talking on his mobile. He grinned and hung up. 'Someone crying off. All the more food for us!' He followed her back out to the garden, where Viv was dancing with the vicar, who was back in his clerical collar and flying around the floor with the best of them. A second later they'd dragged her into their mad stampede, leaving Eve no time to glance at her watch to check the number of hours left until midnight.

Images of Polly's party spooled through Eve's head when she finally sank onto her mattress at two the following morning. Her bed had never felt so inviting. Gus had given her a stern look on her return, like a parent who'd waited up late for their wayward child.

Eve had been on her feet all night. As Viv had said, Robin, Saxford St Peter's gardener and – Eve felt a shock of embarrassed excitement – her secret lover, had not come.

It wasn't a disappointment, because she'd known he wouldn't. He never attended village events where the drink and gossip flowed; the secret he kept was too important. He'd once been Robert Kelly, a detective inspector down in London, until uncovering high-level police corruption had put him in danger from slippery colleagues and their criminal contacts. He'd moved to Suffolk and become Robin Yardley, turning a hobby into his profession. And the vicar had helped him settle. The villagers (mostly) trusted him because Jim Thackeray did.

Eve was nervous of people uncovering their relationship. Robin's background was the topic of much speculation in Saxford, and if people knew they were close they'd be bound to ask her about him. Saying she didn't know would make her look like a gullible jerk, but the alternative would be to lie. Neither appealed, so keeping their affair on the down-low remained the best option.

After all the dancing, and a certain amount of Prosecco, Eve fell soundly asleep. But twenty minutes later she was awake again, her heart thudding.

She thought she'd heard footsteps out in the lane. She blinked and sat upright in bed, to the sound of Gus whining downstairs.

She'd gone to bed half expecting to dream the dream associated with the lane on which she lived. Back in the 1720s, a woman called Elizabeth who'd lived in her house had hidden a local servant boy to save him from the gallows. His crime had been to steal a loaf of bread to feed his starving siblings. A hue and cry had come after him, thudding down Haunted Lane, thumping at the door of the cottage and searching the house. The story had a happy ending.

The men failed to find the boy, Isaac, and Elizabeth smuggled him away to safety. Her grandson had renamed Eve's cottage after her and twice a year, following a long tradition, Eve held an open house, allowing visitors to see the tiny chamber under the cottage where Isaac had hidden. They donated to children's charities in return for the tour and she let them climb down into the space if they liked. There was a torch they could use down there, but Eve left them to it. She was anything but fanciful normally, but entering the space left her breathless with fear, as though she could feel Isaac's emotions, centuries later.

Haunted Lane was named for the thudding feet you were meant to hear after dark – echoes of the ruthless men who'd chased the boy. Hearing the footfalls was meant to signify danger.

Eve could hear Gus on the stairs now, and went to the bedroom door to let him in.

'There's no one there really, Gus. I don't know why we imagine these things.' She knew it was ridiculous. She definitely didn't believe in ghosts. Her pet theory was that the dream came when she was uneasy about cold, hard reality. All the same, her hands felt clammy as she went to pull back the curtains.

A second later, she was laughing. Down below she could see two teenagers chasing each other up the lane. After a moment, one caught the other up and they walked on, arm in arm, kissing outside Hope Cottage, which was diagonally opposite her house.

She guessed they must have been at a party and cut back along the footpath next to the marshes.

'False alarm. It must be them that I heard.' She shook her head. 'I'm getting jumpy, Gus.' But as she settled back down to sleep the dream took hold again, and there were multiple feet, heavy, thudding. And the teenagers had been wearing Converse. She'd never have heard their footfalls.

# CHAPTER SEVEN

Eve felt bleary the following morning, after the party and the disturbed night. She showered and slipped on her neat green dress with the daisy print, walked Gus round the village green, then dosed up on coffee over a leisurely breakfast. There was no point in rushing to fetch the cake platters from Watcher's Wood. She guessed the actors and crew would be having a well-earned lie-in, given it was Sunday. It was also the one day of the week when Monty's opened late, so she had plenty of time before her shift. It gave Eve the chance to browse the death notices online and do some googling, to see if she could spot an interesting subject to pitch to one of the publications she worked with. As usual, she felt frustrated that most media would only be interested in the famous or infamous, despite every life being fascinating.

At last, Eve left the house and walked along a rapidly warming Haunted Lane, bathed in sunlight and birdsong.

She went to find her Mini Clubman by the green. It was stuffy when she slid inside, and she opened the windows. A moment later she was enjoying the gentle breeze as she drove through the village, before looking out for the wooden gate which would give her access to Watcher's Wood. She found it open and went straight through onto the bumpy grass-tufted driveway, bordered by trees.

Eve entered the area the team used as a car park and pulled up next to a towering oak. As she removed her keys from the ignition, she spotted Margot Hale, Rufus Beaumont's personal assistant, dashing between two of the trailers up ahead. At the sound of Eve's engine, the woman looked round and waved to her.

'You've come for the trays?' She smiled. 'I'll get them for you.'

She disappeared from sight as Eve exited her car and closed the door behind her, enjoying the smell of warm earth and grass.

Within seconds, she was slipping between the accommodation trailers again, to reach the clearing they'd used the afternoon before for their cakes and champagne.

To her left, Isla, the producer, was knocking on Rufus's trailer door. In fact, battering might be a better description. 'If you're sulking, Rufus, you can stop it right now. You're wanted.' Suddenly, her eyes lit on Eve. 'Oh. Good morning.' Eve could tell her presence was an irritation.

She explained her mission, then looked away so Isla could carry on haranguing her director while Eve feigned nonchalance. A moment later, though, she glimpsed the producer peering into Rufus's trailer between the curtain and the window frame. Shaking her head, the woman tried the door, which was unlocked.

She disappeared inside but emerged again in an instant. 'Where the hell is he?'

Margot Hale had reappeared with Monty's trays, all wiped clean. As she handed them over, her smile faded. 'I assumed he was in his trailer, though it's not like him to lie in this late, even on a Sunday.' She glanced at her watch and her frown deepened. 'He's not in the office.' The 'office' was another trailer. Eve had seen it when they came for their first run-through.

'Bed doesn't look slept in,' Isla said. Her gaze turned to another trailer, but the costume supervisor, who passed at that moment, shook her head.

'I've seen Saskia this morning. If he's in there he's lying in on his own.'

'Thanks, Brooke.' Isla shrugged and Eve noticed the costume supervisor catch Margot Hale's eye. What was going on?

'Does anyone know where the hell Rufus is?' Isla shouted the query so that people inside and out of the trailers would hear. A couple of doors opened, to reveal puzzled faces. 'We agreed to catch up this morning.'

'Some of the crew went for a walk around the mansion grounds. I'll go and ask them.' Margot moved swiftly.

'I'll check this end,' Brooke said, her silky red hair gleaming in the sun. The heat was intense; it was only half an hour off midday.

'Thanks for the trays!' Eve called to Margot's retreating back. There was no reason to stay, but her legs felt like jelly after the dream. Where the heck *was* Rufus?

She was just moving between the trailers when she heard a shout from behind her.

'Isla! I need to talk to you.'

Margot had stopped in her tracks at the words too, pausing just ahead of Eve and glancing over her shoulder.

It was Drew Fawcett. He shook his head, and a queasiness took hold of Eve's stomach.

'Rufus is in the vestry at the church.' He stood strangely still.

'Well, come on!' Isla was striding forward. 'If you can't winkle him out, I will!'

Drew shielded his eyes from the sun. 'Isla, he's dead.'

Isla's handsome face froze. Her hand went to her mouth, her green eyes unblinking. 'What? What do you mean?'

Drew moved closer to her, his voice quiet and controlled. 'I don't know what happened. A heart attack maybe? He looks peaceful, almost as though he's asleep. He's lying on the floor with his eyes closed. I called an ambulance on my way back here. Just in case… but there's no pulse.'

Margot was walking slowly back towards the clearing now, staring ahead as though she was in a trance. 'How can it be? He was so young.' The cheerful, brisk efficiency she'd radiated the day before had drained out of her. Suddenly, she turned to Eve. 'He said you thought the flowers he'd been given were dangerous. Could they have killed him? If he'd got poison in a cut?'

Eve shook her head. 'I've read about that happening, but I think he'd have had symptoms sooner if there was any harm done on Friday. Unless he kept them?'

Margot shook her head slowly; she looked desolate. 'I made sure he threw them away.' She didn't mention the note. Eve guessed Rufus had kept it secret. He'd hated Eve seeing it. 'But it's an odd coincidence.'

Eve agreed. Too much of one.

'I think we should call the police,' Drew said. 'No one ever admitted to delivering the flowers.'

Isla threw her head back and took a deep breath. 'Hell. Poor Rufus. It goes without saying that his death is a huge blow. But his lifestyle wasn't healthy. He liked a drink and his precious cigars. A heart attack doesn't seem so far-fetched. Surely we don't have to involve the authorities? Every day we lose filming will cost us a fortune. If I shut off my emotions, with my producer's hat on, the last thing I want is a pointless police enquiry. We need to get on and find a replacement director. The flowers seem like the act of some star-struck teenager who didn't know their botany.' She couldn't know about the note either. She turned to Eve. 'You might be able to find out who put them in his trailer. I'd imagine it was one of the villagers. We could try that route instead.'

Eve saw Margot's cheeks tinge a deep red. Isla's attitude made her catch her breath too. She tried to see her views in the round. The pressure to deliver a project on time and to budget must be huge. But she'd literally just heard her long-time collaborator was dead. How could she be so cold?

'I think Drew's right,' Eve said, preparing herself for resistance. 'If the coroner orders a post-mortem it won't be long before the results come through. They'll soon clear you to re-start filming if it was a heart attack. And the paramedics will probably refer it on anyway, with the death being out of the blue.' She didn't want to mention the note. The police might prefer to keep the information under wraps. The sender might give themselves away if they slipped up and admitted to knowing about it.

There was a long pause, but maybe her words had hit home. 'Oh, damnation. All right then.'

As Drew made the call, some of the actors traipsed into the clearing from different directions, moving as though in slow motion. Brooke had reappeared too, her jaw slack, her striking face pale, despite the expertly applied make-up. She must have overheard bits of the conversation.

'Would you like me to go and tell Rick Sutton?' Eve said. 'So it's not a surprise when the police and ambulance turn up?' The press would be clamouring for information imminently too. Rick would need to manage it all, at least in terms of securing the site from unwanted hacks.

'Thanks.' Drew's dark eyes were on hers. 'His office and living quarters are in a chalet beyond the trailers.'

Viv would say she was hanging around for more information, and there was nothing to say that Rufus's death was murder. But in her heart of hearts, Eve was sure there was more to this than met the eye. Walking the site now, to get an immediate impression of the scene, might be useful later.

She felt implicated in what had happened. Her fingernails dug into her palms painfully as she clenched her hands. Rufus hadn't wanted to involve the police over the wolfsbane, but she could have told them about the incident herself. She examined her conscience, wondering if she'd ducked taking it further because of her poor relationship with the local detective inspector, Nigel Palmer. But she could have tried his constable, Olivia Dawkins, or DS Greg Boles, the one member of the local team who knew Robin's history. He was married to Robin's cousin and had enlisted the vicar's help to get him settled in Saxford. But she hadn't been sure, and now it was too late.

She'd need to tell them what she knew, and that wouldn't be an end to her involvement if Rufus's death turned out to be murder. She'd contributed to their investigations before. She'd pitch to *Icon* magazine for his obituary, and if they said yes, she'd be interviewing the same people as the police. Palmer hated her interference, but Eve could never bring herself to step back. And in this case, she was personally involved. She should have trusted her instincts and pushed Rufus harder to report the flowers. If there'd been foul play, she owed it to him to investigate. And she'd been watching for clues ever since she'd suspected some kind of trouble. Perhaps she'd seen something important.

She desperately hoped the death had been natural, for everyone's sake. It would be so much harder for Rufus's wife to know his life had been deliberately cut short. And any police investigation was bound to reveal his affair with Saskia too.

But as she had the thought, she heard voices coming from close to the costume trailer.

'… can't believe it,' a woman said. 'And I passed Brooke on my way here. She said Isla didn't want the police involved.'

Eve slowed her pace as someone else let out a sharp sigh. 'Well, I'm not surprised, after yesterday evening.'

'What?'

'Didn't you hear them, before we set out? Blimey, I thought they'd come to blows. They were in Isla's trailer, so I've no idea what they quarrelled about. I couldn't hear her, but Rufus was really yelling. Isla emerged with her mask intact, but it was after that that Rufus decided not to come to the pub. And there's a rumour the flowers someone left him were poisonous. Who's to say it's not murder?'

Eve had to knock three times on Rick Sutton's chalet door before she heard movement. It was understandable – he likely had the day off and there was no reason he should be ready for visitors. Now, she heard a scuffling and what sounded like something dropping to the floor. Half a minute later he opened up. He was only half-dressed: just jeans and a shirt, three buttons open at the neck. He had one sock on, but no shoes yet. Behind him, beyond his desk and office, Eve could see an open door, and through it a sofa and the side of a television.

Eve was starting to wonder if he'd had a proper job before. She would have made herself more presentable before opening up. She couldn't imagine him taking charge of the circumstances he was about to be hit with.

The custodian's eyes had screwed up against the sun, but now they widened at the sight of her.

'Hello there! What are you doing here?'

'I popped over to pick up our cake trays, but I'm afraid I walked in on a situation. There's some terrible news.'

The young man blinked, his hair flopping forward.

'Rufus Beaumont's been found dead. It might have been a heart attack. His body's in the vestry of the church and Drew Fawcett has called an ambulance and the police.'

'The police?'

Eve explained about the wolfsbane. 'It's just a precaution. But I think they come anyway, when there's been a sudden death.'

'I see, I see.' Rick Sutton was half up on the balls of his feet.

The image made her shiver as she walked back to her car. He'd looked excited.

# CHAPTER EIGHT

Eve managed to grab some lunch and draft a quick pitch for Rufus's obituary before her shift at Monty's. On her way over, she saw a police patrol car skirting the village green, taking the most direct route from Blyworth to Watcher's Wood, she guessed. The site must be crawling with detectives and scientific support officers by now. She had visions of Rick Sutton in the middle of it all, head spinning. Or would he just be thrilled by all the action?

The actors and crew would be getting the third degree. Tension, nerves and sorrow flooding the site. And, if Eve's misgivings were correct, one person would be feeling fear. Both the heat and the chill of it.

Viv spent the afternoon pummelling her for information, while Eve felt frustrated at the lack of it. Many of their customers had heard the news, but no one knew any more than she did.

By the time she returned home, Portia Coldwell at *Icon* magazine had already contacted her, pre-empting her proposal. No doubt she'd realised Eve would be on the spot again. Rufus was well respected in his own right, but Eve could see it was his place in the Beaumont acting dynasty that had really sparked Portia's interest. Eve knew readers would be entranced by the whiff of Hollywood glamour his family brought, but she was determined to pay tribute to Rufus for his own sake. He might be on the other side of a bank of cameras, and in television, rather than film, but the critics loved his work, and so did millions around the globe. The series he worked on had been exported internationally.

There was no word yet on how he'd died, but the possibility that he'd been killed filled Eve's mind as she started to research him.

She focused on the basics first. He'd only been thirty-nine when he'd died – certainly young for his heart to give out, which made Isla's plea to leave the police out of it all the more unreasonable. His partnership with her had been going on for ten years, during which time they'd worked on seven projects, five of which had won awards, either for him, or one of the actors involved. The one before *Lindens* had been *The Pedestal*, which had earned Dot Hampshire a BAFTA, and Rufus great critical acclaim.

Before directing, Rufus had acted. Immediately after drama school, he'd made a big impression on the critics as a supporting actor in *Shadows in the Trees*, an independent film that was a hit in arts cinemas. But after that, from the age of twenty-two to twenty-six, his parts had all been on the small screen. He'd chalked up appearances on a handful of soaps, murder mysteries and the like, but never as a recurring character.

He was the youngest of the three Beaumont siblings. His elder brother Jasper and sister Gabriella were both regularly top-billed in Hollywood movies these days, following in the footsteps of their parents, Magnus and Naomi, who'd each directed, as well as acting. It was mind-bending, as far as Eve was concerned, to have one family produce that much talent. But of course, the Beaumont children had all the right connections. Others with just as much promise might have fallen by the wayside. Despite his privilege, Rufus had taken longer to find his niche than the others. Eve guessed that might have affected him. Made him even more determined maybe, or perhaps feel jealous or small. Eve suspected a combination of all three, from what she'd seen and heard.

She was already aware of Rufus's wife, Cassie, and his affair with Saskia, of course. But as she searched she found there were a couple of other small scandals in his love life that the press had picked up on. One was a steamy affair he'd had with a married actress called Dora Blake on the set of *Shadows in the Trees*, and the other was the death of Emily Longfellow, his childhood sweetheart who'd gone on to attend the same drama school as him. She'd fallen down the stairs in a drunken stupor eight years earlier at the age of just thirty-one. The thought tugged at Eve's heartstrings. They'd broken up in the final year of their studies, but despite the passing of time, the press hinted Emily had never got over Rufus. Eve wondered. It would have been ten years after they'd broken up. She suspected the media had decided she was still heartbroken because it made a good story. Love and tragedy sold papers, unfortunately. The press had raked up the details in an article supposedly focused on the strength of Rufus's marriage. They knew what would hook their readers.

She paused a moment, her mind drifting back to the man's death, and shook her head. It was just too weird that he should die so soon after the flowers. The way Drew had described his body came back to her: 'peaceful', almost as though he was asleep. Would that fit if he'd died in pain of a heart attack? And 'peaceful' didn't imply a man who'd fallen to the ground in an uncontrolled way. Every inch of her was filled with foreboding.

She'd know soon enough. She'd filled Robin in on the developments at Watcher's Wood and was due to meet him a little later. He'd have the most up-to-date information from DS Greg Boles. The pair were close. Greg was frustrated by his DI's shortcomings; it meant he liked to chew cases over with a like-minded outsider. The fact that Robin was a former detective, related to Greg by marriage, had cemented their friendship.

Their association had benefited Eve. In the past, when she'd interviewed the friends and relations of murder victims, inside information from Robin had helped keep her safe.

For now, she concentrated on what she could learn independently, looking beyond the basic information she'd found, oblivious to everything but her subject and Gus.

It was getting dusky by the time Eve headed off to Robin's home that evening. She always took back routes to reach his fisherman's cottage on Dark Lane, to avoid being seen and the questions that would follow.

'We'll head through Blind Eye Wood, buddy,' she said to Gus. He cocked his head and scampered forwards eagerly. The woods in the evening meant Robin, and Robin meant excitement and extra attention. Their feelings were aligned on that score.

She was halfway along Love Lane, alongside the village green, when she spotted Moira emerge from her house, two doors down from the store. 'A last stroll before bed, Eve? I always think that does one good. I just wondered, have you heard anything further about poor dear Rufus? I heard the news this morning of course. Babs Lewis was in. I'm sure it must be *very* upsetting for them all, especially Saskia Thomas. What must she be going through? Though I don't suppose Dot Hampshire will miss him much.' She shook her head. 'So awful that they were at daggers drawn just before he died.'

It was against Eve's principles to feed Moira gossip. She couldn't expect her obituary interviewees – or anyone else – to trust her if she spread their private affairs around the village.

'Nothing further, I'm afraid.'

The storekeeper still looked hopeful. 'I just thought, with you having been there when it happened…'

'Only when he was discovered.'

She sighed. 'Of course.'

Eve felt Moira's eyes on her back as she crossed over to reach Heath Lane. She wondered how long she'd monitor her progress.

'I hope she's not going to wait until we come back,' she muttered to Gus, who gave her a doubtful glance. 'She definitely won't buy the "dog walk" excuse if I'm gone for hours.'

They turned right, into shadowy Blind Eye Wood. The name dated back to when smuggling was rife in the village. The locals knew it was best to turn a blind eye to any odd activity on the coast, or heavily laden ponies treading quietly through the trees after dark.

As Eve picked her way between oaks, hawthorn, beech and holly, she couldn't quell the teenager-ish thrill in doing something illicit. She hadn't rebelled much first time around; it was surprisingly pleasing to make up for it now. Viv had occasionally tried to prise the truth about Robin out of her but the vicar had somehow made her understand that the information was under wraps for a good reason. It meant periodic exasperated sighs were as far as Viv got. She'd asked her a couple of weeks back whether she wouldn't rather be with someone who could meet her in the Cross Keys for fish and chips. The truth was, Eve had had a dream about her and Robin doing just that (only she'd got chicken and ham pie), but she'd banished the vision. It was pointless; if going public put Robin in danger she wasn't going to entertain the idea.

Gus was snuffling his way along the path they'd chosen, distracted by a multitude of interesting smells. Somewhere nearby, Eve heard the churring of a nightjar, rising and falling in the quiet of the evening. That moment of peace made her think again of the description of Rufus in death and suddenly, the familiar woods didn't feel so comforting. There was no one else about.

'C'mon, Gus. Let's get going.'

At last they came to the gap in the hedge, next to a mature blackthorn tree, and squeezed through to Robin's garden and along his hawthorn border, past an abundance of sweet peas, honeysuckle, love-in-a-mist and old roses. The fragrant smell of night-scented stock drifted towards her as she approached the stable-style back door. Through a window, the glow of lights looked welcoming. Gus leaped up before Robin had opened up.

'You'll ruin the paintwork!' Eve said, as the door was pulled inwards and her dachshund launched himself at Robin's legs, receiving a laugh and a pat in return.

A second later she was inside both the cottage and Robin's warm embrace. He raised his hand to her cheek as he let her go. 'I'm sorry about Rufus Beaumont. It must have been a shock this morning. Did you like him?'

She put her head on one side. 'He was talented, and charming on the face of it, but his temper was uncertain and he had his enemies. I'm wondering if he was a serial philanderer, too.'

'That sounds potentially relevant.'

She looked at him questioningly.

'I'll fill you in while we eat. I thought I should prepare something light in this heat.'

The tiny table in the centre of his kitchen was already laid for two and in moments, Robin had served up smoked salmon, wedges of lemon and piles of thin toast, with a side salad and good-sized glasses of Viognier.

His eyes turned serious as he sat down to join her and ground pepper over his fish. 'It's confirmed now. It was murder.'

# CHAPTER NINE

Of course, Eve had guessed Rufus's death had been unnatural, but the reality still hit her in the gut. She paused, her toast and salmon halfway from the plate to her lips. 'What happened?'

'Thanks to the pathologist and forensics, we know someone slipped him a strong sedative. That would have put him under. Then it seems the killer smothered him with a cushion in the vestry. The crime scene investigators found it smeared with traces of saliva. Greg says he'd been drinking heavily all evening. There was a whisky bottle, two-thirds empty, in his trailer.' Robin met her eyes. 'His PA says it was full when she went to talk to him before everyone left for the pub. Someone heard him swear at her when she tried to persuade him to come out.'

Poor Margot.

'But analysis shows neither the whisky nor anything else in his accommodation was drugged, so the police's theory is that he was lured to the vestry, where his killer slipped him the drugged drink, then finished him off. He must have been pretty far gone already.'

Eve put her fish and toast back down on her plate and took a sip of her wine.

'I'm sorry.' Robin took her hand when she put down her glass. 'And someone's mentioned you to the police, apparently – the way you went to Rufus's trailer after the wolfsbane was delivered, and you being there this morning. So I guess you'll get a visit from Palmer too.'

Eve closed her eyes for a moment. 'I feel I should have reported the flowers.'

'You suggested it to Rufus. If he didn't pay you any heed, Palmer wouldn't have either.'

'I overheard some of the TV crowd saying Rufus had a very audible argument with the producer, Isla Quinn, early yesterday evening. I wonder if that's what made him hit the bottle.'

'Could be. Any idea what the row was about?'

Eve shook her head. 'But the word is it was Rufus yelling at her, not the other way about. They were clearly at odds, but it sounds like he was the one who lost control.'

'Quinn told the police it was a disagreement over future projects. I'd guess that's half the story at most.'

'From the description of the argument, I imagine you're right. So what are DI Palmer's thoughts so far?'

'That the killer's female. Based on the fact that Beaumont was drugged, rather than overcome by brute force, and the floral element.'

Eve felt her blood pressure rise and opened her mouth.

'I know. But he's never had much imagination.'

'It could be a man who doesn't conform to his expectations, or one who's just trying to convince the police the killer's female. That would fit. The whole thing seemed so stagey.'

Robin nodded. 'I agree, but if so, his plan's worked perfectly on Palmer.'

He took a bite of his food and at last she followed suit, swallowing mechanically, irritation making her stomach tense.

'What are your instincts?' Robin said. 'Who might have wanted him dead?'

Eve knew he liked to have her thoughts unclouded by the police's findings. She explained why Dot Hampshire and Kip Clayton had caught her attention. 'They'd be my initial focus. There's a feeling of brute force about Kip. It's hard to envisage him doing all the preparation and planning, but I've no doubt he was seriously angry with Rufus. I think that could have been enough to make him pull out all the stops. And although I couldn't imagine him delivering the flowers, using them in an attempt to put the police off the scent doesn't seem so far-fetched. As for Dot, she strikes me as more organised and controlled, but now I know the wolfsbane was a precursor to murder, I'd almost say it was too obvious for her.' She frowned, picturing the scene in the vestry. 'It's hard to imagine Rufus sitting down to drink with either of them under the circumstances. But truth to tell, I could see Dot coming up with a ruse to get him there.' She shook her head. She liked the actress but she had to be honest. Not let her feelings about her and Toby influence her thinking. 'I wouldn't rule Kip out though. He and Rufus had a score to settle, and Rufus was a proud man. I guess he wouldn't have shied away from meeting him, even if Kip had been aggressive in his request.'

Robin nodded. 'That's all useful. Anyone else spark your interest?'

She frowned. 'There's something odd about the site custodian, Rick Sutton. He looked excited when I told him the news this morning. I get that it's dramatic and he's young, but I think it's more than that.

'I even wondered about Isla Quinn, especially after I heard about the argument. She didn't want to call the police when Rufus's body was discovered.' Eve frowned, remembering. 'But she was hammering on his trailer door this morning. She looked genuinely surprised that he hadn't appeared. So, what have you been told?'

He pulled a notepad and pencil from his jeans pocket. 'The time of death's quite precise, which is useful. Beaumont signed into internet banking at eight forty-five on his laptop in his trailer. The tab was still open. Apparently he cancelled a direct debit to his wife at eight fifty. The five-minute gap might imply he was debating what to do. Or that he was so drunk it took a while.'

Eve raised an eyebrow. 'Either way, it sounds significant, especially given the timing.'

He nodded. 'It's something the police team will be looking into. And it means he couldn't have arrived at the vestry before eight fifty-three at the earliest. That marks the beginning of the window when he might have been killed.

'Then, luckily for Palmer, his weekly alarm to call his wife was still flashing unsilenced on his phone, which was in his pocket. It was set for half past nine. The audible alert had stopped by the time he was found but apparently it would have carried on for several minutes. The theory is that Rufus was dead and the killer gone by the time it sounded, otherwise they would have dismissed it to avoid unwanted attention.'

The thought was chilling. Images of what had happened in the peaceful church spooled through Eve's head: a bold and stealthy killer welcoming Rufus Beaumont, weakened by drink, and ending his life in the space of thirty-five minutes.

As the cold, frightening thoughts subsided, the reminder Rufus had set to call his wife drifted through her head. It was no wonder he couldn't remember to ring her unassisted. Not with Saskia to distract him. And what kind of time was nine thirty? One that suited him, she guessed. Probably interrupting Cassie Beaumont's evening, just as she was settling down to relax.

Eve took a slightly larger sip of her wine. She felt sorry for Rufus's wife, but she had an obvious motive for murder. And what had prompted him to cancel a regular payment to her last night? 'Does Cassie Beaumont have an alibi?'

Robin shook his head. 'She's down in Hertfordshire so the local police have been with her, then Palmer and Greg went to see her this afternoon. She says she was home alone, working in her office on a design for a multi-millionaire down in London.'

'It would have been a risk to creep onto the Watcher's Wood site. People would have known she wasn't meant to be there, whereas any of the others flitting about wouldn't have attracted attention. And if she delivered the flowers, she'd have taken that risk twice.'

Robin nodded. 'True, but if she was pushed to the limit she might still have done it. Greg says she was livid when Palmer mentioned Saskia Thomas, but he thinks it was a reaction to the way he dealt with the topic, not at the revelation.'

Palmer made Eve livid too. 'They think she already knew about Saskia?'

Robin nodded.

So jealousy could have built up, especially if Saskia was just the latest in a long line of women. She needed to know what Cassie Beaumont was like. 'I want to see if she'll talk with me. My article will be off balance without her input.' But she guessed Rufus's wife would put up barriers, what with the hacks and the police quizzing her too. 'Even if her opportunity was less immediate than that of the cast and crew, she might be aware of the layout of Watcher's Wood, or have visited even. But I guess the same won't be true of other outsiders, so presumably they're less likely. And they'd have no way of knowing the place would be almost deserted last night.'

'True.'

Eve cast her mind back to the previous evening. 'A lot of the actors and crew must still have been at the Cross Keys when Rufus was killed. But I saw some of them leave early.' She'd been clock-watching, thanks to trepidation for Polly's party, so the timings were clear in her head. She'd have to note them all down. 'Isla and Drew went off together muttering about work, then Dot and Kip slipped away moments later, before Viv and I left for Polly's party. Viv mentioned Rick Sutton had been there too. She says he disappeared the instant he heard Saskia wouldn't be putting in an appearance. And of course, she never left the site, as far as I know.'

Robin nodded. 'Beyond them, there are one or two underlings who skipped the drinks. Their day-to-day dealings are with Drew rather than Rufus, so they seem unlikely. The police will need to rule them out, but overall Palmer's excited to have the field of suspects narrowed down. The bulk of the gang went home from the pub en masse, arriving at around ten fifteen, so they're all out of it.

'Apparently Rufus's PA and Brooke Shaw, the costume supervisor, left early too, but they were together and walked back via the beach. A constable going door to door found a couple in a cottage beyond the stables who saw them pass at nine twenty. I understand they were laughing, so they attracted attention. They couldn't have got back to the site before nine thirty, the end of the window when Rufus was killed, so they're out of it.'

It was interesting that the pair seemed to be buddies. They were opposites in many ways: Margot seemed mature, smart, professional and caring, and Brooke firm, a little cynical, young and overtly sexy.

Eve thought back to Brooke's words about Rufus Beaumont. She'd said he had a vile temper when the mood took him. Swearing at Margot Hale proved that. Eve visualised the PA's bright smile and calm demeanour. He'd been lucky to have her.

'And Isla Quinn and Drew Fawcett alibi each other too,' Robin went on. 'She told Palmer she wanted Fawcett to run through the next day's filming. Dot Hampshire heard them talking in Quinn's trailer when she got back to the site.' He glanced at some notes. 'She says that was at eight forty-five. Greg says Quinn sounds like a control freak.'

Eve nodded. 'That ties in with my impression, and the plans they were making at the pub.' But few alibis were watertight. If she found either of them had a motive, she'd think again.

Robin glanced at his notebook. 'Dot Hampshire says Drew Fawcett asked if she could try to persuade Kip Clayton to leave the pub early rather than getting drunk and disorderly.'

Eve nodded. 'I remember Drew whispering to her as he left. He might have figured she could talk him round better than anyone. They had a shared dislike of Rufus.'

Robin nodded. 'Makes sense. According to her, she escorted Kip back to his trailer. He wanted her to go in for a drink, but she said he was "being obnoxious". She stayed long enough to tell him so, then left.'

'That also figures.'

A flash of a smile crossed Robin's face. 'But here's where it gets messy. She told Palmer and Greg she went off for a long walk afterwards, because she was in a foul mood. She was able to give them a fair amount of detail about where she went, and as a consequence, Palmer's smelled a rat, real or imaginary: he thinks she was too well prepared. And that it's convenient she effectively went AWOL at the start of the window when Beaumont might have been killed, and didn't return until after the end. She couldn't remember precisely what time she got back, but if she went where she said she did, Greg reckons it couldn't have been before Beaumont died, even if she jogged it. The place she walked to was at least twenty-five minutes away.'

'Heck. That does sound a little well arranged.' And Palmer probably realised Rufus had been the source of Dot's bad temper too. It wasn't a great excuse to give. That said, it made her seem frank, but Eve could imagine that being a double bluff.

Robin swigged his wine. 'So, Dot's one of Palmer's chief suspects. He admits Kip's got plenty of motive, but Greg says he's not taking him seriously enough. He's convinced the killing had "a woman's touch".'

'Oh dear. But Kip doesn't have an alibi either?'

Robin shook his head. 'Says he was out for the count in his trailer, apparently, so Palmer shouldn't ignore him. Still, you and Greg are on the case too. And if you agree to treat me as a consultant, I'll be curious to see what you come up with.'

'Deal. I'll write some notes and email you a timetable covering the bits I know.'

'Excellent. Two other things you need to know.'

Eve picked up more of her toast and salmon. 'Yes?'

'Palmer's discovered Saskia Thomas wanted Beaumont to divorce his wife.'

'Really? Their affair can't have been going on for more than a couple of months. She was with Kip Clayton before that.'

'It sounds as though things got intense very quickly. Palmer's every bit as interested in her as Dot Hampshire. He thinks she could have killed Rufus if he refused to go along with her wishes.'

'Seriously?'

Robin raised an eyebrow. 'Rufus sent her a romantic text, saying he loved her and they belonged together forever. Saskia replied, suggesting he leave Cassie.'

'He walked right into that one. Did Greg mention Rufus's replies?'

'The standard stuff about it not being the right time. The last one was a couple of weeks back. Palmer wonders if she'd taken to tackling him about it in person and he'd told her it was no go.'

Eve shook her head. 'That makes no sense. Moira says they were still kissing passionately while we were on site. That doesn't say game over to me. And if Rufus hadn't ended the affair, I'll bet Saskia would have kept on wheedling. Either that or bided her time and had another go later. Killing him would be seriously counterproductive.'

Robin gave a quick laugh. 'It's all right – I believe you. Though it's worth just bearing in mind.'

'Consider it borne. Albeit grudgingly.'

'It's only because I care. I assume you'll be interviewing them all soon.'

Eve nodded. 'I hope so. I've already emailed Margot Hale to give my condolences and ask if she'll put feelers out to see who's willing to talk.'

'Palmer's given you a helping hand there.'

'That sounds unlikely.'

He gave her a fleeting smile. 'The church is cordoned off of course – for now – but he's asked the entire cast and crew to continue to live on site while he conducts the investigation. You won't have to go further than Watcher's Wood for your interviews.'

'That's handy. What was the second thing you wanted to tell me?'

'Saskia Thomas saw Rick Sutton peering at her through her trailer window. He was hiding in the undergrowth.'

Eve shuddered. 'How horrible. I thought there was something creepy about him. Does that mean they can alibi each other?'

Robin shook his head. 'It wasn't until nine forty-five. Saskia drew her curtains when she saw him staring. She says she stayed in her trailer all night.'

'She didn't spend any time with Rufus?'

'Not by her account. Palmer was suspicious about that. And about Rick Sutton hanging round in what would have been the immediate aftermath of the murder, as you can imagine. But Sutton claims he went straight to her trailer from his chalet and returned there the moment he realised he'd been seen. He said he wanted to ask for an autograph and was plucking up courage to go and knock on her door. But when she drew the curtains he guessed he wouldn't be welcome.'

'How very astute of him!'

'So where does all this leave your plans?'

Eve slipped her notebook from her handbag and shook her head. 'Complicated.' She was about to say Kip was top of her suspect list, but she forced herself to face facts. He shouldn't occupy that position alone. If anything, Dot Hampshire was ahead of him. 'I need to find out more about Dot and Kip.' There was real animosity there. From both of them. 'It's odd, the way Dot stuck around to act in *Lindens*, despite being given a lesser part. I guess you have to take the work, but you'd think she'd have found something comparable elsewhere after her BAFTA. And she comes across as proud. Not the sort to knuckle down and button her lip. I'd put Cassie Beaumont a little further down the list. Her motive's good, but her opportunity is less straightforward. I'll need to quiz them all.'

Robin nodded. 'And I guess even Rick Sutton's worth considering. If he's obsessed with Saskia, killing Rufus would have amounted to removing his rival.'

# CHAPTER TEN

The first interaction Eve had the following day was with Toby Falconer from the Cross Keys. He was out as early as she was, each of them on dog-walking detail. As Gus bounded after Hetty through the trees of Blind Eye Wood, Toby's anxious gaze met Eve's.

'You're writing Rufus Beaumont's obituary?'

She nodded as they turned to follow their dogs. '*Icon* is keen.'

'I hear he was murdered. Sent poisonous flowers, then drugged and smothered.'

'I'm afraid so.' As usual, she couldn't quote Robin.

'And you'll be looking into who might have killed him, I guess, as well as his life history.' He bit his lip.

Was he worried about Dot? Her and Rufus's feud would be the talk of the village, especially after the director's death. She could imagine people speculating in whispers that she might be guilty. And if that had started yesterday evening in the pub, Toby was probably aware.

'That's right. I'll keep my eyes and ears open. I don't trust Palmer. He's too blinkered.'

Toby nodded. 'I suppose Dot will be amongst the suspects. I keep thinking...' His voice trailed off but at last he spoke again: 'I'm sure she wouldn't do it.'

Eve watched his chest rise and fall. 'What were you going to say, before that?'

'I just remember my mum warning us about wolfsbane once, when Dot was here in Saxford, visiting Babs. We found some growing in a ditch and Dot said how pretty it was and picked some for me. We got back to my flat and put them in a vase, and Mum happened to drop in while Dot was still there. She made us wash our hands.' He smiled for a moment. 'She's always been a worrier.'

Eve had only met her once. She and Toby's dad had moved to County Durham shortly before Eve arrived in Saxford.

Toby's eyes met Eve's. 'I mean, I don't suppose Dot even remembers that now. It was a few years ago.' He was twisting his watch absently with his right hand.

But Eve didn't agree. Picking the flowers implied she'd fancied Toby back then, even if it was only a holiday flirtation. Accidentally giving him a poisonous present would have stuck in her mind. 'Even if she does, I'm sure plenty of other people would recognise the plant too. The papers seem to have articles warning about poisonous flowers each summer. And she's not the only one to have fallen out with Rufus.'

The vulnerable look in Toby's eye made Eve want to reassure him, but the talk left her uneasy. If he was truly convinced of Dot's innocence, he wouldn't have felt the need to offload the story about the wolfsbane.


Immediately after breakfast, Eve wrote the notes she'd promised Robin, covering everything they'd discussed the day before in detail. She looked at the timeline she'd created:

**7.40 p.m. (approx.):** Isla Quinn and Drew Fawcett leave the Cross Keys (after agreeing to go over the following day's schedule)

**7.45 p.m. (approx.):** Dot Hampshire and Kip Clayton leave the Cross Keys (Kip pretty drunk)

**8.45 p.m.:** Dot and Kip arrive back at Watcher's Wood (According to Dot. Long walk, and Kip was drunk. A brisk walker could have done it in fifty minutes, but sounds plausible.) Dot sees Drew and Isla in Isla's trailer

**8.45 p.m.:** Rufus signs into internet banking in his trailer

**8.48 p.m.:** or thereabouts. Dot leaves for her long walk, assuming she only spent a few minutes bundling Kip into his trailer (and that she's telling the truth)

**8.50 p.m.:** Rufus cancels direct debit to Cassie

**8.53 p.m.:** Rufus reaches the vestry. (Earliest possible time. And he was drunk. Might have been slower.)

**9.20 p.m.:** Brooke and Margot pass house beyond the stables on their way back from the pub. (Seen by occupants. More than ten minutes' walk away from Watcher's Wood. Couldn't have arrived back before Rufus was killed.)

**9.30 p.m.:** Rufus's phone alarm goes off. (Police guess he was dead by this time and his murderer gone from the vestry.)

**Later than 9.30 p.m.:** Dot arrives back from her walk. (If she's telling the truth about where she went and how quickly she left. The point she reached was at least 25 minutes away.)

**9.45 p.m.:** Saskia Thomas sees Rick Sutton peering at her. (He claims he went straight to her trailer from his chalet and returned there immediately afterwards. She claims she never left her trailer.)

The timing was all so tight. Surely that had to trip the murderer up, sooner or later? And what if Rick Sutton had lied about going straight from his chalet to Saskia's trailer? He could have been involved in the killing, or if he hadn't, he might have seen something vital.

Not long after breakfast, Detective Inspector Nigel Palmer came to bother Eve. She'd ceased to be amazed at how often he visited her when he must be busy, and a detective constable would be more appropriate. She knew he'd want to warn her off in person. He probably imagined he'd have more effect than his subordinates, but he was wrong. Eve couldn't let this case go. Whatever she thought of Rufus, she might have saved him if she'd acted decisively, and the case affected her friends too. Toby had looked seriously anxious that morning. His previous connection with Dot might have been fleeting, but he was clearly fond of her.

Gus fixed the inspector with an unfriendly stare the moment he showed up on the doorstep. That and the suspicious way he sniffed the inspector's shoes said a lot about the way the dachshund viewed him.

*You and me both, buddy.*

Eve stood back to let the inspector in and he sank down onto one of her treasured couches, causing its springs to groan in protest. There was a distasteful, meditative look in his eye as though she was a fly on his bowl of trifle and he was working out how best to swat her.

'So, here we are again, Ms Mallow. I understand you were at Watcher's Wood when Rufus Beaumont's body was found.'

Eve nodded. He made it sound as though she'd been lurking behind the trailers, carrying the cushion the director had been smothered with. 'I was fetching the cake trays Viv Montague and I had left there the day before.'

He fixed her with a beady stare. 'The timing was very convenient.'

Eve tried to relax her shoulders. 'It was chance.'

'Tell me exactly who you saw, where they were and what they said.'

Eve ran through the order of events. She could remember every detail now, having noted them down and relayed them to Robin.

'You sound almost rehearsed,' Palmer said.

Just like Dot Hampshire. His tone made Eve's teeth grind. 'As you can imagine, it's been playing on my mind. It was such a shock.'

Palmer looked at her, his head on one side. 'Yet from what I understand, you were already worried for Mr Beaumont's safety. You immediately recognised the flowers he'd been sent as' – he glanced at his notes – '*Aconitum*, otherwise known as wolfsbane or monkshood. How is it that you're so familiar with them? I understand there's some talk in Saxford of you having slipped them into Beaumont's trailer yourself.'

Blast Moira and whoever she'd talked to. 'I didn't.'

'It wouldn't be unnatural. You're single after all.'

Eve shot up out of her seat before she could stifle the instinct. It wouldn't be quite so bad if he was trying to goad her to get a response, but Palmer really did think like that. 'I resent what you're suggesting. I'm very happy with my life and I didn't have a crush on Rufus Beaumont. If I had, I wouldn't have risked his or my safety by gathering such a dangerous plant.'

'Unless your feelings weren't reciprocated, perhaps.'

'I barely knew him.' She sat down again now and tried to appear relaxed, though she knew it was too late for that. The thought that she'd betrayed her anger infuriated her.

'Can you think of anyone else who might have wanted him dead?'

'I didn't want him dead, so the use of "else" is inappropriate.' Eve thought of Dot Hampshire and Kip Clayton. 'And no, I can't.'

'Very well then, that's all. For now.'

Eve half expected him to tell her not to leave town, but he stuck to warning her to mind her own business after asking if she'd be writing Rufus Beaumont's obituary.

She wouldn't cooperate on that, either.


Eve stomped round Elizabeth's Cottage, getting ready for that day's shift at Monty's and slamming things to try to rid her system of the adrenaline Palmer had caused. She snapped out of it when she accidentally made Gus jump.

'Sorry, buddy.' She bent down to cuddle him. 'You had to suffer him too and your behaviour is exemplary. I shall follow your example.' *As best I can…*

For a moment, she wondered if she should have told Palmer what she knew about Dot and Kip, but on reflection her conscience was clear. The tensions had been plain for all to see. Palmer wouldn't be depending on her for information.

A little later, Eve left for Monty's, ready to do her shift. She tried to relax her shoulders as she walked; she didn't want the Palmer-induced tension to affect her concentration.

She was just about to cross Love Lane towards the teashop when she saw Saskia Thomas emerge from a white Renault. She looked bent under her sorrow, her long hair lank and falling forwards. If she was heading to the village store, Moira would be beside herself. In Saskia's place, Eve would have opted to shop elsewhere, but she probably didn't know who'd be lurking behind the counter.

Eve glanced at her watch. She was ten minutes early for her shift. Well, twelve, actually. It was par for the course. She felt triumphant. At times like this, her cautious nature paid dividends. She had time to follow her instincts, and this was too good an opportunity to miss.

By the time she'd reached the store, Saskia already had her basket half full. She must be in a hurry, or maybe Moira's questions were increasing her sense of urgency. The young woman turned as the old-fashioned bell jangled when the door opened, and murmured a greeting to Eve. Her eyes were red and bloodshot.

'Ah, Eve, you're here too.' Moira sounded disappointed. She'd probably envisaged a solo grilling session. 'I was just expressing my sympathy to poor, dear Saskia. What a thing to happen, especially now the police have confirmed it's... Well, anyway, if there's anything at all we in the village can do,' she turned to the actress, 'you've only to ask.'

Saskia nodded her thanks. Eve had a feeling speech was beyond her. Maybe Moira realised it too. She gave the actress's hand a quick motherly squeeze when she reached the counter, and Eve remembered why, deep down, she was fond of the storekeeper.

Moira rang up Saskia's items on her old-fashioned till.

'Let's see, that's five pounds ninety for the flowers,' she paused, 'seven fifty for the wine' – more tapping – 'two seventy-five for the cordial, three pounds for the grapes, and... just seventy pence for the newspaper. All done. So that'll be nineteen pounds eighty-five all told.'

Saskia paid, her head low, hair falling forward over her eyes. Eve saw her lips move as she turned to leave, but her farewell was inaudible.

'Poor dear,' Moira said with a heavy sigh as they watched Saskia head towards her car. 'You know, I honestly don't think she should be driving in that state.'

Eve felt guiltily opportunistic. It was the perfect excuse to go and talk to the actress, and Moira was probably right. Accidents were common after a bereavement. Saskia hadn't far to go if she was heading back to Watcher's Wood, but the lanes were narrow. She might land herself in a ditch.

'I'll go and have a word with her.' Eve returned the bottle of milk she'd been about to buy to the fridge. 'Maybe she'll agree to a cup of tea at Monty's before she heads off. Or if she has the right insurance, I could drive her.' Eve knew Viv would forgive her lateness under the circumstances. 'I'll come back for my shopping.'

Moira bit her lip as Eve turned to leave the store. Eve knew her kind instincts, genuine though they were, would be mixed with a good dose of fear of missing out. Eve was just the same, of course. She wanted information for other reasons, but neither she nor the storekeeper were pure.

A moment later she'd caught Saskia up as she put her shopping into the boot of her Renault.

'I'm so sorry. I don't want to intrude when you're grieving, but you look so upset and it must all be a terrible shock. Would you like me to drive you back?'

Eve saw the young woman swallow. 'No. But thank you.' Her voice was very low.

'Or you could pause for a cup of tea at Monty's to steady you?' Eve indicated the teashop behind her.

'I heard you're writing Rufus's obituary.'

Eve could imagine how she must have come across: a sneaky hack, after the dirt. And how could she expect Saskia to think anything else?

'I am, but I'll only interview people who're happy to talk. It's against my principles to trick people into giving confidences.' Not in order to put them in print, anyway. To solve a murder, she made her morals a little more elastic. 'I don't have to sit with you. I'm due to start my shift there in a minute.' Saskia really did look wrung out.

But at Eve's words the actress took a deep breath. 'No, I'd like to speak with you. The police asked me so many questions yesterday I thought I'd never want to talk again, but this is different. I want to be quoted in Rufus's obituary. There are things I'd like to say.'

# CHAPTER ELEVEN

Eve and Saskia crossed the green, the smell of grass and earth rising in the sun.

Outside Monty's, the white-painted ironwork tables were already set, ready for the first customers. The colourful bunting in the bay windows gave the place a permanent holiday atmosphere. Inside, Eve found the space was relatively cool. Someone had propped the front and rear doors open and a large fan stirred the air. The cerise tablecloths shifted slightly in the breeze.

Viv shot them a glance when they entered the teashop, then whispered something to her son, Sam, who nodded quickly and smiled at Eve.

'Mum said you might like the table nearest the river. And she insists you're not to worry about the schedule.'

The schedule that Eve herself had created, which said she should be working. Eve usually stuck to it fiercely and felt shifty now, though she knew there was an element of self-interest in Viv's suggestion. The more information Saskia shared, the better the quality of news she'd get later. And Eve couldn't help noticing that Sam's girlfriend Kirsty was on duty, as well as Angie, one of their regular college-student helpers. Kirsty hadn't been on Eve's rota. Viv must have requested backup, to give Eve time to gossip. It wasn't the first time she'd pulled that stunt.

Saskia refused cakes. Eve knew it would perturb Viv, but she followed suit. She couldn't munch her way through the teashop's summer selection when Saskia was suffering so badly. Sam took their order for a pot of Assam. At least it ought to give the woman time to recover herself a little.

'Margot says the obituary will appear in *Icon*?' Saskia sat forward in her chair, her head in her hands, elbows on the cerise tablecloth, which matched Viv's current hair colour.

'That's right. I do a lot of work for them.'

The actress shook her head. 'I'd never have guessed you were a journalist. I know you and your friend as suppliers of cakes – I thought that was your job.'

Viv happened to be passing at that moment and nodded her approval. She was occasionally tormented by people who regarded her vocation as some kind of light-hearted hobby that happened to make money.

'The two jobs provide a good balance, but it's Viv who's the creative genius behind this place.'

Her friend was beaming now.

A second later, Sam delivered their tea. The stylishly mismatched crockery they were given was a Monty's trademark. The pieces were expertly chosen by Viv, and went together perfectly. In the centre of their table sat a jam jar decorated with a shocking-pink ribbon, containing cornflowers.

Saskia slumped forward in her chair, elbows on the table, as though her whole body felt heavy. 'What do you normally ask people?'

Eve took out her notepad. 'It would be great to know how you met Rufus. Was it when you came to audition?'

Saskia shook her head. 'He came to see me before that, in a play called *Highs and Lows*. I couldn't believe it when he asked for me at the stage door.' Her eyes were glistening. 'He said I was the best young actress he'd seen in years. He just wanted to tell me. The excitement I felt... And then, when *Last of the Lindens* came up, he contacted my agent to ask me to audition.' She shook her head. 'I could see him and Isla arguing over it after I'd tried out. Immediate whispers, subtle, but not subtle enough. But he convinced her, and she's a tough cookie. I felt invincible when he won her over; I was soaring.'

Eve could see how high she still felt from that intense start to their association, but it was all down to him recognising her talent. She didn't mention fancying or even liking him immediately. But Eve guessed it might be easy to feel a strong attraction to someone who championed your work and propelled you into a new world, one you'd always wanted to occupy. She could imagine Saskia confusing passion for her future with passion for Rufus.

'What was he like as a person?' Eve poured tea for them both.

Saskia took a deep, juddering breath. 'Exciting. Inspiring. Demanding. He opened me up to new ideas.'

All comments on their working relationship. 'And when you weren't talking about acting?'

Saskia's eyes widened. 'We were always talking about it.'

It seemed to confirm Eve's opinion. If it hadn't been for Saskia's drive and Rufus's belief in her talent, would their relationship have developed? 'The method acting sounded exacting.'

Tears filled her eyes. 'It was such a novel idea to me: to go to those lengths. His passion for art made me feel that same willingness to make sacrifices. I suddenly saw my chosen career as a calling. It was as though he'd given me permission to treat it seriously. Not that I didn't work hard before, but that kind of commitment is different.' She pulled a tissue from her pocket and blew her nose. 'I was glad to do it. My family understood. And he held out the promise of a spectacular career.'

Eve nodded.

Saskia's right hand was clenched tight now, her knuckles white. 'I know word's got out that we were close.' She looked at Eve, her eyes damp. 'But that was irrelevant to our working relationship.

He didn't make a habit of sleeping with his lead actresses. He was a decent man. And a workaholic, he and Isla both.'

At the words 'decent man', Eve thought of his wife, but she pushed away snap judgements. All the same, it made her feel Saskia was blinkered at the very least. If a man had been unfaithful once, why would you assume it wasn't his habit? Saskia struck her as someone who'd been on cloud nine and failed to look down. But maybe Eve was just being cynical. Either way, the actress's words gave her the opening she needed. A chance to dig for concrete personal information…

'It was so unlucky that Moira spotted you and Rufus together. You must have been very careful up until that point, assuming your relationship had been going on for a while?'

Saskia tucked a strand of her long, straight hair behind one ear and sipped her tea before nodding. 'Two and a half months.'

The sort of duration you could still measure in weeks; not dissimilar to Eve and Robin. Saskia could probably quote the number of days. And it wasn't as though they'd been friends beforehand. There'd been no time for them to really get to know each other. Certainly not outside the pressure-cooker atmosphere created by filming.

'It was unlucky,' Saskia went on, 'being caught kissing like that. I'd had some bad news, and his sympathy for me overcame his usual reticence.' She shook her head. 'I even held back – it felt wrong to be comforted – but I gave in.' She bit her lip, then took a deep breath and met Eve's eyes.

'That's understandable. I'm sorry about your news.'

Saskia nodded, but didn't elaborate.

Under the circumstances, it seemed telling that they hadn't been together while everyone was at the Cross Keys. Assuming Saskia was telling the truth.

Palmer's suspicions about the actress ran through Eve's mind. She still hadn't seen her motive for murder. But if they hadn't made plans to spend the evening together, maybe the police were right and they'd fallen out before Rufus's death. And love that was built on shared passion, that had flared up so quickly, might not last. It was worth pushing to get more.

'I'm so sorry for your loss. You must wish you'd arranged to be together on Saturday night.'

Saskia nodded. 'I hoped he might come to my trailer, at least by late evening, but I wasn't entirely surprised when he didn't.' She took out a fresh tissue from a packet in her bag and dabbed her eyes. 'He'd had this awful row with Isla before she went off to the pub. Several of us overheard him shouting at her.

'And then I glimpsed him leaving her trailer and he looked awful. White-faced, really upset. I saw him like that once before, after some horrible negative press in one of the Sunday papers. It was best to leave him be when he was in that frame of mind.' She shook her head. 'I wish to God I'd gone to find him now.'

It meant their instinct hadn't been to talk to each other in times of trouble: he after his row, she after her news. Rufus had kissed Saskia to comfort her, but his support hadn't gone deeper. 'I'm so sorry.' Eve topped up their teas. Saskia sounded honest, but Eve reminded herself she was sitting opposite a first-class actress.

'Saskia,' Eve leaned forward, her voice low, 'you won't know this if you didn't realise about my regular work, but I've written obituaries about murder victims before.'

The actress leaned towards her, her eyes widening a little.

'It tends to put me at the heart of some very strained situations, and I tread carefully, as you can imagine. I find it's best to prepare myself. Do you have any idea who might have killed Rufus?'

If he'd confided in her, even if it was only about other people on set, she might have crucial information.

Saskia swallowed. 'It's so hard imagining anyone doing such a thing, but I know how jealous Kip was. People keep saying Rufus had a temper, but Kip does too. I could imagine him losing control.' She looked down at her lap. 'Kip behaved like he owned me. If I'd understood his character better, I'd never have gone out with him in the first place.'

Eve waited a moment, then asked gently: 'Do you think Kip knew you were in a relationship with Rufus before Moira gave the game away?'

'I don't know. It's possible.'

If so, Kip must have kept his feelings under wraps, despite the temper Saskia described. It didn't seem likely to Eve, but maybe he'd released his pent-up feelings in secret, just as he had when he'd spat in the director's drink. It wasn't impossible.

Saskia's eyes were on the river now. 'If it weren't for Isla's alibi, I'd wonder about her too. She's been down on me and Rufus. And whatever she said to him the evening he died, he looked all but destroyed by it.' She turned back to Eve and her jaw was tense. 'But it can't be her. And in all honesty, I don't really believe Kip did it either. Losing control is one thing; carefully planning a murder is another.'

Eve let the silence ride for a moment. There were an awful lot of tensions in the team. Finding out the real cause of the argument felt crucial.

'You mentioned there was something you wanted to tell me. For the obituary, I mean.'

Saskia closed her striking blue eyes for a second, then nodded. 'It feels wrong in some ways. I know Rufus's wife must be devastated after what's happened, but equally our affair's likely to come out anyway. It was all round the site half an hour after your friend saw us together.'

Eve wondered what she was building up to. 'I'm afraid you're right. I certainly won't pass it on, but things like that have a habit of leaking out.'

In truth, knowing about it put Eve in a conflicted position. She was against airbrushing the history of people she wrote about, but equally not a fan of making the lives of surviving relatives more upsetting than they already were. Her solution would likely be to say something general about the relationships Rufus had had over his lifetime, so people got a sense of his character without knowing the specifics.

Saskia looked earnest now. 'I guessed it would end up in the papers,' she said. 'And that being the case, Cassie Beaumont will hear about it anyway. So, I wanted to let you know, for the record, that Rufus was going to leave his wife for me. Not immediately, I don't mean, but that was the plan. He was waiting for the right moment to tell Cassie, but we were going to marry. I'd like people to know. It was part of his history and if I don't speak out, it will feel like I'm denying the seriousness of our relationship.'

Five minutes later, Eve watched Saskia Thomas walk from the teashop, back to her Renault by the village green. She drove off, heading out of Saxford towards the Old Toll Road, rather than back in the direction of Watcher's Wood.

'I love it that you skipped off work to talk to an interviewee. Does that mean I can muck around with the schedule too?' Viv had moved to stand next to her.

'Only if it's because there's been a murder. Besides, you already did, today, when you brought Kirsty in.'

'Touché. What's up anyway? You look like a mole that's had a flashlight thrust in its face.'

'Gee, thanks. And not here. You still haven't honed your whispering skills.'

Viv tutted and scurried after Eve into the kitchen, where she filled her in as she put on her apron. Everything that had come from Robin she passed off as 'rumour'.

Viv whistled. 'So, the police think she was hassling Rufus to get a divorce and he was putting her off, but Saskia says it was game on.'

Eve nodded.

'Conclusions?'

She shrugged. 'She might be talking out of pride, I suppose. It's clearly what she wanted. But honestly, she spoke with such conviction, I had the impression she believed it. If that's right, she'd hardly have killed him, but it almost seems like she's out of touch with reality. She keeps saying what a decent man Rufus was, yet they'd only been in a relationship for two and a half months. And their affair seems based entirely on professional thrill – his at finding someone so talented, I guess, and hers at being spotted. It sounded intense, but not founded on anything solid. That will be enough to keep her on my radar.'

Viv nodded sagely. 'I see your point. Anything else?'

'She was using patterned tissues but the design doesn't match the one I saw in Kip Clayton's bin. She could have bought a new packet, but she was clearly fixated on Rufus and done with Kip. So I think he slept with someone else, the night before I sneaked into his trailer.'

'Nice deduction.'

'Thank you. And finally, I'm curious to know where Saskia's just driven off to. Not back to the production site, clearly.'

'The police station in Blyworth? They might have called her in.'

'But then why do her shopping on the way?'

Viv frowned. 'True.'

'Either way, she's just made things more complicated, not less. She was right down at the bottom of my list of suspects, but I wonder if I was too hasty.'

# CHAPTER TWELVE

Once Eve had added an unattractive blue hairnet to her outfit, in addition to her apron, she was ready to start baking.

'You're on raspberry cupcakes with the dark chocolate ganache, by the way.' Viv was giving her a recipe she'd done many times before. It was another tactic she used when she wanted Eve to focus on passing on gossip.

'Yes, ma'am.' Eve began to weigh out her flour as Viv set to chopping some pistachios.

'So, now you need to fill me in on everything you found out yesterday afternoon.'

Eve started off with the most concrete details, such as who had been at Watcher's Wood at the time of the murder, and who had alibis. Once again, she glossed over where she'd got the details. The Saxford rumour mill was a useful standby, and she explained Palmer had been to visit. He often let things slip too.

'And then, through my research, I got some interesting background. Rufus attended the Ryland School of Drama – not unnatural, I suppose. He was following in the footsteps of his parents and elder siblings.'

'Yes.' Viv snorted. 'I can't imagine him going into accountancy.'

'Quite.' Eve raised her sieve high over her mixing bowl and began to sift the flour. 'But in fact, he didn't act for long. He was offered a good supporting role in an art-house film just before he finished his degree. He rolled straight from studying into that. But by the time he was twenty-six he'd switched to directing, like his mother.

Only for Rufus, it was much earlier in his career and to television rather than film.' She shot Viv a sideways glance. 'He was crazily young to land such a key role and there were some nasty rumours about the way he got it. His mother was close friends with the producer who hired him, apparently. But everyone acknowledges how good he was.'

Viv was preparing to weigh some butter now. She'd had it on the worktop and her knife slid through it without pressure. The day was even hotter than the one before. 'I wonder why he made the switch to directing.'

'I found an interview on YouTube where he was enthusing about it; he said he loved creating a whole package.' Eve visualised Rufus as he'd spoken, sitting back in a deep red sofa, one leg crossed lazily over the other. He'd chuckled and said he enjoyed being in charge too. The woman interviewing him looked caught up by his charm, laughing when he laughed, touching her hair. *Honestly…* 'But maybe it was a combination of things. Although he got that early part – to rave reviews – his acting career seemed to coast a bit after that. Lots of small roles, but nothing earth-shattering.

'But it feels like he landed on his feet with the career switch. He's got a reputation for backing complete unknowns for leading roles and getting them to produce something brilliant. It looks as though he was about to do that with Saskia, and he did it with Dot too. Though obviously they each brought their own talent to the party.'

'You don't think he gave Saskia the part just because he fancied her then?'

Eve frowned. 'No. I'm not saying he wasn't influenced by that, but I don't think he'd have risked basing his judgement on anything but professional promise. His career meant too much to him.' Eve could relate to that at least. She never compromised with her obituaries either. She'd do her absolute best, every time she took on a job. 'The interesting thing,' she went on, 'is that he seemed to distance himself from the stars he nurtured as soon as they made it big.'

Viv pushed her hairnet up with the back of her hand. 'Perhaps he got bored – felt his work was done?'

'Maybe, but I've got it noted as oddity number one. It seems a bit self-defeating. He and Isla could have kept up relationships with a host of talented artists. Instead, they're off making their mark elsewhere. Cecilia Dunwoody's a case in point.'

Viv raised an eyebrow. 'She was one of theirs? Didn't she win an Oscar?'

Eve nodded. 'And she still does TV as well as film, yet she's never featured in another Quinn and Beaumont production. And it's not just her: Dot's the first successful actor I could find who's worked with them twice, and her new role is a demotion, which is oddity number two.'

'Maybe she's difficult to work with. I get that it must have been hard to take Rufus's criticisms, but she seems pretty bolshy.'

'True. But if she's that bad, why cast her at all? Either she's such a good actress that Isla and Rufus put up with her temperament, or maybe she's not the problem.' Eve added baking powder to her flour and began to crack eggs into a bowl.

'But if it was Rufus causing trouble, then here's oddity number three. Why did Dot agree to take a lesser part and stick around to be browbeaten? She got amazing reviews and her BAFTA after she played the lead in *The Pedestal*. I'd have thought she'd have her pick of roles.'

Viv frowned. 'It does seem odd. Maybe things changed between them. Could they have had a fling that fell by the wayside when Saskia appeared on the scene? In fact, if it's mainly actresses we're talking about, maybe that accounts for the breakdown in relations with the rest too. Perhaps he's a serial womaniser.'

'I'd wondered that.' Eve added the eggs and some caster sugar to her mix. 'Whatever the case, I think Dot had an odd relationship with Rufus and there's a lot more to uncover.

'Speaking of him being a womaniser, I did find some information about Rufus's love life. It doesn't relate to the people he cast, but it might support the idea of him as a heartbreaker.'

Viv shook her head. 'I had a feeling he might fall into that category.' She was working with eggs too, breaking them into her mixing bowl without looking, an action that always made Eve feel inferior.

Eve passed on the story of Rufus's steamy affair with the married actress, and the one about his alcoholic ex-girlfriend, Emily, who'd died falling down the stairs. 'She acted too, but their connection was personal, not professional. The article which mentioned her quoted a producer, Stefan Meyer, who said she would have made it big if it hadn't been for her problems.'

'And they put those down to Rufus?'

Eve nodded. She could still visualise the photograph of the dead woman: slender and blue-eyed in a strap top, her elegant neck emphasised by a black leather necklace with a silver bead. She'd been a little like Saskia, physically.

'That's so sad.'

Eve nodded. She wondered how Cassie Beaumont had felt, reading the piece. The writer had presented it as a profile of her and her husband's successful marriage, yet dredged up those details. Cassie probably didn't like journalists much, which would make Eve's job difficult when she came to ask for an interview.

Viv was busy with her whisk. 'So, on the upside, we think Rufus was charming, as well as devoted to promoting new talent. But he was also a probable philanderer who made people jealous. And his odd relationship with his actresses might be related to that.'

'*Mostly* charming. But on the whole I'd say that sums it up nicely. It means I mustn't lose focus on Dot or Cassie – despite

Cassie being further flung, geographically. And I guess it suggests it's possible there was some problem between him and Saskia too. But I didn't see any hint of it in her eyes. My hunch is not.

'But it'll be a challenge, working out who's telling the truth. Even Isla's got acting experience – I wouldn't be surprised if most of the crew have stepped on stage at one time or another. They're probably all experts at fooling people.'

As Eve left Monty's, she glanced at the village store and spotted Moira peering out. Of course, Eve had whisked Saskia from under her nose, which must have left the woman frustrated. A moment later, she emerged onto the pavement opposite the green and waved. Eve considered just waving back, but it was too cruel. Some kind of non-committal update was in order.

'Thank you for looking after Saskia,' Moira said breathlessly as Eve approached her. 'How did you get on? You had a long chat about the obituary, I suppose?'

Eve nodded. 'I think talking might have helped. She seemed calmer when she left.' She wanted to avoid specifics. She wasn't sure what she'd write yet; it all depended on what other information came out. Balancing evidence would allow her to form a judgement.

'I wondered,' Moira went on, 'only, I've had a couple of members of the production team in, and of course there's been gossip.'

Moira would have done her utmost to extract it. 'I guess it's natural.'

The woman nodded. 'It's not just them, of course. Half the villagers have visited to tell me what they think.' She shook her head. 'Poor Babs.' There was just a hint of pleasurable speculation behind her concerned mask. 'Most of them are convinced Dot Hampshire must be guilty. And although I really am sure she would never…

well, of course she wouldn't, but… Anyway, you can see why they think that. She made her dislike of Rufus so very clear.'

Eve's stomach twisted in sympathy for the actress. But what Moira said was true. 'And what about the people from the production?'

'Oh yes!' She leaned forward, appearing to remember her purpose. 'One of them told me dear Saskia was hoping Rufus would marry her. Poor girl. I mean, I'm not "of that world" shall we say, but I do hear a lot via Babs Lewis and I know there are an awful lot of affairs in showbusiness. I imagine Rufus Beaumont had a series of lovers.' She put her head on one side. 'He was very good-looking of course, but I suspect Saskia would have been disappointed by him in the end.'

'You mentioned more than one person coming in?'

The storekeeper nodded. 'Well, that's right, and it was honestly quite painful to watch the other gentleman. It was Kip Clayton, you know, the camera operator. He came in first thing. I understand he was Saskia's boyfriend until she took up with Rufus. Though I'm honestly not sure she'd have been any better off with him.' She frowned as though someone had put her in charge of the problem, then shook her head. 'He bought two bottles of whisky and lit a cigarette the instant he got outside, before the door was even closed. And this was at seven thirty in the morning, if you please.'

'He might have been planning ahead.' Eve didn't imagine he'd manage two bottles at breakfast time. 'And meaning to share the drink with the others at Watcher's Wood, perhaps?' Though after his performance at the Cross Keys, perhaps not.

Moira frowned. 'It's possible, I suppose.' She hesitated. 'I happened to go outside just after he left, to adjust the store's sign.'

She did that, when there was anything interesting going on.

'And he was making a call on his mobile. As he walked off, I heard him say, "Saskia!" in a desperate way, but then nothing more. A moment later he looked at his phone and then threw it on the ground! I imagine she must have hung up when she heard his voice. It's not that I don't feel for him. No one's ever called me unsympathetic. But you know me, Eve: I'm good at reading people's feelings,' she shook her head, 'and he clearly has trouble controlling his anger.'

Eve would have picked up on that too.

# CHAPTER THIRTEEN

Back at Elizabeth's Cottage in the early afternoon, Eve went to the kitchen and opened the back door. Gus pottered towards the garden, his paws tapping on the brick floor.

A short while later, she followed him outside and sat at the ironwork table with the coffee and sandwich she'd made. Close by, a blackbird was singing in her gnarled old apple tree and the air was heady with the scent of roses, honeysuckle and jasmine.

She frowned. 'I definitely need to interview Kip Clayton, Gus, but I doubt he'll be keen on the idea. It might be best to make the request in person. If he's prickly I can try to talk him round.

'As for Saskia, I've had second thoughts since we went to see Robin. I wonder if she became obsessed with Rufus and developed a skewed view of their relationship.' But did the facts point to her killing because of it?

Eve reviewed the order of events. She was kissing him passionately the day before he died, then half an hour later he found the wolfsbane in his trailer. She sighed. 'I suppose it's possible Saskia gave Rufus the flowers if he'd told her he'd never leave his wife. Passion's a strange thing. She might have been sufficiently fixated to give in when he tried to kiss her, yet still have hated him enough to kill him the following day. And Moira did say she held back initially. But I still don't think she'd have got that despairing, that quickly, despite her intensity. If he'd been stringing her along for years, it would be a different matter.'

Gus had been looking at her intently, which left her feeling gratified, but now, in the middle of her sentence, he turned and darted towards the hedge at the bottom of the garden. It was one of his favourite places: full of intriguing rustles made by creatures who stayed just out of his reach.

Eve sighed and got up to follow him. His front half was obscured by hedge, his rear end sticking out, legs tensed.

'And then there's Kip. Delivering the flowers as a jealous reaction to Rufus and Saskia's kiss just doesn't make sense. It would have taken time to gather them, and I can't see his first reaction being to dash off into the woods to gather poisonous plants.'

But Kip could have got wind of the affair earlier. He might have had the flowers ready, chosen to point the finger at a woman. Eve could imagine him having a stereotypical idea of the opposite sex, but picturing him doing the planning was still hard. So perhaps it was Dot then – ground down by Rufus's behaviour. Her mind flitted again to Toby's tale of how she'd unwittingly gathered wolfsbane a few years ago.

Whoever was responsible, they needn't have picked the flowers immediately before delivering them. The accompanying note had been damp in one corner. Maybe they'd been kept in a vase for a while.

As Gus reversed out of the hedge at last, looking thwarted, Eve's mobile rang.

A number she didn't recognise came up on the screen and when she answered, it was Dot Hampshire herself on the line.

'I hear you're writing Rufus's obituary,' the actress said. 'Can we meet?'


Eve walked with Gus to reach the beach by Watcher's Wood, where Dot Hampshire had suggested they talk. Eve imagined she wanted privacy. She'd heard the main site entrance was crowded with press, clamouring for quotes and craning for photographs. Inside, the atmosphere was probably just as oppressive. Eve imagined the rumours and accusations were flying.

She walked Gus through the trees, close to the beach, the smell of warm earth and leaf matter stirred up by their feet. It was interesting that Dot had called her up so quickly. 'I wonder if she's got an agenda, just like Saskia Thomas,' she said out loud.

Ahead of them, through the sun-dappled space, they could see the sea. Gus tore ahead of her now. She guessed he'd caught the smell of salt on the wind, like she had. She dashed to catch up and spotted Dot Hampshire's lone figure on the shingle-strewn sand. Glancing round, she judged the actress had made it there without any reporters in pursuit. Her fair hair was blowing in the breeze. She wasn't classically beautiful like Saskia, but just as attractive. Her face was expressive, full of character and interest. She was wearing a black shift dress and sandals.

'Thank you for calling me,' Eve said. 'It'll be great to get your memories of Rufus.' At Dot's wry look she held up a hand. 'I gathered you weren't his number-one fan, but it's my job to give a balanced view. I'll be glad to hear your thoughts, whatever they are.'

'Thanks.' The woman gave Gus a quick pat, then started up the beach. Eve kept pace with her.

'I was keen to talk to you, to set the record straight,' Dot said. 'I've been in and out of police interviews since Rufus died, being constantly interrupted and having my words twisted.' She raised an eyebrow. 'And I know what they're saying about me in the village. My aunt's friends are the worst of the lot. The fact that they've known me for years counts for nothing.' She gave a bitter laugh, but it sounded strained. Eve had a hunch she was genuinely hurt. 'Or maybe it's the impression I've created. Either way, I'm top entertainment as far as they're concerned. But Toby told me I can trust you – that your reputation's good. And that you've written about murder victims before. Worked out the truth. I thought it might be refreshing to meet someone who hasn't made up their mind yet.'

'Thanks.'

'You might have heard I went off for a walk when I got back from the pub the night Rufus died. You can bet your life I wish I hadn't now. The local detective inspector thinks it's suspicious, but it happens to be the truth. Rufus had been winding me up, and then I felt duty-bound to try to get Kip back to his trailer before he disgraced himself in front of the extras. Drew asked me if I could manage it. By that stage I was fuming. I just needed an hour or so to walk off my mood. I'd never have slept otherwise.'

It rang true. Eve might have taken a similar approach if it had been her. Running up the beach with Gus was one of her top ways of letting off steam. But Dot had been livid with the murder victim, the night he'd died. Eve couldn't ignore that.

She asked her about playing the lead in *The Pedestal* and was shocked at the similarity between her and Saskia's stories. Rufus had waited outside a studio after a previous performance because he *had* to speak to her. He'd been so excited about her talent. And Eve could see how thrilled she'd been too – at the time. Her eyes sparkled as she remembered.

'And it was great, working with him, at first. Maybe he went off me because I wasn't compliant enough.' Dot turned and gave a quick sardonic smile. 'Saskia's been following his every directorial whim, but I put my foot down when it came to shooting the closing scenes of the show. It was meant to be five years on from the original action and I was supposed to be half starved and close to death. I dieted and everything of course, the weight loss looked realistic and costume got me clothes that accentuated my boniness. Plus there's a lot that can be done with make-up: sunken eyes, hollow cheeks, and all the rest of it. But Rufus said I shouldn't bathe for three weeks before filming, or wash my hair, and to stay up half the night so I was permanently sleep deprived.' She laughed and the sound was harsh. 'I told him I could *act* being a wreck instead. That was kind of the point of my chosen career. And it was too late for him to do anything about it by that stage. It's not as though he could send me packing in the middle of filming. But he was angry.'

'Wasn't he won over when you got such amazing reviews?'

'That was when his behaviour towards me got worse.'

'Because you'd been right, and managed a star performance without following his instructions?'

That sidelong glance again. 'Maybe; though I never told anyone we'd crossed swords, or showed him up. And he lapped up all the adoration as usual. Yet I could tell that our working relationship would never be as good.' She sighed and her shoulders rose and fell. 'There's no point in me pretending we were bosom buddies. Everyone knows that's not the case. If I could have seen the future I might have held on to my temper, covered my feelings, but it's too late now. Heigh-ho. So the police – and probably my aunt and her friends – all think I'm a murderer.'

'It's very early days yet.' Eve paused a moment. 'Who do you think makes the most likely suspect?' Dot knew her background; there was no point in holding back.

The actress paused and dug the toe of her sandal into the sand, her eyes on the horizon. 'Unfortunately, it's probably me. Along with Kip, who's never struck me as a giver of flowers. But if I had to guess who's really guilty?' She sighed. 'I don't know. Rick Sutton makes my skin crawl. He was bouncing around like a schoolkid when the police turned up, though he looked nervous when he realised they wanted to interview him too. He seems very naive. Why he'd deliver the flowers, then kill Rufus, I don't know, but I'd say he's got a passion for drama.'

It was an interesting point. 'Did you see him after he'd finished talking to the police?'

Dot nodded. 'He was grinning inanely again, so he must have thought the exchange had gone well.'

And that was even more interesting. The police had faced him with Saskia's accusation, that he'd been seen outside her trailer, and he'd admitted it. Yet he was still nervous before and happy afterwards. If he had a secret, that told Eve he'd managed to keep it. And what could it be? She'd need to dig deeper. Find out his background, try to work out any previous connection he might have had with Rufus or Saskia.

She turned her mind back to Dot's relationship with the director. 'What made you take a part in *Last of the Lindens*, if working with Rufus was already difficult?' Eve might have understood if she'd been offered the lead, but why suffer for a lesser role?

The actress shook her head. 'For a start, I didn't realise just *how* tricky he was going to be. And although we had our spats, I didn't hold it against Rufus. He still gave me my big break. It was no one's fault that we didn't work well together.'

Eve found it hard to take her at her word. She'd seen how angry the director made her.

'But I also stayed out of loyalty to Isla,' Dot went on. 'I liked the idea of working with her again and I knew it might lead to more opportunities in future.'

But probably not while Rufus lived. He and Isla had come as a pair for the last ten years; he'd have blocked her progress.

'And then there was my reputation. I didn't want to come across as some prima donna who'd only take starring roles. It's an interesting part and totally different from my last one. It was another good, solid opportunity.'

'Good' and 'solid' had a lukewarm feel to them, although Eve knew the profession was an uncertain one, and it could be a risk for any actor to turn down a good job offer. Had that really been enough to convince her, though? Eve didn't quite believe it. Dot was hiding something.

At last, Dot spoke again. 'Of course, the news of Rufus's affair with Saskia is going round like wildfire now. The police think I was jealous of her and angry with Rufus because Saskia had supplanted me in more ways than one, but I sure as hell never slept with him. He was good-looking, but I don't go in for that kind of arrogant swagger. Not my style.'

That, Eve could believe, but it didn't make Dot innocent. She'd still been rejected and that smarted, especially when it was unjust. For a moment, Eve's mind strayed to the day her ex-husband had walked out, but she pushed the thought away.

Dot was a tough cookie with exceptional acting talent, yet her career was stalling. And Rufus seemed to be at the root of that.

# CHAPTER FOURTEEN

That evening after supper, Eve settled down on one of the couches at Elizabeth's Cottage, with each of the leaded casement windows open. A faint breeze stirred the air as she put her feet up and Gus came to join her, squeezing himself between her seat and the coffee table.

'There's no hiding Dot Hampshire's bitterness,' Eve said to him. 'And I can only think she was happy for me to see that. She could have acted her way out of it if she'd wanted. My bet is she's cutting her losses. Everyone saw her clash swords with Rufus so there's no point denying it. If she has something to hide – murder included – being frank about her feelings is probably the best way to seem innocent.'

Gus put his head down on the floor and closed his eyes.

'Tactless.' She sighed. She'd liked Dot. There was something pleasingly robust about the way she dealt with life, but she could still see her cracking in response to constant criticism from Rufus. She had a temper and Eve believed she'd nurse a grudge too – enough to do the planning involved rather than just lashing out. And she was hiding something. Eve didn't buy her reasons for staying on for *Last of the Lindens*, however much Dot respected Isla.

Was there any chance Dot had taken the part so she could keep close to Rufus in order to do him harm? It wasn't impossible. Once again, her thoughts turned to Toby, and the sight of him and Dot chatting over the bar at the Cross Keys. A twinge of anxiety twisted in her chest. She mustn't let her feelings cloud her judgement.

Eve had already updated the obituary and murder-suspect spreadsheets she'd created, and sent an email to Cassie Beaumont, trying to convince her that obituary writers were a whole lot nicer than other journalists. Maybe she'd grant her an interview.

Now she turned to her final job of the day. She was going to watch *Shadows in the Trees*, the film where Rufus had had a supporting role, just after he'd left drama school.

Eve found it hard to switch off after the film had finished, unlike Gus who'd been snoring rhythmically for the past hour. Rufus had played a man devastated after a relationship break-up and Eve had become completely wrapped up in his character's anguish. Instead of going straight to bed, she looked up reviews for the work. A lot of them were stellar (though one or two had said he'd overacted). But as she'd noted before, he'd never garnered the same level of approval again, and had switched to directing instead. Every time he'd been interviewed he'd raved about his career behind the camera, saying how much he preferred it to acting, but Eve suspected he'd made a virtue of necessity. Maybe he wasn't cut out to act. And that might have been hard to take, coming from a family of award-winning stars of stage and screen.

At last, she got up off the couch and went round the ground floor of Elizabeth's Cottage, closing the windows and drawing the curtains. She was in her dining room, unhooking the window catch as she faced the dark back garden, when she caught movement. A shifting of shadows, down in the bushes.

Her heart rate ramped up instantly. She couldn't see anything now, but the shape had seemed way too large for the type of creature Gus normally went after.

A person? She swallowed and peered out. 'Who's there?'

But the only noise she heard was Gus barking. She must have woken him.

With hands that shook, however much she wished they wouldn't, she fastened the window, wishing it had a lock, and pulled the curtains closed.

In seconds she was in the kitchen, shushing Gus and opening the drawer where she kept a torch. The curtains in that room were already drawn, the kitchen in darkness, apart from the light that drifted in from the sitting room. She eased the curtains back and pressed the torch flat to the window to avoid reflections. An instant later the bottom of the garden was bathed in light.

Nothing. The only sound was an extra bark from her dachshund.

Eve dashed upstairs now, with Gus chasing at her heels. All the rooms were unlit, and she looked out of a back window.

By the light of the moon, in the fields that lay behind her house between the estuary and the village, a dark shape was moving swiftly.

It was a long time before Eve managed to sleep that night. She thought about calling Robin but there was nothing he could do, so she emailed him instead. It was relevant information, but it would wait until the morning.

Eve loved her garden, but for the first time ever she wished it had a high wall at the bottom, rather than the hedge and low mesh that stopped Gus going walkabout. They were no match for a determined intruder and the cross-country route provided the perfect way to approach unseen. She spent hours staring up at her bedroom ceiling in the darkness.

The following morning brought a call from Robin, triggered by her email.

'Don't worry. I've calmed down now,' Eve said in response to his concern. 'But I'm going to install a security camera. If they come again, I'll be able to identify them.'

'*Good move. Have you looked for anything they might have left behind? I guess it's too dry for footprints.*'

'Uh-huh.' Eve had been down the garden as soon as it was light, but she'd found nothing.

'*You should report it.*'

But Eve couldn't bear another visit from Palmer. He wouldn't take her seriously, and would make sure none of the others did either. He'd probably be glad if someone finally came and did away with her. She was a thorn in his side.

She rang off. Anger at the intruder, mixed with fear, caused her to feel breathless. Had it been Rufus's killer? Dot and Saskia knew she'd been involved in murder investigations before; word might have got around. Was the guilty party keeping an eye on her?

But it made no sense. They couldn't tell if she was making progress by peering at her from a dark garden. In fact, she couldn't imagine what the intruder's agenda had been. It was yet another mystery to add to her list.

# CHAPTER FIFTEEN

Just after breakfast, Margot Hale called with a catch in her voice to say Isla Quinn would be free for an interview that day. She'd be essential for Eve's obituary of course, but she was an interesting witness for the case too. Despite her alibi, she might shed light on the other suspects, and her argument with Rufus played on Eve's mind. Any drama might be related to his death.

Visiting Watcher's Wood would allow Eve to talk face to face with Kip Clayton too – see if she could persuade him to do an interview. The trouble was, he'd only have negative feelings to share and she guessed he'd be reluctant to detail them, given he was a murder suspect.

Eve would want to speak with Margot at some stage too. Rufus's PA probably knew more about him than most people, but it would have to wait a day or two. She was the linchpin in the production team, busy working on staffing, now they had no director, managing the press and liaising with the commissioning TV company over delays. Apparently the insurers were refusing to cover the production until the police made a breakthrough. It meant the TV company had put their weight behind Palmer's orders for the cast and crew to stay put in Suffolk until the case was solved.

Eve's email to Cassie Beaumont had worked though. She'd received a rather terse reply offering her half an hour the following day. She'd make every minute count.

*

Eve travelled to Watcher's Wood on foot. As she approached the site's main entrance she could see the press were still camped outside, but she managed to hitch up the rose-coloured dress she was wearing and climb over a wall to avoid them. She decided to announce her presence to Rick Sutton before finding Isla. She'd got no excuse to interview him, so invented reasons to chat were useful.

But when Eve reached his chalet, in the clearing beyond the cast and crew's campsite, close to the cool canopy of trees, she found his office door ajar and the room unoccupied.

'Rick?' She stepped inside. Maybe he was out the back in his living quarters. 'Rick? Mr Sutton?' He was around the same age as Eve's son, Nick. It felt weird to address him as 'mister'.

Everything was quiet. Perhaps he really was out after all. He was clearly careless about security, though the door to his accommodation was locked when she tried it. Not that she would have gone in without permission, but it was interesting to know the score.

The sight of his office left her twitching. An in-tray sat full of unopened post. He must have let it accumulate for weeks. After all, most people emailed their messages these days. The screensaver was showing on his computer, so Eve couldn't see what he'd been working on, but instinct told her not much. The light on his answerphone was flashing too, filling her with the urge to play his messages and note them down in order of priority.

Eve moved forward a little and noticed there was a magazine of some sort on his chair, tucked under his desk. The seat was the only thing put away neatly. Glancing over her shoulder, she pulled it out so she could see what it was.

A copy of *Treading the Boards*. The cover featured a close-up of Saskia Thomas, looking straight to camera, her eyes huge.

Eve shivered. It was natural to be star-struck with actors on site, and to be interested in the latest showbiz gossip, but to try to hide your interest and home in on just one person was creepy. She made up her mind to talk to Saskia.

Eve left Sutton's trailer and walked back towards the production team's campsite, cutting through the trees. It was only as she got close to the clearing that she heard raised voices.

Isla. Talking to – she peered round the side of a trailer – Drew Fawcett.

Eve slowed her pace automatically.

'I hadn't expected disloyalty!' Isla was standing tall, her whole body taut. 'We'll talk again.'

Drew stalked off to one of the two-apartment trailers and let himself inside. So, Isla would be in a foul mood for their interview. For a standard obituary, Eve would regret that, but after the murder it might help. She was more likely to speak frankly if she was rattled.

Isla glanced up and saw her then. 'Apologies. A little administrative problem. Come in.' She held the door to her trailer open and Eve stepped inside.

The place was far smarter than Kip Clayton's accommodation. The room Eve entered had a state-of-the-art kitchen area with under-unit lighting and a gleaming built-in oven. The space also had room for a smart dining table for two, a flat-screen television, sofa and a couple of swanky black-and-aluminium chairs besides.

The accommodation said 'top dog'. It was interesting. Glancing round the camping area, Eve had noticed Saskia had a trailer to herself too, whereas Dot, in her supporting role, had one of the smaller apartments in a shared vehicle. It was a very physical way of reminding everyone of the pecking order. Dot could have got herself a leading role on another production, surely, and lived in luxury like Saskia.

'Coffee?' Isla was still on her feet as she motioned Eve to take a chair and moved towards a pot that was already full.

'Thank you. Just black.' Eve took out her notebook and pen.

The woman nodded and poured for the pair of them. 'I'd like to get one thing out of the way immediately.' Yet another person with a message to broadcast. 'I know the rumour mill's going crazy after the row I had with Rufus the evening he died.' She put Eve's coffee on the low table in front of her and sat down on the sofa. 'But there's nothing sinister about it.' She shook her head. 'We were arguing over a future project and Rufus got ludicrously het up about it. I regret that our last conversation ended in a row, but that's what it's like if you're passionate about what you do. I'd rather that than everyone agreeing all the time, which often leads to bland results.'

But the more Eve thought about it, the more the facts didn't fit. If you were arguing the toss over something, you'd expect both parties to raise their voices, not just one. And wouldn't anger and irritation be the natural reaction if you couldn't talk the other person round? Rufus's extreme upset, as witnessed by both Saskia and Margot, seemed to jar with Isla's explanation. He'd drunk himself almost to oblivion, before his killer finished the job.

Isla was watching her closely and Eve wondered if she could guess her thoughts.

A moment later, the producer shrugged, with what Eve judged to be carefully feigned nonchalance. 'We didn't always see eye to eye. And Rufus could make a big deal out of small things. Take the choice of this location for *Last of the Lindens*. He really dug his heels in. He was dead against Suffolk, but you can see for yourself how perfect it is. So lush, green and intense with that feeling of separation from the rest of the world.'

Eve remembered Brooke, the costume supervisor, mentioning Rufus hadn't approved.

'We had a hideous meeting the day after we came for the site viewing,' Isla went on, 'back in the office in London. Everyone argued for this place while Rufus sat with his arms folded saying it had the wrong atmosphere.'

'I must admit, I'd heard that mentioned and I was surprised.'

The producer gave an irritated sigh. 'Naturally. It's a great location. But Rufus wasn't always honest about his reasoning, even to himself. I never got to the bottom of it but I suspect it was something about him, and not Watcher's Wood.'

Bones of contention led Eve neatly to one of the key questions she wanted to ask. 'I wondered what you thought about Rufus's habit of distancing himself from actors once they'd made it big,' she said. 'Was it hard to see Cecilia Dunwoody go on to win an award for another producer?'

Isla raised an eyebrow. 'Moving on wasn't a set policy of his, just tittle-tattle put about by the press. Some reporters have overactive imaginations.' Her tone was carefully controlled, her hands clasped together. 'Cecilia wasn't free to work with us on our next project. But promoting new talent was a shared passion. We became known for it and that makes me proud. Rufus was good at spotting raw promise.'

Eve frowned. This was something she'd need to come back to. She'd drawn the same conclusion as the 'imaginative' reporters. But if it had been Dunwoody's choice not to work with them that might lend weight to Rufus being unprofessional. Once again, Eve wondered if he was a serial womaniser and Cecilia hadn't wanted to stick around.

'Of course, Dot's presence proves we don't excommunicate artists once their careers are established!' Isla went on. 'She's a genius and I'm delighted to work with her again. People will watch *Lindens* simply because she's in it.'

'You and Rufus didn't think she was right for the lead?'

Isla cocked her head. 'No. She doesn't have the ethereal quality we were looking for.'

That was fair enough, but the situation was still weird. Eve wondered how hard to push. 'It's great that Dot stayed on, despite the lesser role. Obviously, I saw the strained side of her relationship with Rufus, but I guess she must have had a lot of time for him underneath it all.'

'I'm sure she did.' Isla folded her arms and Eve could tell that line of enquiry was at an end. Whatever had gone on between Rufus and Dot, the producer didn't want to discuss it. Maybe it would reflect badly on her too.

'So how did you and Rufus come to work together?'

Isla shifted on the sofa, relaxing. 'He approached me about a project. *More Fruit in the Orchard*. You remember it?'

Eve nodded, glad that she'd revised her and Rufus's output as part of her initial research.

'I normally initiate my own projects, then pick my team, but I was caught up in his passion for the idea.'

'It was an amazing series.'

'Thank you.' She waved a hand, almost impatient at the compliment. She must hear them so often. 'Anyway, we worked well together and the partnership endured all these years.'

As the interview progressed, Isla gave her lots of useful memories of Rufus: little vignettes that told her how he'd worked.

She said he'd often stay up all night working through ideas, and that everything else was a blur for him. He'd reach for odd socks without noticing and forget to put milk on his cereal.

He came across as proud, intense, committed and creative. But Isla's hints that he wasn't honest with himself – that he buried difficult feelings – fitted with Eve's impression of the man. He'd had a dark side.

It was all great material for her article, but for her investigation, Eve wanted more on Rufus's relationship with Saskia. She hesitated a moment. 'I'm not muckraking, but I wondered, did Rufus often develop relationships with people on set? I talked to Saskia yesterday and she said it was unusual.'

'It was.'

Eve put her coffee cup down on the table. She realised she'd taken it for granted that Saskia was being naive. 'She even told me things might have moved forward between the two of them if Rufus had lived.' She didn't want to break a confidence, but it was highly relevant – both to the obit and her investigation.

Isla tucked her wavy blonde hair behind one ear, revealing a blue and orange Perspex designer earring, abstract, with geometric shapes. 'She told you they were going to marry?'

Eve nodded.

Isla shook her head. 'I advised her not to mention it to anyone.'

'It was true?'

'Oh yes. Rufus was head over heels, seemingly.' There was a note of distaste in her voice. 'He asked me for the name of the divorce lawyer I used. That must have been a week or two ago now. He said he'd been playing for time when Saskia asked him to leave his wife, but he suddenly realised you only get one life, blah, blah, blah.'

So she'd known about their affair well in advance of Moira spotting the couple then. Her lips were white.

'You didn't approve?'

'Absolutely not. For a start, it was ridiculous. They'd only known each other for five minutes. More importantly, it would have been a quick way to ruin Saskia's career. I had her in here to talk about it. If she insisted on marrying him, I warned her to delay starting a family.' She shook her head; quick, sharp movements. 'But she said they'd already discussed it and she wanted to have children while she was young. And she was convinced she could step out of acting and walk right back in after a couple of years. That might be true if she had more of a track record. As it is, she's either naive or arrogant. Or maybe it's what Rufus told her.' She shook her head. 'I can't remember what it's like to be young.'

Eve was struggling to process the new information. She'd almost convinced herself Saskia was some kind of obsessive, living in an invented reality. She'd seemed so young and starry-eyed. Eve was interested in Isla's attitude too.

'I had the impression you didn't like Saskia much.'

Isla's look was withering. 'Because I was harsh in the pub, when I said her histrionics were affected? I wouldn't bother criticising her if I didn't think she was worth it. She's got a marvellous career ahead of her, but she needs to grow up.'

'Did you tell the police about her and Rufus's plans to marry?'

Isla's eyes were flinty, her chin held high. 'No. As I say, I advised Saskia to keep it quiet. The critics will only say she got her part because Rufus fell for her. Why let him ruin her chances?'

'It might convince DI Palmer that she's innocent. And she's bent on making their relationship public anyway.'

The woman huffed with irritation. 'So be it. I'll confirm her claims, but she's a fool.'

'It must have made things difficult here, when Kip Clayton found he'd lost her to Rufus.'

Isla waved her words aside, her smile grim. 'It's nothing he won't get over. Just hurt ego. I suspect Rufus got careless once he decided to leave Cassie. It was no longer such a big secret. All the same, I warned him to keep it quiet, because of the potential fallout. I could have kicked him for kissing her with a load of extras on set.'

'He'd already told his wife?'

'You'd have to ask her. It's none of my business.'

Eve wanted to know who Isla thought might be guilty, but she was sure the producer wouldn't tell her. And she had a feeling being so direct would scupper her chances if she wanted to ask any follow-up questions. The stability of Isla's production was simply too important to her. Running a tight ship would be impossible if word got out that she was pointing the finger at her employees, and she had no reason to trust Eve's discretion.

Eve was thoughtful as she left the trailer. The producer was still holding out on the cause of her and Rufus's argument. Why was that? And there was no missing the underlying anger. It had been there, simmering, obvious in her white lips and taut movements. The careful control in her voice.

Just how reliable was her alibi?

# CHAPTER SIXTEEN

Before Eve left Watcher's Wood, she went to knock on Saskia's trailer door.

The young woman opened up, her face pale in the bright sunlight.

'I'm sorry to bother you,' Eve said quietly. 'It's nothing to do with the obituary. I was hoping for a quick word about Rick Sutton.' After viewing his office, Eve felt more uneasy about him than ever.

Saskia's blue eyes widened and she pulled back the door to let Eve in.

'I just wondered if the police had said anything more about him. He might have nothing to do with Rufus's death, but if he's bothering you, someone needs to focus on that too.'

Saskia shook her head. 'Thanks. It's not uncommon for me to get inappropriate attention from fans. Rick's actions seem like part of that, I guess.'

'Has he sent you anything?'

She put her head in her hands. 'Not that I know of, but a lot of my fan mail is anonymous, so it's hard to tell.' Her hollow-looking eyes, full of pain, met Eve's now. 'The one recent gift I got was from Kip, not Rick.' She reached to pick up a clear plastic bag with a photo inside that had been torn to shreds. 'It was him and me together.' She took a deep breath. 'He left it tucked into my name plate outside. He's been trying to talk to me but I blanked him and this is the result.' Eve saw Kip had scribbled *poisonous* on the bag in permanent marker.

'I'm sorry. Have you told the police?'

Saskia shook her head.

'I think you should. I've met some of the local officers. Olivia Dawkins and Greg Boles are really good.' But Eve wasn't sure Saskia would go through with it.

On her way back to her car, she passed Kip himself. He was slouching outside his trailer, with Isla standing over him. Her upright stance made her seem taller than him, though Eve guessed they were equal in height.

'I did you a favour,' Isla was saying. 'You'll come to realise it in time. And I suppose you're happy now, at any rate!' She turned her back on him and walked off.

Eve was beyond the trailers opposite the pair, but Kip looked up at that point. He must know she'd heard. The look he shot her was full of pent-up anger. It wasn't the ideal moment to ask him for an interview. She took a deep breath and walked up to him anyway, a business card in her hand.

'Margot might have mentioned I'm writing Rufus's obituary for *Icon* magazine.' She handed over her contact details.

'And you want me to help you big him up?' He laughed harshly. 'What are you? Crazy? Get out of here. I don't want to talk.'

Eve stood her ground. 'It's my job to give an honest portrayal of his life and character. That means interviewing enemies as well as friends. I can't give a balanced view otherwise. Dot's spoken with me.'

Kip jerked his chin up, turned to one side and spat on the ground. *Charming.* She wasn't sure if the action was in response to her pitch, or if he and Dot had had a falling-out.

'If I go ahead without you, I'll only be telling part of the story.' She doubted he'd be flattered, but it was worth a go. 'Maybe you could just consider—'

He looked at her levelly. 'Or maybe I just couldn't.'

*Right.*

*

The walk back to Elizabeth's Cottage helped Eve unwind. It was crazy to let Kip Clayton get to her. When her adrenaline rush finally subsided, she prepared a lunch from the crusty white bread Toby at the pub baked for the village store. She topped it with artichoke hearts, olives and hummus and prepared to enjoy it, despite the irritation she still felt. Gus pottered in from the garden and drank noisily from his water bowl.

As soon as she'd eaten, Eve reviewed the notes from her interview that morning. Isla's testimony had returned Saskia to the bottom of her suspect list. However surprising it was, it seemed she and Rufus really had made a commitment to each other. Any barriers he'd put up to start with had been abandoned. And Eve had seen no hint of reservation in Saskia's eyes as she'd spoken about the man. As far as she could see, the actress had no motive; just the opposite, in fact.

Eve decided to dig deep to find out more about the other suspects instead. She started her research with Rick Sutton. What was his story, and did it relate to Rufus's death? He'd mentioned only being in post for a short time, so she searched to check if the advertisement for his role was still online. It would be interesting to see the sort of experience the site owners had been after. What had made them choose Rick?

It didn't take long to find the details. The vacancy didn't look that exciting on the face of it: a lot of admin, with the added joy of sorting out the campers who normally occupied the site the production team was using. And the pay was terrible, even allowing for the free accommodation. Eve wouldn't fancy that chalet either. It was all very well in summer, but it would be bitter and expensive to heat come the colder months of the year.

It was only when she noticed the date of the advert that she started to wonder. It was just six months previously, and filming had started two and a half months before.

She frowned. Rick had told her how excited he'd been to book the production team in, as though he'd brokered the deal himself. That had to be a lie. These things must be planned many months, if not years, in advance.

She googled *Last of the Lindens*, looking for key dates in the production schedule, and big announcements in the press. In moments she had it. Proof that Rick Sutton had misled her. The booking of the Suffolk site had happened months before the job had been advertised. The previous custodian must have dealt with it. There was an excited splash in the *Eastern Daily Press* about the choice of location.

So… so maybe Rick Sutton had only taken the job because he knew it would get him close to Saskia Thomas. And he was clearly in the habit of covering up his preoccupation with her, hence his fib and the magazine on his chair, tucked under his desk. Perhaps he'd resign as soon as the TV crew departed, leaving the thin-walled chalet before winter. And he was even younger than Eve had thought. His LinkedIn page only showed six months of 'assorted' bar work after finishing a degree down in London. He was still of an age where he could follow his whims, with no responsibilities to anyone else. All well and good, but loitering outside Saskia's trailer wasn't on. It made Eve's skin crawl. She wondered if Rick had ever met her in real life before his arrival in Suffolk. Saskia clearly didn't remember him, but that meant nothing. She must see lots of people. Faces would blur. Eve made a note to look into the matter.

At that moment there was a knock on the cottage door which made her jump, she'd been so deep in thought. She breathed a sigh of relief when she opened up and found it was only the guy delivering her security camera. She paused to set it up before carrying on with her work. She'd never relax otherwise. Luckily, it was easy to install, just as the marketing claimed, though the accompanying app was a double-edged sword. Her phone felt like a ticking timebomb. She'd set up human motion alerts (the instructions recommended it, to reduce false alarms). If the app was triggered it wouldn't be a rabbit or a bird, but a genuine intruder, creeping onto her land.

She tried to push the thought from her mind. When she finally returned to her seat, she focused on Isla Quinn; in particular, the argument she and Rufus had had the night he died. Eve was sure she was lying about the cause of their disagreement. And that it had been serious – or at least Rufus had thought so. She did some more research on the producer–director partnership, and on each of them individually. Between writing her notes, theories filled her head, but each one fizzled out when the facts wouldn't fit. At six, there was another knock at the door and still the right ideas hadn't come.

Viv stood on the doormat, smiling ingratiatingly.

'Hungry for the latest news?' Eve stepped back as Gus mobbed her friend, jumping up and scampering in circles.

'That and some nuts or crisps if you have them,' Viv said. 'Long day.' At last Gus withdrew so she could get through the door.

'And I daresay you could be persuaded to accept a gin and tonic as well?'

'The chances are good. And I haven't only come to bother you for information. I'm here to help. I am your Watson, your sounding board; Gus and I can do it jointly. Coming to see you is a self-sacrificial act of loyalty.'

'You can lay it on too thick, you know.' Eve went to prepare the drinks and slid sea salt crisps into a large bowl. She was sure the flavour would be just the same as standard salt, but it was what Moira supplied.

'So, what gives?' Viv took several crisps at once.

Eve filled her in on the morning's events and that afternoon's research too. 'The stuff on Rick Sutton was especially interesting, but there were other, smaller things as well.' She sipped her gin, the fizz of the tonic tickling her nose. 'Not so relevant to the murder, but very much so to the obituary.' A moment later she'd flipped her laptop open and twisted the screen so Viv could see the quote from Rufus's school report that had found its way into *Real Story* magazine.

'"On stage, I'm afraid to say Rufus is disappointing and shows none of the promise of his brother and sister." Blimey. Where did his school get their teachers? What a thing to write.'

'I know. I found some hateful gossip about him out there too. Hints that even his place at drama school was a favour to his famous parents. But I watched the one film he acted in and I found it really moving.'

'I guess there's a lot of competition out there. Maybe he was good, but just not good enough. It must have been galling when his parents and siblings were so successful. So what's next on your list?'

Eve frowned. 'I think I missed something during my talk with Isla.' She pulled out her pad and re-scanned the notes she'd taken as she'd talked to the woman.

'Let's see.' Viv craned forward. 'Wow. Your writing's got worse.'

'It's a sort of shorthand I use when I'm interviewing.' Eve was secretly glad Viv couldn't decipher it. She couldn't bear it if she saw something Eve had overlooked before she managed to work it out.

'Would you read it out to me?'

'All right.' Eve put her shoulders back and tried not to feel self-conscious.

She reached the end without either of them saying anything, but she could feel that tingle again: the sense that something was on the edge of her mind.

And then suddenly she had it; like spotting the solution to an anagram that had been staring her in the face.

'What does this bit say to you: "He'd frequently stay up all night, working on ideas. The rest of the world was a blur. He'd pick odd socks in the morning and forget to add milk to his cereal."'

Viv blinked at her. 'You've lost me.'

'The scene Isla painted is pretty domestic, isn't it?'

Realisation flooded Viv's face. 'Of course. It would be one thing to say he wore odd socks, but saying he picked them implies she was there when he made the selection.'

Goosebumps snaked their way along Eve's arms. 'Exactly.'

'You think she might have had an affair with Rufus herself?'

'Maybe. And perhaps it was a long-standing one. If he was occupied with her each night, it would explain how she knew he didn't make a habit of sleeping with other members of the crew.'

They both sipped their gin and tonics.

'So she could have been jealous of Saskia.'

Eve nodded. 'Absolutely, and it fits the way she was trying to persuade her not to marry Rufus. Apparently for the good of her career, but maybe that wasn't the real reason. She's been pretty harsh about her in my hearing. And she said Rufus went to her for details of the divorce lawyer she used. That was colossally insensitive, assuming he broke off their affair.'

'But she has an alibi, right?' Viv said. 'So even if she was jealous of Saskia, she's innocent?'

'If Drew's telling the truth.'

Viv raised an eyebrow. 'You think he'd lie?'

Eve visualised Isla, suggesting they didn't call the police after Rufus was found dead. 'We know they went back to her trailer just after the pub. If he left after a bit, she could have said how ironic it was that they weren't together at the crucial time. I could see her asking him to stretch a point to save her from hours of police interviews. Whether he'd have agreed to it is another matter. I haven't interviewed him yet; I don't know him well enough to say.'

'But I suppose it's possible, if he trusted her.'

'And I don't know who will replace Rufus either. Isla said Margot Hale is sorting everything out, but maybe Isla promised Drew a step-up as a sweetener.'

'You have a nasty mind,' Viv said, grabbing some more crisps. 'But it all sounds plausible.'

'The worrying thing is, just before I went into Isla's trailer for the interview, I overheard her talking to Drew. She was saying something about disloyalty.'

'You think he might be having second thoughts, if he provided her with a false alibi?'

Eve nodded. 'And if so, he could be in danger.'

The moment Viv left, Eve called Robin to share her hunches and asked him to alert Greg. She had no proof, but she couldn't wait if Drew Fawcett might be under threat.

# CHAPTER SEVENTEEN

The following day, Eve was sleep deprived. Although there'd been no motion alerts from her new camera overnight, the app gave her a live view of her garden. She'd found it impossible to resist peering whenever she stirred. It wasn't a recipe for relaxation.

Maybe she'd frightened her visitor off. All the same, she felt better having the camera in place. But she still couldn't work out why anyone – including the killer – might want to monitor her movements.

After she'd washed and dressed, she took Gus for a walk around the village green. It was crowded with children thanks to the school vacation. There were parents present too, sitting on the green's wooden benches, keeping an eye on the little ones. As she passed, Eve heard a woman mention Dot's name. The guy next to her, who was holding a pink toddler's drink bottle, nodded.

'She seems most likely to me too. Poor Babs Lewis…'

*Poor Dot.*

Gus got distracted as someone kicked a football past his nose.

'Not your game to play, I'm afraid, Gus,' she said, as the laughing boy who'd come to fetch it swiped it from under his chin. The dachshund looked indignant.

'But you'll get to see Angie soon! Your number-one fan.' Gus jumped up giddily at the mention of the student's name. Eve was due to interview Rufus Beaumont's wife, Cassie, a little later on. She lived down in Hertfordshire, so Eve would be gone a while. Angie undertook dog-minding duties regularly for Eve when she wasn't working at Monty's or in college. 'She's going to walk you along the beach.'

Nothing would please him more, she knew. It was slightly hurtful to come second best. Actually probably fourth or fifth best after the equally exciting Viv, Sam and Robin, but she was glad he was happy. 'It's lucky for you I'm such a noble owner,' she said as they crossed Love Lane, back towards home.

She was outside her neighbours' house, Hope Cottage, when her mobile went. Robin's number flashed on her screen.

She wondered if he'd had more thoughts on her theories about Isla and picked up as she strode towards her garden gate.

'Hello. Everything all right?'

'*I'm afraid not.*' Eve's insides pulled taut. '*Greg's just been in touch. Isla Quinn was found dead this morning. Have you got time to come over?*'

As Eve approached Robin's house via his back garden her hands felt cold and clammy and her heart rate was soaring. Even Gus seemed disconcerted. He must have picked up on her reaction.

She tapped on Robin's back door.

'I'm sorry.' Robin kissed her then pulled her close as she stepped into his kitchen. 'It must be a shock. Especially after talking to her only yesterday.'

Eve nodded. 'I can't take it in.' How was it possible that such a fierce and vital force was no more? 'Do the police think it's the same killer?'

Robin pushed the back door closed behind her. His kitchen was warm but Eve was shivering. 'It's likely, but they can't be certain yet. It looks like the same MO. She was discovered in a clearing in the woods, next to a picnic table. One of the crew found a cushion tossed into the trees. The murderer must have thought it was safest to dump it rather than try to dispose of it elsewhere. First indications are that she died yesterday evening, sometime between eight fifty, when a couple of the crew saw her strolling through the site, and eleven. But Greg's hunch is it was towards the start of that period. She was wearing a thin shift dress – just as she was when the witnesses saw her – and not carrying anything except a phone in her pocket. Nothing to keep herself warm, despite the evening sea breeze. And the phone torch would be all right for lighting the way, but not for illuminating the seating area while she had a drink. It's well away from the trailers and the church. Greg can't see her heading out like that after dark.'

'Sounds logical.'

'He says she looked peaceful, just like Beaumont. No sign of a struggle, so they're guessing her killer drugged her there, then laid her down and smothered her.'

Eve nodded. 'So it looks like someone lured her away for a private chat, maybe. And there was clearly a preconceived plan.'

'Yes. Greg wanted to know if I'd heard anything useful. In particular anything you'd turned up.' Greg knew Robin was seeing Eve on the quiet.

Eve frowned. 'I feel I'm all hunches and no proof, and Isla's death proves that. I was convinced she might be guilty last night.' She shook her head slowly. 'This turns everything on its head. Dot, Kip, Rick Sutton and even Saskia, if you believe Palmer, had motives for killing Rufus, but none of them look as likely for Isla. If I'm right about Isla and Rufus's affair though, this second death puts Cassie Beaumont even more squarely in the frame.' She shivered. 'Her opportunity was less straightforward, but I could see Isla sitting down to drink with her. It would be hard to turn a bereaved woman away. And she might have been less cautious with her too, if she'd assumed Cassie was off-site when Rufus was killed.'

Robin nodded. 'She's definitely worth watching. And I take your point. The previous suspects don't seem to fit for Isla. But I doubt our information is complete. And now the Beaumont–Quinn partnership has been wiped out, it seems likely the killer's someone with a longer-term association with them. A person who'd had time for any resentments, jealousies or rivalries to build up.'

Eve could see his point. 'I suppose that covers Kip, Dot and Drew.' She felt automatic resistance to the idea. She'd been happy to see Dot lose her status as suspect number one. 'And as you say, there might be more to uncover.' The sinking feeling intensified.

'Drew's looking less likely.'

Eve paused for thought but then nodded. 'I see his alibi's worthless, now Isla's dead. And they argued of course. She called him disloyal. But it was she who seemed angry with him, not the other way about. And besides, it was Drew who persuaded Isla to call the police when Rufus died. At a pinch he could have killed Rufus if he thought he'd get his job, but removing Isla as well?' She shook her head. 'It makes no sense.'

'I agree.'

'And assuming it's one killer, and Isla was innocent, she had no reason to make a pact with Drew over the alibi either. I can believe she'd have dreaded all the police interviews – she'd have seen them as a waste of time – but not to such a degree that she'd have risked shielding a potentially guilty man.'

'That all makes sense, and for what it's worth, Drew was seen heading off towards the manor house last night before Isla died – the opposite direction to where she was found. By all accounts he's been working his way through this crisis, planning for when filming restarts. He'd told Margot Hale he was going to rethink the set layout and the security system bears that out. The alarm was deactivated at eight thirty and re-set at ten. It doesn't prove he wasn't involved but it adds to the picture.'

'What about Dot?'

Robin's eyes met hers. 'She told Greg she was reading in her trailer.'

'Still, she says she stayed on to take part in *Last of the Lindens* out of loyalty to Isla. I didn't completely buy that. I doubt she'd take on something so time-consuming as a favour. But Isla was singing Dot's praises too. She was confident people would watch *Last of the Lindens* simply because she's in it.'

'What are your thoughts on Kip?'

Eve sighed. 'He had good cause to hate Rufus. And I could see there were tensions between him and Isla too. She had a little dig at him at the Cross Keys.' Eve visualised the dead woman's ironic smile when she'd asked Kip if he was still sulking. 'It was tactless and a bit cruel. And yesterday I overheard an odd conversation between them. Isla was saying she'd done Kip a favour and she presumed he was happy now. I couldn't help feeling she meant now Rufus was dead. But the favour couldn't have been killing him. She'd never have referred to something like that in public.' Thoughts of their conversation had been nagging at her ever since her visit to Watcher's Wood the day before. 'Kip certainly has an aggressive temperament. But I don't think anything I've seen is strong enough to give him a motive for this second murder.'

So that was two of Eve's top suspects relegated. Yet it was a coincidence if Dot and Kip's hatred of Rufus was irrelevant to the case. Once again, Eve tried to imagine Rufus sitting down to have a drink with either of them. Kip, a man whose sometime-girlfriend he'd seduced, and Dot, a woman he seemed to despise. But one of them could have come up with a story to get him to the vestry. The need to confide, to report something perhaps. And it was even more plausible with Isla, after the first death. She'd surely be keen to speak to any member of her team in confidence if she thought they had information. But why accept a drink from them?

'I suppose it's just possible it's a copycat killing,' she said at last. 'If Isla murdered Rufus as a result of their break-up, someone could have stolen the sedatives from her and killed her in revenge.'

'You're thinking of Saskia?'

Eve nodded. 'I'm not sure her and Rufus's relationship would have lasted – or that I'd even call it love – but I think her feelings were passionate. Worryingly intense. And Isla told me she'd had private conversations with Saskia about her relationship with him: advised her not to waste her career by marrying. If I'm right, and Isla and Rufus were once in a relationship, Saskia might have got wind of that somehow and guessed her guilt. When I interviewed her on Monday she told me she'd have suspected Isla if it weren't for her alibi. Maybe that thought developed.

'She could have found an excuse to visit Isla's trailer after Rufus's death. If the sedatives were tucked away in the bathroom she could have pinched them without being seen.'

'I suppose there's a chance that's right.'

Eve closed her eyes for a moment. 'Perhaps I can put the theory about Rufus and Isla's affair to the test. If it was long-standing, Cassie Beaumont could have been aware of it. I won't ask her outright, of course, but I can draw her into conversation and lead her in the right direction. She might give something away. It would add to the picture.'

'All right.' He stroked her hair and Eve felt warmth spread through her that seemed entirely inappropriate considering the topic of conversation. 'But take care, won't you?'

Eve swallowed. 'I'll watch what I drink.'

'What about someone killing Isla because she was too close to the truth about Rufus's death?'

'I imagine she'd have gone to the police if she had any inkling. The production was everything to her and once the killer's arrested I understand the insurance company will give them permission to carry on.'

He nodded. 'But someone could have panicked before she had the chance to tell: if Isla had come very close to the truth maybe. Or if she'd said something that made them think she'd clicked.'

Eve bit her lip. 'True. I could imagine someone like Rick Sutton getting flustered. He strikes me as careless and impulsive. He's an outsider, but I've got plans to dig for more on him. I want to know if he'd connected with Rufus or Saskia before he came to Watcher's Wood.'

She'd have to pursue that, once she'd dealt with Cassie Beaumont: the woman who likely had a strong motive for both murders. But who was well down Palmer's list, thanks to her location. Would she have travelled to Suffolk with the flowers? Could she have sneaked onto the site unseen to deliver them? And then twice more to end her husband and Isla's lives?

But there'd been plenty to distract the cast and crew and no doubt times when people's backs were turned. And Rufus might have betrayed her trust, over and over again. If she'd decided to kill him – an unimaginably drastic action – it seemed crazy to imagine a couple of hours in the car would deter her.

# CHAPTER EIGHTEEN

As Eve drove to Hertfordshire nerves tickled her stomach. She'd need to play the interview carefully. She wondered if Palmer would already have sent the local police to talk to Cassie about the latest killing. But presumably she'd only be a suspect if Eve was right about Isla and Rufus's affair and the police were aware of it too. It might be a figment of Eve's imagination.

Cassie might not even know Isla was dead yet. Unless she'd killed her herself.

It left Eve wondering how to approach the interview. Her immediate goal was to find out if it was likely Cassie had killed both victims out of jealousy. But if she was innocent, she might still contribute to the investigation. If she knew anything about Rufus's philandering, it might help Eve understand the love triangle between Rufus, Saskia and Isla. Phrasing her opening sentences in the right way might surprise Cassie into admitting what she knew.

Eve felt her adrenaline ramp up further. The conversation would take her onto dangerous territory. She'd put an alarm in her bag, in case anything went awry.

Whatever happened, the interview was likely to be difficult. The news about Saskia's affair and her and Rufus's possible marriage had made the papers now.

Cassie's home village was full of wide leafy roads. Having researched her a little just after Rufus's death, Eve had gathered she had her own office on the site of their shared house, so there was no commute for her. As Eve mounted a flight of steps to the front door of the arts and crafts building, she could see what must be Cassie's studio on the other side of a large garden. The grounds were full of mature trees, with a couple of hammocks mounted between them, and an inviting-looking swimming pool. The situation set her nerves on edge. Who would hear her alarm if she set it off?

When Cassie answered the door, Eve recognised her from the articles she'd seen. She was elegant in a smoke-grey dress, with thick dark hair and slate-grey eyes. The look she gave Eve was wintery.

'I bought your pitch about not being a standard reporter,' she said, opening the door and stepping back so Eve could enter a large, square hall with whitewashed walls. 'I hope you're not going to disappoint me. I won't hesitate to cut our meeting short, and I know you've come a long way.'

Eve silently cursed whichever members of the press she'd been dealing with since her husband's death. 'You're right. Obituary writing's different.' She followed Cassie through to a light room with a long oak table at its centre. The space felt modern, yet sensitive to the period property – precisely what you'd expect from a renowned interior designer. A carafe of iced water with slices of lemon floating in it sat on a mat next to two tall glasses. Cassie managed to offer her some without speaking, nodding at the vessel and raising her eyes.

'Thank you.' The woman had no reason to wish her harm at present. Eve wasn't worried about accepting. 'My work involves giving as true a report of a person's life as possible, in a way that will enlighten and interest my readers. I won't gloss over the facts, but equally I don't try to trip people up. And it's against my rules to pressure them.'

'That sounds refreshing. I've had hacks standing on my doorstep, asking personal questions. Muckraking all the way back to Rufus's drama-school days, wanting to know about Emily, the girlfriend who died, who I never even met. They just hope I'm a one-stop shop who'll save them time and trouble with no thought for my feelings. And as I reply I get twenty flashing cameras thrust into my face.'

'It sounds terrible to cope with at any time, especially when you're grieving. I'm so sorry for your loss.'

And at Eve's words, Cassie did look sad. But it wasn't the sorrow Eve was used to seeing when she interviewed spouses of the dead. There was something more detached about it. She motioned Eve to take a seat at the table, and perched on a chair opposite her.

'I'm especially grateful to you for agreeing to see me, under the circumstances.' Eve felt her pulse quicken as she prepared to deliver the line she'd planned in the car. 'I wondered if the police would be with you again after Isla's murder. I would have understood if you'd had to cancel.'

She watched the woman carefully. No shock at the mention of the producer's death, but a frown and a subtle widening of the eyes.

'Why would the police want to talk to me about Isla?' Her gaze met Eve's, but a moment later her shoulders went down. 'Ah. You know about her and Rufus. I'm assuming the authorities don't though; I haven't heard from that appalling detective inspector. It was Margot Hale who called to tell me Isla was dead. We've got to know each other well over the years and I'm one of the few outsiders who knows all the people involved. Margot's under a lot of strain.'

'I can imagine.'

'Have you told the police about Isla and Rufus?'

Eve's mind was racing. Cassie now had a definite motive for both killings. Was she checking whether the secret would die with Eve?

The truth was, she'd asked Robin not to tell Greg about the possible affair until she'd found out more.

At last, she shook her head. 'But I'm afraid it might get out. I'm not the only one who knows.' At least Viv and Robin were aware of her suspicions. 'I didn't tell DI Palmer. We don't get on.'

The woman's lips twitched in a tiny smile. 'I'm glad we agree on the inspector.' She stood up, turned away and walked towards the window. Eve watched her shoulders rise and fall. 'I was so angry with him I could hardly speak. Marching in here, treating me like the wronged woman, assuming I'd kill Rufus because I couldn't live without him. As though that was a natural assumption to make.' She turned to face Eve. 'What do you think?'

*Heck.* She felt like she was being tested and the wrong answer might end the interview. She wracked her brains, fighting through the fog to respond to the question honestly. 'You were already living without him,' she said at last. 'He was hardly ever here.'

Cassie's movements were less stiff as she walked slowly back to the table. 'Thank you. Exactly. I've been independent a long, long time.'

She said the words with such emphasis that Eve knew there was a whole story to uncover here. It might unlock the case and it would certainly be first-class content for the obituary. She wanted it desperately, but one wrong word and it would be beyond her grasp.

'Will you write everything I say in your article?'

Eve took a deep breath. 'Not if you tell me it's off the record. I won't break your confidence.'

Cassie nodded. 'Thank you. I need to think. I didn't give the police the background. The inspector had so clearly made up his mind that I was too furious to spend time explaining. But I'd like people to know the truth. It's relevant to Rufus and who he was, and I'm damned if I'll let *Icon*'s readership see me as a victim.' Her fist was clenched tight, her eyes fiery.

'So, here's the bit the police will fixate on, if they find out: Rufus began an affair with Isla four years ago. Then, weeks after they broke up, he got his hooks into Saskia Thomas. What do you say to that?'

Once again Eve felt she was being offered a riddle – a test where she must prove herself to unlock the next bit of Cassie's puzzle.

If she could show she was in sympathy with the woman – on her wavelength – then she'd be rewarded.

Eve thought of what she knew, reviewing the director and the producer's history. And four years previously they'd started an affair…

'It seems surprising in a way. Rufus and Isla worked together for a long time before anything happened between them.'

Cassie nodded. 'That's significant. So, here's the bit the police would never guess. The bit they might not believe. Four years and two months ago, I told Rufus our marriage wasn't working. I'd had a fling with a work colleague, but it was symptomatic of the problem, not the cause of it. Rufus was never here and although I still loved him, it was more as a friend.

'I suggested a trial separation but Rufus begged me not to move out. He pointed out all the aspects of our marriage that worked for us both, from the fondness we had for each other to much more practical things like the security of our house, life in the community, shared finances.' Cassie looked at Eve. 'Even the fact that I got a lot of business through his rich contacts. A lot of publicity too. Celebrity home makeovers are great for getting features in upmarket glossies, and that means more commissions.'

She shook her head. 'I know this will sound mercenary, but I thought about it and it made sense. And I *was* still fond of him. I felt sorry for him and his desperation accentuated that. So I gave in and agreed to stay.' She sipped her water. 'He wasn't in love with me then either. It was the act of being left that he couldn't stand. The articles in the papers held our marriage up as a success. Think of the humiliation! His ego was like a cobweb: painstakingly constructed but easily destroyed. At that point, we agreed to have an open marriage and within weeks, after never looking further afield, he'd started seeing Isla. I'd swear he'd never even been tempted before that.'

'They must have been very discreet. It's not widely known.'

Cassie nodded. 'I believe that was an insurance policy on Rufus's part – in case it didn't work out. He didn't tell me, but he was so transparent that I guessed. He was suddenly more upbeat when we spoke, the confidence was back in his voice. And then, when he came home, he left his mobile on the table when he went to answer the door and I saw a message from her flash up. And although he'd never risen to the bait, she'd always given him the come-on. I'd seen her at it when we were at parties together, so it all made sense.'

'But you decided not to leave him?'

'That's right.' Cassie poured herself more water from the carafe. 'The status quo still worked for me and I carried on seeing whoever I liked on the side too.' She pushed the water towards Eve and she topped up her glass.

'And then Rufus and Isla broke up?'

Cassie nodded. 'She dumped him, shortly before filming began on *Last of the Lindens*. It was unfortunate timing, because I've finally met someone I really mind about. I was about to tell him I wanted to end our marriage.' She put her head in her hands. 'But he was already in an awful state. Of course, I didn't officially know about him and Isla breaking up, but it was obvious what had happened. He was suddenly around a lot more and miserable as hell.' She chewed her lip. 'It was inevitable though. Isla was a hard-bitten cynic with two marriages under her belt already. I couldn't see her settling down again, and certainly not with someone she worked with. I'm sure she'd have found it far too claustrophobic.'

'Did you go ahead and tell him you wanted a divorce anyway?'

'I skirted round the subject: hinted. I wanted to break it to him gently. And each time I built up to saying more he'd make an excuse and disappear. But he knew what was coming when he went off to start filming *Lindens*. And just a couple of weeks later, he was more cheerful again. I guessed he'd embarked on another affair. And now, thanks to the papers, I have all the details. He was making arrangements to leave me before I left him.' She gave a wry smile. 'A speedy marriage proposal to his new starlet. Quite something.'

Eve paused. She couldn't admit she had inside knowledge of the police investigation, but she really wanted to ask more. 'I heard a rumour that the marriage was Saskia Thomas's idea, and that Rufus rebuffed her at first: telling her it wasn't the right time.'

'And then suddenly he decided he was madly in love, and that it was something he just couldn't fight?'

Eve could hardly meet her eyes. 'Something like that.'

'Well, what sort of impression would you try to give, if you were in Rufus's situation? If he'd seemed careless of my feelings he might have put Saskia off. And besides, Rufus is a past master at lying to himself. I'll bet he went to his grave thinking our final break-up would have been down to him. He could cope with it that way.'

Eve was just about to wrap up her questions when a man walked past the open door to the room they occupied. 'I'm just going to pick us up something for supper.'

Eve caught a glimpse of a long-limbed figure wearing round wire-framed glasses, jeans and a black T-shirt.

Cassie followed him into the corridor. It was a moment before she was back.

'Clive,' she said, nodding after him. 'We're engaged. I was with him last night, so if that detective does come knocking, he can forget the accusations this time.'

# CHAPTER NINETEEN

Eve drove home, her mind full of the interview with Cassie Beaumont. Palmer wouldn't take what her new partner said at face value, but Eve found herself trusting the woman. Her frustration at being misunderstood seemed genuine. And the extent of Rufus's crippling insecurity was believable. It matched the defensive anger in his eyes when she'd seen the note that was left with the flowers. Something that proved he was hated. And it fitted his position in his family too. The sibling who'd never quite made it as an actor. Who worked in television, rather than in Hollywood. Whose parents had (maybe) used their influence to get him work. And she guessed Cassie's alibi was solid too. Why bother telling Eve about it otherwise? It wasn't as though she was the one who needed convincing.

The woman's account even worked with the romantic text Rufus had sent Saskia, saying he loved her and that they belonged together forever. Eve had thought at the time that he'd almost goaded her into suggesting he divorce his wife. Judging by Cassie's insights that had probably been his intention. By egging Saskia on to persuade him, he could pretend to himself that the marriage break-up was his decision. And his initial reluctance would have convinced Saskia he took his relationships seriously. It was messed up, but it figured.

But still, Eve felt she was missing something. If Rufus had guessed Cassie was finally determined to end their marriage weeks ago, why cancel the direct debit the night he died? Something must have triggered that move. It would have been an effort when he was drunk and upset.

Even without this unanswered question, Eve's trust in Cassie wasn't enough. She'd need evidence to back up her version of events. If Cassie became Palmer's favourite suspect he'd argue that she was lying to hide her motive for murder. And if Eve verified Cassie's account, it wouldn't just benefit her. It would show that Isla had had no reason to kill Rufus out of jealousy, nor Saskia a motive to kill Isla in revenge. They were outside possibilities, but ones that needed striking from the list.

She might focus on Isla and Rufus's affair. She wanted to know why the split had happened when it did, and if it related to the row they'd had.

Her mind turned to the other suspects – the ones she'd have to focus on if Cassie was definitely out of the running. It was Dot who came to the fore. Could her staying on in such odd circumstances really be irrelevant to the murders? And her character struck Eve as significant. She wasn't the sort to pander to Rufus. Instead, she'd challenged him. Not really bought into the award-winning Rufus Beaumont method. Could she have threatened his feelings of self-worth? And if Isla had taken sides, was she part of the unhealthy dynamic too?

One thing looked certain: Rufus was pathologically defensive. Sensitive about his standing to an abnormal degree. It meant he'd go to extremes to avoid looking small. Eve guessed he'd retaliate forcefully if anyone threatened his status. Perhaps someone who'd seen his shortcomings had struck back in turn: a fatal blow. Dot fitted the profile she was imagining perfectly.

Crawling along in thick traffic on the A12, Eve's mind turned to Saskia. She doubted Rufus had really loved her. But the fact remained, he'd been set to divorce Cassie, and whatever the truth about their relationship, it didn't seem likely that she'd try to stop him.

Two hours later, she parked next to the village green in Saxford. A scientific support vehicle and a police patrol car drove past her, heading away from the coast, over the Old Toll Road bridge. She doubted the day was over at Watcher's Wood, either for the investigators or the suspects. She could barely imagine the tension. She hoped she'd be able to approach the cast and crew again the following day but what would it be like, talking to them? The place must be a powder keg by now.

Gus bounced on the doormat as Eve let herself into Elizabeth's Cottage, performing ballet with some impressive leaps.

'Can I actually come in?' She bent to hug him and they accidentally knocked heads, which seemed to sober the dachshund. 'Sorry!' She went to replenish his water bowl and made herself some tea.

Once they'd spent some time in the garden together, Eve settled down to research Rick Sutton. Was he simply a star-struck man, young for his age, who'd developed a crush on Saskia when she'd arrived at Watcher's Wood? Or was he an obsessive super-fan who'd followed her there?

She knew his LinkedIn was no use. It only told her he'd done assorted bar work before the custodian job, so she resorted to Instagram for more detail. On the upside, his account was public. But he posted a *lot. Heck.* Eve wondered he had time to do any work or follow Saskia around. She scrolled back and back until at last she found a selfie of him serving in a bar. It looked plush, with gilt furniture, and red swagged curtains in the windows to one side. But otherwise it was anonymous. The only caption was 'New job!' He hadn't named the venue and the comments and location tag didn't give it away. All the same, it looked theatrical. Eve's mind turned to the theatre where Saskia said she'd been performing when Rufus had spotted her.

It probably wouldn't work, but she saved a copy of the image and searched for a match using Google. She found herself holding her breath.

To her surprise, a result came up, but it wasn't what she'd expected. The bar belonged to a television studio, Hope Cross, in

London. *Lindens* was Saskia's first job in TV. He couldn't have been working there to get close to her after all. For a moment, Eve felt thwarted, but of course, Quinn and Beaumont were old hands... She put the producer and director's names and Hope Cross into Google. In a second, she had it: proof that Rick had being doing bar work at the studio where Isla and Rufus and their actors and crew had been wrapping up work on *The Pedestal*, the production before *Last of the Lindens*.

Eve felt goosebumps rise on her arms as she got up to make some supper. She was barely conscious of her actions as she cooked.

It couldn't be a coincidence, surely. But what did it mean?

# CHAPTER TWENTY

Eve spent some time after supper updating Robin by phone. He told her the police had questioned Drew Fawcett about his heated conversation with Isla the day before. Drew said she'd accused him of disloyalty when he'd criticised her handling of Kip Clayton. He'd felt she was winding him up instead of smoothing the way. It figured. Eve had thought the same at the Cross Keys, when Isla had laughed at Kip and accused him of sulking.

After she'd rung off, it was Rick Sutton who occupied her thoughts as she took Gus out for a last airing. They walked past St Peter's church, inky black against the moonlit sky, the ruins of the older church that lay on the same site casting eerie shadows on grass that had lost its colour in the darkness. Gus was sniffing round the tumbledown cobble-flint walls of the ruin when she noticed a tall, bulky figure behind her, moving heavily. Her dachshund stiffened suddenly and Eve moved closer to the lamp-post, even though the green was bordered by cottages on three sides. Her mind was instantly back on the dark shape she'd seen in her garden; the person who'd spied on her.

As the figure emerged into the pool of light cast by the street lamp, her pulse quickened. It was Kip Clayton.

'Good evening.' *Good evening?! How ridiculously formal did that sound?* And she could see by his scowl that it wasn't good from his point of view. Why would it be? His boss had been found dead that morning, he and his colleagues were probably all under suspicion of murder and even if he was innocent, his girlfriend was lost and his future uncertain. She guessed he'd come out for a walk after a day of dealing with press and the police. He'd got no motive for killing Isla as far as Eve knew, but she couldn't write him off. And innocent or not, he might have vital information. She had to try.

'I'm so sorry about Isla.'

He grunted, his face in shadow now the street lamp was beyond him.

'You must have had an awful day.' She thought again of the patrol car she'd seen and imagined Clayton sweating as he'd waited for his turn to talk to the police. Even if he was innocent, it would have been tense. 'Can I buy you a drink at the Cross Keys?' She nodded at the pub. 'I don't suppose the press will be in there. Not with all the action being centred at Watcher's Wood. We don't have to talk about Rufus but the offer's still there if you'd like to tell me your experience of him for the obituary. As I said, I really want to make it balanced but I don't have to quote you directly if you'd rather not.'

Kip looked at her meditatively. 'Seriously? You expect me to believe that, even though you're a journalist?' He folded his arms, muscly under his long-sleeved T-shirt. 'And you've done work for the police too. I'm surprised anyone ever talks to you. The information you gather could go anywhere.'

Eve actually laughed. 'I can't imagine what the local detective inspector would say if he heard you. I don't "do work" for the police. I stick my oar in if something really important and incontrovertible comes to my attention. And DI Palmer hates it. And me.'

There was a pause, but Kip's shoulders relaxed very slightly. 'Join the club. Shan't be sorry if I never see him again.'

'Same. But I know I will. He pays regular visits to warn me off. Gus and I don't like having him in the house.' She nodded at her dachshund, who looked sternly up at Kip. It was probably because he was a hulking and faintly threatening presence, but it looked like a response to the mention of Palmer, which was handy.

'Your dog's got taste,' Kip said.

'And I can understand you being wary about talking to journalists. You've probably been hounded since Rufus's death, but we do vary. If I have an interviewee who doesn't want to be quoted, I use their information to inform my overall article. Or I can allude to what they tell me generally. You know the kind of thing. "Some contacts of Rufus Beaumont say…" I'm just concerned with painting a fair picture. Otherwise it will be wall-to-wall flattery for him.' She knew she was goading him into saying his piece, but he might yet be a murderer or have vital information about who was. A bit of manipulation was justified.

At last, Kip sighed. 'All right. You've won me over. And I could do with a whisky after today.'

Eve remembered his alcohol consumption the night Rufus died. She was determined to get the interview done before he got to the belligerent stage. There was no way she was seeing him back to his trailer like Dot had done.

Toby Falconer raised an eyebrow as Eve approached the bar with the camera operator. He'd guess what she was up to. Of the three pub co-owners, Toby was the intuitive one, offering calm words and a friendly smile: the peacemaker when Jo the cook was at her fieriest, and the responsible one when his brother Matt got carried away.

Kip asked for a double Scotch, and Eve went for a gin and tonic. She intended to ignore it until she'd finished talking, but after seeing Kip insult Drew over his puritanical drinking habits, she felt he might be more forthcoming if she appeared to join him.

It was late, and the pub wasn't busy. All the same, Eve guided Kip to the table she and Viv always picked when they wanted privacy; it was tucked away and far from the nearest table. She delayed taking her notepad from her bag. Anything too formal might set him on edge again.

'So,' she said, 'when did you first meet Rufus?' Non-controversial questions first…

'I was taken on for the last-but-one Quinn Beaumont production.' He rubbed the back of his neck then took a swig of his whisky. 'It was all right back then.'

'You and Rufus got on?'

'"Got on" might be taking it too far. He always struck me as an old phoney. It was like he was acting all the time. Always bigging himself up, but deep down he knew he was a loser. You only had to mention some bit of media coverage about his brother or sister and you got a flash of the real man.' He shook his head. 'The look of anger in his eyes… it's no wonder he kept arguing against Watcher's Wood as the location for *Lindens*. We're only a stone's throw away from his parents' country home. He was *that* sensitive.'

*Interesting.* Eve made a mental note of the location. As for Kip, he'd noticed a lot. Eve wondered how many times he'd pressed on that open wound, once he'd identified it. That could have set a battle in motion that had ended in Rufus's death. But did Kip have cause to kill Isla too? Eve still didn't think so.

'But anyway,' the camera operator went on, 'we had a decent working relationship. I did what needed to be done and professionally he was all right, I suppose. Together we got results that won acclaim and awards.'

Eve took a deep breath. 'So things only went downhill recently?' She wanted him to mention Saskia first. He might walk out if she did.

He took a large draught of his Scotch. The double wouldn't last long. 'That's right.' His eyes met hers, as though weighing up how much to say. 'From when I told Rufus about Saskia, who was my new girlfriend at the time. It was one night at the pub, after a day filming *The Pedestal*.'

That was the series Dot Hampshire had starred in, the production before *Last of the Lindens*.

'I said what a great actress she was. She was in a production of *Highs and Lows* at the time.' His eyes were far away, and despite the hard-man demeanour he tried to present, she could see the emotion in them. But then his fists clenched. 'Rufus was interested, and – if you can believe it – I was pleased. Told her later I'd put a word in for her. She was delighted.'

Saskia hadn't mentioned that. It seemed Kip's role was long forgotten.

'You probably know the rest of the story if you've talked to her,' Kip went on, closing his eyes for a moment. 'He went to see the play, and was – apparently – as stunned by her performance as I was.'

'You don't think it was genuine?'

Everything about Kip was tense, from his jaw to his fists, but at last he sat back in his chair. 'She's a great actress, but she's also very beautiful. I don't suppose that went unnoticed.'

He was probably right. And if Kip had taken to mentioning Rufus's siblings to taunt him, maybe Rufus had been out for revenge too. Gut instinct told her neither of them would have behaved well. Rufus had gone to extremes to protect his self-esteem, and Kip seemed laddish: the sort to look for weak spots in others to enhance his standing.

'From then on, he paid her a lot of attention, all under the guise of preparing her to audition for *Last of the Lindens*, ready to win Isla over. Suddenly, when I asked Saskia out for dinner on one of her rare nights off, she'd knock me back because she "had to see Rufus" to discuss her part. We were still an item, but when filming finally started, she was well and truly in his thrall. She thinks she was in love, but I don't buy that. He promised her fame if she followed his guidance. *That's* what she was after.'

He might claim to be lovelorn, but his opinion of Saskia was clearly poor. Eve imagined Isla had been right, and that it was mainly his ego that had taken a hammering, not his heart.

'To cut a long story short, Rufus told her she should stop seeing me "for the duration of filming" and rather than protest, she calmly told me the plan. Next thing I know they're clearly carrying on together and far from planning to come back to me, she was hoping to marry him.' He shrugged. 'How does anyone expect me to feel? It doesn't mean I killed him.'

Kip shook his head. 'He damaged people, that's the truth, but it wasn't just me and Saskia. You can trace the trail right back. There's that drama-school girlfriend, Emily, who drank so much she died falling down stairs, years after he'd left her. She might have been the first, but she was just one in a long line. There's no need for everyone to home in on me.'

But his hurt was recent. He had a massive motive for Rufus. Eve could see how angry and humiliated he felt and how the battle lines had been drawn. She'd have to work out how to use his information fairly in her obituary.

'Drew Fawcett suggested we use you.' He leaned forward across the table.

'Excuse me?'

'We've all read about the way you've solved mysteries before. He thought you might be able to find out the truth. The pressure's terrible at the moment.'

'He hasn't asked me about it.'

Kip shook his head. 'Isla wasn't in favour. Thought we should keep our dirty linen to ourselves. Though I don't think she had much faith in the detective inspector. Maybe she should have listened to Drew, but she never took anyone else's advice.'

Kip hadn't liked her, that much was clear from his tone. Maybe he was guilty after all, and checking for signs that she knew. His fiery eyes made her nervous.

'The press have exaggerated my role in the past. I don't have the resources of the police.' Eve wasn't going to tell him she'd been working on the case all this time and got nowhere. 'And I don't actively dig for clues. I just pass on concrete information if I get it.' She crossed her fingers under the table.

His look said he didn't believe her. She needed to focus on him, but Isla's reaction was interesting. Eve imagined she'd have wanted the case solved as quickly as possible, so that filming could continue. Yet she'd rejected Drew's idea, even though she felt Palmer was failing. Was there any chance she might have guessed the identity of the killer after all, but decided to keep quiet for some reason?

Eve frowned. A desire to protect someone *might* outweigh Isla's keenness to see the case solved. But if she'd been on the right track she'd never have accepted a drink from them, or failed to keep an eye on something she'd poured herself. Eve tucked the thought away for later.

'You've probably got a better idea of who's guilty than I have,' Eve said at last. 'It must be scary, not knowing who to trust.'

Kip shrugged. 'I don't frighten easily.'

She'd expected that response. Fed him the line to make him feel good. She smiled. 'That's just as well. I'd be looking over my shoulder all the time if it were me. What's your gut instinct about who's guilty?'

He stiffened, but at last leaned forward, his elbows on the table. 'That Rick Sutton's been bothering me.'

'He's an unusual sort.' Best to be non-committal.

'Certainly is. Lurking round Saskia's trailer. But there's more to it than that. I keep thinking I've seen him before somewhere.'

Eve felt the goosebumps she'd experienced earlier rise on her arms again. 'Down in London, you mean?' She didn't want to admit she knew Rick had worked at the bar where Kip, Isla and Rufus had filmed *The Pedestal*. He'd know just how involved she was getting in the case and that might make her vulnerable.

He nodded. 'I keep wondering if he was one of the crowd of fans who used to hang around the stage door, leering at Saskia when we were first going out. He's a creepy so-and-so.' But of course, Eve knew why he'd look familiar. Kip liked his ale. She was willing to bet he spent plenty of time in the bar at Hope Cross TV studios.

The camera operator shook his head. 'But he might not have anything to do with it. He might have been jealous of Rufus, but I don't see why he'd kill Isla. Plus he's wet behind the ears.

'But you might be interested to know that Dot didn't like either of the victims.' He gave her a meaningful look as he drained his whisky.

'Really? I knew about Rufus, of course. But I thought she admired Isla.'

Kip gave a harsh laugh. 'If that's what she told you, she's lying. You should have heard Isla after Dot miscarried.'

Eve frowned. 'I heard something about Dot breaking up with a long-term partner when they were filming *The Pedestal*, but nothing about her losing a baby.' It hadn't made it into the press. And Eve guessed Dot's aunt hadn't known either, or it would have been all over the village.

Kip nodded. 'But that was when it happened. She and her bloke split up immediately after the miscarriage.' He shook his head. 'In the aftermath, one of the crew overheard Isla talking about it. She said something like: "In all honesty, thank God. She'd have been starting to show by the end of filming. Any delay whatsoever would have been a disaster. I just hope she doesn't mope for long. We can't afford to carry her while she pulls herself together."'

He whistled. 'Oh boy, were there ructions after that! Her comments got back to Dot, and the guy who overheard and spread the news was out within twenty-four hours. Isla never pulled her punches. It was her fault, but the bloke who overheard who suffered. So yeah, Dot's not Isla's number one fan.'

And presumably Kip wasn't Dot's, either. There was a smile on his lips as he stuck the boot in, showing Eve exactly why Dot had good cause to hate a recently murdered woman.

Eve's heart ached at the actress's story. Losing a baby and partner so quickly, and knowing it made her boss see her as a liability, must have left Dot full of sorrow and rage. What the heck had Isla been thinking? But it fitted with the producer's character.

And who had Isla been talking to when she said those awful things? Rufus, most likely.

A quiver of uneasiness fluttered in Eve's stomach. Isla's attitude had been unforgiveable but it meant Dot Hampshire was back on her radar. All this had happened many months back, but grudges could intensify over time and it was clear Dot had been antagonistic from the moment she'd started work on *Lindens*.

Maybe Eve was getting to the heart of the reason she'd stayed on: to get revenge on a man who'd passed her over for a new actress and a woman who'd treated her like a workhorse – only useful if it could carry its load, however bad its injuries. She might have needed the work too, but Eve bet she'd have moved heaven and earth to find an alternative part in preference to working with Quinn and Beaumont again. On paper, Dot now looked like an excellent fit for murderer. The thought settled like a cold weight inside her.

# CHAPTER TWENTY-ONE

The following day, just after breakfast, Eve received an email from Kip Clayton. She'd asked him to get in touch if he remembered anything else he wanted to share and oh boy had he delivered. He'd found a photo he'd taken of Saskia in the theatre where she'd acted in *Highs and Lows*. She was in the bar, beaming, with a gaggle of people queuing up for autographs. And there, skulking at the back, was Rick Sutton.

*Knew I recognised the little creep*, Kip had written.

So he'd been right after all. Rick had been keeping a close eye on Saskia, even back then.

And he'd been a barman at Hope Cross TV Studios at much the same time. The question was, which came first? Did Rick latch on to Saskia initially and then get the bar job? Eve checked the date stamps on Kip's photo and the one on Instagram. Yes, it had been that way round. He'd only fetched up at the studios towards the very end of filming for *The Pedestal*.

Eve's thinking was that one had maybe triggered the other. Kip said Rufus was already muscling in on his relationship with Saskia by then: meeting her frequently to talk about *Last of the Lindens*, taking her out to dinner so they could discuss her part. If Rick Sutton had been dogging Saskia's footsteps, he'd probably spotted the burgeoning relationship as well.

It seemed to Eve that his reaction had been to get himself a job where his rival was working. It was hard to be sure, but if she was right, perhaps his jealousy had driven him to investigate Rufus, to see if he was worthy of Saskia. Sooner or later, Rick could have discovered the director was married and his heart's desire was being played. In the eyes of an obsessive, perhaps it had been a capital offence.

And what about Isla? Saskia had said herself that Rufus had had to argue for her to be given the lead in *Lindens*. And whatever Isla's true feelings, she'd spoken harshly about Saskia in Eve's hearing. If she'd done the same in front of Rick Sutton, he might have a motive after all. It all depended on how deep his obsession went. His presence at the two locations in London suggested it went pretty deep. In an email to Robin, she suggested Greg might like to look at Rick Sutton's work history in more detail. She also replied to Kip, suggesting he share his photo with the police, but she couldn't force him. He'd shown it to her in confidence.

She filled Robin in on Dot Hampshire too. She realised she'd devoted a lot of space to Rick Sutton as murderer, despite the hazy facts. After a moment, she forced herself to cut and paste the evidence against Dot so that it came first. She liked the woman, and Eve's feelings for Toby went deep too, but she was a professional. She couldn't be blinkered. There it was in black and white in front of her. Strong reasons to hate both victims, no alibi for either murder, just the tale of an improbably long walk at the time of the first one. The cool intelligence to plot and plan. The patience to wait for an opportunity. And although Eve still couldn't imagine Rufus eagerly sitting down to share a drink with her, she'd have the necessary guile to arrange it, Eve was sure.

She shook herself. There was more legwork to do. As Robin had pointed out, now Rufus and Isla were both dead, it seemed likely the killer was someone who'd had an ongoing connection with the pair of them. Someone who'd had time to build up a grudge. And although it was probably someone at Watcher's Wood – given the flowers left in Rufus's trailer – that wasn't a certainty. It would be interesting to find out more about their working relationships outside the cast and crew. Eve did some googling, unearthing contacts at TV companies, agents, actors, crew and even suppliers they'd dealt with. Anyone who might secretly harbour a grudge. After that, she cross-checked the names methodically, putting them into Google with Isla and Rufus's names in turn, looking for mentions of them in the gossip columns of industry publications.

Eve had the impression that scandals and feuds tended to go public sooner or later in the circles they moved in. After all, people were living in each other's pockets for months on end, or wrangling over decisions that cost hundreds of thousands of pounds and could make or break careers. But though Eve found odd mentions of disagreements, and in particular Isla's 'forceful' personality, when she dug deeper each instance fizzled away. She found no one who really rang alarm bells. She managed to track down details of Emily Longfellow's family too. Her parents might have blamed Rufus for her death, egged on by the media. But they were both dead and she had no siblings. Eve even looked up the woman Rufus had slept with on the set of the film he'd acted in. Her husband must have been jealous, and it was possible he'd only discovered the affair more recently, when it was dredged up by the press. But internet stalking showed they'd divorced five years earlier and he was now living in California. Unless he'd returned to England to kill over it, he was in the clear. And neither he nor Emily Longfellow's relations would have any reason to kill Isla anyway.

As she prepared to conduct the interview she'd arranged with Drew, she was back to thinking about Rick Sutton, and, most especially, Dot Hampshire. Eve had been clutching at straws, looking for an outside contact to rival her as a suspect. Her heart felt leaden and that only got worse as she walked across the village green. She overheard not one but two sets of people mention Dot's name in hushed tones when her aunt was seen entering the village store.

*

Eve sat with Drew inside the eighteenth-century manor house on the Watcher's Wood site. The garden would have been a nice spot for the interview, but a couple of press photographers had been hanging around the gates when Eve turned up, staring hungrily up at the manor in search of stray cast or crew. Eve could see why Drew preferred to be indoors.

All around them were signs of the production. Rows of set lights gleamed in the sunlight that streamed through the leaded window.

They each had Cokes with ice and lemon from the fridge in the building's vast kitchen. It was just what she needed to help her think and was refreshing in the heat. Drew had called to say it would be more relaxed to talk there, rather than at his trailer with constant interruptions.

'The police interviewed me yesterday' – his way of speaking seemed to match his personality: quick, purposeful and full of pent-up energy – 'so I'm not needed today, and the atmosphere at the camp is claustrophobic. People keep knocking at my door to talk, but there's nothing to say. None of us has any answers. I think we all thought Rufus's murder was a one-off, so although it was horrifying, it didn't lead to panic. Now everyone's looking over their shoulders.'

Eve tried to imagine bedding down each night, knowing the murderer was in their midst. The tension must be dreadful.

'Well, thank you for seeing me, anyway,' she said. 'You must be fed up with answering questions by now.' She wondered what Palmer made of him. 'So, how did you meet Rufus?'

'I first came across him at drama school. He was in his third year when I started my first. We didn't mix, but Rufus was from such a famous family that everyone was aware of him.' His dark eyes met hers. 'But we only met properly when he hired me. I joined him for *The Pedestal* and stayed on.'

'You don't remember anything particular about him from your student days? Who he mixed with, that kind of thing?'

Drew gave her an apologetic look. 'Not really. I was busy finding my feet and trying to bond with the other first years.'

Eve remembered that feeling. 'And what was he like to work with, once you re-connected?'

Drew sipped his Coke. 'Single-minded, dedicated. Lived and breathed his job. He'd sacrifice anything for it. I was interested – I learned a lot from him. But the debacle with Saskia was problematic. I was surprised Isla didn't put her foot down sooner about that. I bet she knew. She watched us all like a hawk.'

But perhaps she was glad to see him move on. A happy, occupied Rufus had probably been better than one drooping about the place dolefully, looking at her with doe eyes. Of course, it might not have been like that, but Eve could imagine it, if Cassie's account were true.

'We'd just started to tackle the problem of getting Kip to focus on work again when Rufus was killed,' Drew went on, 'but it was an uphill struggle. And Rufus was in no position to pick him up on it. I had a go, but in the end, Isla said she'd take care of it. I guess she knew being lax with Rufus had allowed the problem to surface in the first place and felt responsible.'

'I hadn't thought how much people-management there must be.'

Drew flashed her a brief smile. 'Oh yes – a lot. And since we arrived it hasn't just been Kip. Dot's been out of sorts, and we've even had to manage Rick Sutton, the custodian. Saskia saw him again, near her trailer in the shadows. Isla went to his chalet to give him a talking-to on the back of it.'

So Rick and Isla had had recent, direct contact before she'd died. Eve would need to consider the implications once the interview was done.

For now, she kept her focus on Drew's answers to her questions, but though they'd be useful for her article they didn't help with the case.

At last Eve said: 'What will happen about the production now? Had Isla approached you to take Rufus's place before she died?' She felt as though her reason for asking was written in neon above her head. Had Drew any reason to kill Rufus? Would he gain by his death? And was there any chance Isla had offered him the new job in return for alibiing her? She could still have killed Rufus out of jealousy if Cassie was lying about how their relationship had ended.

But Drew shook his head. 'No, she hadn't. She was after Arielle Jones, which I thought was a long shot. Margot Hale and I were working on it, but we'd only left messages. She hadn't responded when Isla was killed.

'As for not choosing me, it wasn't personal.' He must have read the surprise in Eve's face. 'Boasting apart, I've perfected my role and Isla's used to me in it. If she'd asked me to step up she'd have had another hole in her team, and two people in unfamiliar roles instead of just one.'

It made sense. She imagined he might have been frustrated at Isla's attitude, but it scotched a professional motive for killing Rufus. And it backed up the other evidence she had: Drew's suggestion that they should call the police when Isla died, and even floating the idea of recruiting Eve to help solve the case, according to Kip Clayton. He must want a return to normality too.

'What's the situation now?' Eve couldn't imagine what would happen in such circumstances.

'Everything's on hold until the police make progress and the insurers give us the go-ahead to carry on,' Drew said. 'But of course, the crew's headless now so even if it was appropriate, we couldn't just get on with filming.' He shrugged. 'Everyone's still in shock and our contact at the TV company is… let's say, stressed. Time will tell.'

'Of course.'

They each finished their drinks and washed up their glasses before Drew set the security alarm and locked the house again.

She watched him walk off up the lane, back towards the woods, church and trailers. They must all wish they could escape back to their homes, but with pressure from Palmer and the TV company that wasn't an option. Eve felt the value of the freedom she had as she walked back towards the village.

She used her journey to take stock. So Drew had no obvious motive for killing Rufus or Isla and his future was uncertain. But the interview had made her wonder again about Rick Sutton. Between Rufus's death and Isla's, Isla had been to visit him in his chalet to warn him off stalking Saskia. What if Rick had killed Rufus? She imagined his jumpiness and immaturity. He might easily have worried he'd given something away. She could imagine him killing Isla under those circumstances, even if she'd never suspected him. And if Isla had been disparaging about Saskia during her visit, that might have got to him too. Eve might have to treat Dot as suspect number one, but Rick was still a definite possibility. She must find a way to unlock his secrets.

Back at Elizabeth's Cottage, Eve made a black coffee and took it out to the garden, where the scent of honeysuckle filled the air and a blackbird's sweet song came from the branches of her magnolia tree.

Gus pottered outside to join her and she gave him a pat.

'I'm sure I'm missing something overarching. I'm homing in on suspects, but I still don't know the answer to some basic questions.' Why had Isla and Rufus really argued the night he died, for example? And what had made Rufus cancel his regular payments to his wife? She shook her head. She didn't honestly believe either Isla or Cassie had killed him, but such seismic events just before his death had to be relevant. She needed to focus on them and the information Cassie Beaumont had given her.

Gus was lying down in the sun with his eyes closed. She decided to assume it meant he was concentrating. 'My feeling is that Cassie's information is accurate. She came across as someone who'd been bearing the weight of her secrets for a long time. And why lie to me? It's not as though I've got any sway. So, let's assume it's true that something made Isla leave Rufus after four years. Things might just have petered out, but my bet is there's more to it than that. And it might relate to the row they had, the night he died.' Vaguely, Eve remembered Saskia comparing his reaction after the argument to when he'd received an especially bad review. That brought Cassie's comments about his ego to mind. Had Isla bruised it again? Eve was starting to gather just how badly he'd have taken that. Yet Isla had already dumped him weeks earlier, according to his wife. He could have been trying to persuade her to take him back, but that seemed unlikely, given his relationship with Saskia. So presumably the row hadn't been about personal matters…

'Unless…' Gus opened half an eye as Eve leaped up from the table. 'I need to get my laptop.'

Minutes later, she'd found the replacement director Isla had wanted for *Lindens*: Arielle Jones. And moments after that she had an office number and was on the phone, asking to speak with the woman.

'*I'm afraid she's in meetings for the rest of the day,*' the man who answered said. '*May I take a message? I'll be taking in her coffee imminently if it's urgent.*'

He must have picked up on Eve's tone. 'That's okay, thanks. I'll try again. Or maybe I'll email if she's likely to get my message before she leaves?'

There was a pause. '*Her diary says she won't be through until six, so it may be tomorrow morning.*'

'Thanks. No problem.'

In seconds, she was upstairs in her bedroom, changing into a summer suit: a sky-blue shift dress with purple trim at the neck and a jacket it might be cool enough to wear by late afternoon. As she finished, she called Viv's son Sam and asked if he could come in to make a fuss of Gus and give him his supper.

Her dachshund had stirred himself in response to her activity and come indoors. He glanced at her questioningly as she descended the stairs.

'Impromptu trip to London,' she said, bending down to cuddle him. 'I ought to be back by mid-evening, but Sam's coming to give you your food, yes he is!'

Gus bounded about ecstatically as she combed her hair in front of the mirror by the door and reapplied her mascara.

It was a long way to go on spec but ringing again wouldn't do. It was too easy to hang up. Eve never normally doorstepped people, but if she caught Arielle as she left her office, it might unlock the case.

# CHAPTER TWENTY-TWO

By six that evening, Eve was standing on a crowded dusty London street close to an anonymous-looking door next to a Caffè Nero. The door led to the premises where Arielle Jones worked. Eve had looked her up on the Internet Movie Database during her train journey down to the capital and found she was currently engaged in the final edit for a new television series. There was no information about her next project.

Eve went to get herself a coffee, then perched at a table just outside the café. It gave her a good vantage point. She'd be sure to see Arielle when she left. She was a distinctive person: tall with jet-black close-cropped hair.

By six thirty, Eve was starting to feel shifty and wishing she hadn't had the coffee. If she disappeared inside Caffè Nero's loos now she'd probably miss her quarry. For all she knew, the director's last meeting might have been cancelled or the venue changed. She might be halfway across town.

But at last, ten minutes later, the woman appeared.

Eve got up, put her shoulders back, and went to introduce herself. 'I'm so sorry to bother you. My twins live in London, and as I was passing through I wondered if I might be able to catch you.'

The woman was pulling away, suspicious, wanting to get home after a long day. Eve would do just the same in her position. She felt bad about using her children as part of her ruse too.

'I'm writing Rufus Beaumont's obituary.' She handed over her business card.

Arielle paused, an uncertain look in her eye.

It was time for Eve to take a chance. Pretending to know more than she did might work, but if she was wrong, their talk would be over.

'I gather Isla Quinn was about to end her partnership with Rufus and embark on a new project with you.' Was Eve right? It certainly fitted. Isla had immediately asked for Arielle when Rufus died, with some notion that she might have capacity and be willing. And she'd given Rufus some unwelcome news, the night of his murder. Not ending their affair; she'd done that already. But ending something, Eve guessed. Something that had floored him and sent him drowning his sorrows at the bottom of the bottle of whisky. Even cancelling the direct debit to Cassie made sense. He was probably angry with her if he knew she'd finally decided to leave him, and then his income had been under threat. He could have logged on and made the change as a drunken gesture, but also for practical reasons.

Arielle turned to face Eve properly now. 'I didn't know Isla had told anybody. Apart from Rufus, that is.'

'You knew she'd passed the news on to him? Several people overheard the row they had.'

Arielle's shoulders sank. 'Isla said how upset he was. But it convinced her she was right to make the break, though it was horrific that he was killed that night. She didn't like the idea of him leaning on her; needing her in that way.'

'That fits. Look, I'm sure you must want to get home, but I wonder, could I possibly have five minutes of your time? I'm trying to get a picture of Rufus in the round, and of course because of the horrific events I can't ask Isla for details now. Perhaps I could buy you a glass of wine?'

There was a bar just opposite where they stood. Still Arielle hesitated.

'If you'd prefer to talk off the record I can just use your information to guide my sense of who he was. I give you my word I won't use specifics if you don't want me to.'

At last the woman nodded. 'All right. Let's talk, and I'll work out what I'm happy to put my name to.'

They took a table on the pavement outside the bar and Eve bought them both white wine spritzers.

'I'm so sorry about Isla,' Eve said. 'It must have been a terrible blow.'

The woman nodded; her clear dark eyes were calm. 'We'd known each other for years and I admired her enormously. It would have been an exciting new venture for me.'

'I gather she was hoping you might stand in for Rufus for the remainder of *Last of the Lindens*, too.'

She nodded. 'I'd had a message about that. But I'm still tied up with work on my previous project, so I was going to decline. I knew I'd need to make my boundaries clear from the start.' She smiled ruefully. 'Isla was great – utterly dedicated – but she'd take whatever people would give. She could be a fierce champion of her actors and crew, but if you crossed her the tables could turn. I didn't have the time to leap to it and fill in on *Lindens*. Spreading myself too thinly, then letting her down, would have been worse than saying no.'

Eve nodded. 'That makes sense. I wondered, did Isla ever give you any idea why she decided to end her partnership with Rufus?' It could have been because their relationship had gone sour, but something told Eve that wouldn't be the reason. All Isla's moves seemed to be driven by her professional concerns.

'This is where I need to go off the record.' Arielle's eyes met hers.

'That's no problem. Rufus is a puzzle. If you've got clues to unlock his personality, I'd really appreciate it.'

'All right. As you can imagine, when Isla approached me, I wanted to know why she was suddenly abandoning her favourite director. If there was bad blood between them, I made it plain I wanted to understand what I was walking into. That type of dynamic can cause a lot of fallout. I thought I might have to cope with some of it, so I felt I had a right to know. Isla told me, in confidence, that she found out Rufus had lied to her.' She took a sip of her wine. 'You might remember Cecilia Dunwoody rose to prominence after appearing in a Quinn and Beaumont production?'

Eve nodded. 'Of course. All the way to an Oscar.'

'Right. Well, despite Isla's commitment to nurturing new talent, she wanted to work with Cecilia again. Rufus claimed he'd approached her and she wasn't interested. So then Isla wanted to contact her direct, of course. She was determined to talk her round. But Rufus said she'd been headhunted by a rival and implied Cecilia had never liked Isla. In the end, Isla got angry and left it.

'Then, a few months ago, she ran into Cecilia at an industry do. Isla said she'd had a few drinks, and as she still felt aggrieved, she went right up to her and asked what her problem had been.'

Eve held her breath.

'And here's the thing,' Arielle sipped her drink, 'Rufus had given Cecilia a mirror version of the story he'd told Isla. He'd made out that Isla didn't want her back, implied it was personal and that she shouldn't try to audition for their next production.' She shrugged. 'Whatever his motivation was, he made sure Dunwoody's relationship with Quinn and Beaumont was cut short.'

His behaviour had been bizarre. Eve thought of the woman's talent. 'Isla must have been livid.'

'She was. But as ever, she was practical. This all happened shortly before production was due to start on *Lindens*, so she didn't tackle Rufus immediately. She waited to minimise the impact on filming but when he started talking about future projects the night he died, she told him. Of course, she'd had time to work up to it, so she was perfectly controlled, but he had no warning. And I gather he didn't react well.'

Eve hesitated. 'Did you get the impression Isla and Rufus had been more than friends?'

Their eyes met. 'You know already, don't you?' Arielle's expression was wry. 'Yes, I knew they were. And although Isla waited to break the news about ending their working partnership, she couldn't bring herself to carry on sleeping with him after what he'd done. There's only so much you can fake, I guess.'

'Thank you. Like I said, I won't use any of your off-the-record comments, but this puts everything else in context.'

'I appreciate that. Isla wanted to keep what Rufus had done quiet. It would reflect badly on her as well as him, make her look like a fool. She trusted him instead of doing everything personally and she kicked herself for that. "Never again," she said.' Arielle put her head in her hands. '"Never again" were two of the last words I heard her say. I can't get them out of my head now. I hope to God they find out who killed her.'

# CHAPTER TWENTY-THREE

Early the following morning, Eve was strolling through Blind Eye Wood, arm in arm with Robin, the heath and the sea to their left, Gus scampering ahead of them. The murders aside, she couldn't remember when she'd last felt happier. Sunlight sparkled on the waves and Robin leaned in so her head was against his shoulder. She'd forgotten how joyous that feeling of closeness could be.

And there was nothing more helpful than talking through ideas with him or Viv, either. She'd already filled him in on her interview with Arielle Jones.

'So, what next?' Robin asked.

'A rethink. It seems clear that Isla finished the affair with Rufus, just as Cassie claimed, and now we know why they argued the night he died. Her decision to break off their partnership was completely justified but it was one more blow to his ego and he might have ended up out of work too. Isla was clearly furious with him, but he'd have been out of her life within months, leaving her free to start an exciting new chapter in her career. So, if further proof were needed, I definitely don't believe she killed Rufus, or that anyone killed her out of revenge.'

'Agreed. So it confirms a single murderer is more likely.'

'Yes. And with Cassie's story verified, my gut feeling that she was innocent looks more certain as well. She knew Isla had already dumped Rufus and she'd got her new partner anyway. They were already acting like a couple when I was there: talking about the shopping. I think she'd moved on.'

'So we're left with the excitable Rick Sutton and the intelligent Dot Hampshire.'

'That's right. And the feeling that Rufus's hang-ups controlled everything he did. My guess is Cecilia Dunwoody did something to make him feel small and he made sure she never came back. For her, the future was bright, despite his interference, but most of his actions had negative consequences. He made a dead set at Saskia to bolster his ego after Isla dumped him, and Kip Clayton was the casualty. And then Dot suffered when he passed her over for the lead in *Lindens*. I'd guess he couldn't take it when she questioned his methods. But although Dot looks like a strong suspect on paper, she's not in quite the same boat as Kip. She could have walked away, had her pick of excellent parts, I'd imagine. So maybe Rufus didn't damage her as badly.'

Robin put his head on one side. 'But on the other hand, Dot has a strong motive for killing Isla as well as Rufus. Whereas Kip Clayton doesn't.'

Eve bit her lip. 'As far as we know.'

His eyes met hers.

'No, I know. You're right. I need to be objective. I just feel for her. And for Toby and Babs Lewis too. The entire village is whispering about Dot, but I can see they might be right.'

'Do you have a plan?'

'I need to find out more. I'm worried Dot might have stayed on specifically to take her revenge. She might have decided she needed the work, but her stock's high, and my guess is she could have accepted alternative offers. Better ones, most likely – I imagine her agent must have been irritated if that's the case. I might give the guy a ring and see what gives.'

Robin dropped a light kiss on her head. 'Sounds good. I'm living my sleuthing life vicariously through you, so tell me what happens.' He grinned but then his eyes turned serious. 'And watch your back.'

*

Dot Hampshire's agent was a man named Alastair Finch. He looked around fifteen in his photo and Eve felt guilty for planning to lie to him.

She opted to use the call box outside the village store to make contact. If Finch decided to call her back she'd rather she was untraceable, and his office might not pick up if she withheld her number.

'You'd better stay here, Gus.' She bent to stroke his ears in the sitting room at Elizabeth's Cottage. Call boxes felt very small when shared with energetic dachshunds and any barking would raise suspicions in the agent's mind.

Five minutes later, Alastair Finch's PA was putting her through as Moira came outside to 'adjust the sandwich board' which detailed some of their stock. She glanced curiously in Eve's direction. There'd be questions later...

'I know this is going to sound crass,' Eve began once she got through, 'but my boss asked me to call you. We've heard the awful news about Isla Quinn and Rufus Beaumont, of course. And he was curious, does this mean Dot Hampshire will be free after she's done with filming *Lindens*, assuming it goes to completion? Only we'd heard she'd signed up for another project with them next.'

That ought to rile him if he was cross with her for taking suboptimal roles with Quinn and Beaumont.

'Another project?' Finch sounded bemused, not irritated. 'No, I think that's just gossip. She hasn't discussed anything with me. But your boss would like her to try out for something? Shall we set up an appointment?'

Eve felt herself blush. She hadn't anticipated that reaction. 'Um, I'd better just update her and then we can give you a call.'

'Okay.' The agent sounded disappointed. 'Though we can sort out a provisional date if you'd like?'

'Thanks, but it's all right. I'll be in touch.' She crossed her fingers behind her back and felt sorry for him as she hung up.

Moira wasn't the only one keeping an eye on her dealings. Viv nipped out from the teashop as Eve recrossed the village green, past a group of kids playing cricket.

'Just spotted you using the call box.' She smiled brightly.

'The customers!' Eve knew Viv and Sam were on their own until Tammy – another regular student helper – came to join them at eleven. She had each schedule she created for Monty's off by heart.

Viv waved a hand. 'Sam knows I'll be back in just a second. Assuming you share your news promptly, that is.'

'All right.' If she didn't get on with it, Moira would probably come and join them too. She explained the conversation with Dot's agent.

'So?' Viv's cerise hair gleamed in the sun as a cricket ball narrowly missed her shin. They moved further towards Monty's to get out of the line of fire.

'I just wanted to know how much resistance Alastair Finch had put up when she decided to take an inferior role with Rufus and Isla. I guessed he'd get angry if I hinted she'd been planning to do it again, but he didn't. She's clearly stuck for work. It sounded like "my boss" could have snapped her up. Finch was so eager he didn't even ask me who I represented or what the production was.'

Viv's brow wrinkled. 'Maybe she really *is* difficult to work with.'

'Maybe.' But Eve's mind was on the way Rufus had pulled strings to alter the course of Cecilia Dunwoody's career. Was there any chance he was behind Dot's current situation? Maybe he'd gone further than simply refusing her the lead role in *Lindens*. Nerves tickled her stomach again. She'd wanted information that would make Dot look less likely as the killer, not more. 'You'd better run along,' she said to Viv.

Her friend tossed her head. 'You're no fun.' But she bounded back towards the teashop all the same.

Back at home, in the garden of Elizabeth's Cottage, Eve sat at her ironwork table as Gus snuffled around the flowerbeds. She wished he wasn't quite so interested in bees. She monitored his interactions with a particularly large bumblebee that had caught his attention.

As she watched, she reviewed her call to Dot's agent. Something had gone wrong with her career. There was more work to do, but that afternoon might help. Margot Hale had emailed. The police and forensics teams had left and she was clear to go back on site. Meanwhile, Dot herself had been in touch. She wanted to see Eve again and the desire was mutual.

But there were other ways she could snoop for information before her trip to Watcher's Wood. She thought through the contacts she had in the world of drama. She'd got on well with Kim Carmichael, the veteran actress, when she'd interviewed her for another case. The woman was irreverent, unconventional and fun.

In another moment, Eve had her on the phone.

'*Mind you ringing? Of course not! It's perfect.*' The woman's crackly laugh came down the line. '*I've got the grandchildren here. I was about to have to play little ted has a picnic for the fourth time in a row. You are my salvation. And I've been following your progress in the papers.*'

Eve blushed. She hadn't confessed to Kim that she'd been moonlighting as an amateur detective when she'd visited her last. She'd see right through the questions Eve asked this time around.

'It's just background stuff, relating to the obituary I'm writing of Rufus Beaumont.'

'*Understood!*' Eve doubted Kim believed her. She was the one with the acting skills, not Eve.

'I was curious about Dot Hampshire staying on for *Last of the Lindens* after her starring role in *The Pedestal*. I assumed she'd want to go off and spread her wings with a bigger part.'

'*Ah, yes, me too!*' Kim's voice was interested. '*She's a rare talent. And interesting. Magnetic, not boring-pretty. But the word is, Rufus found her absolute hell to work with. So much so that he put the word out on the circuit.*' She paused. '*I didn't know he was behind the rumours at first, but I was so curious I took a contact out to dinner and plied them with booze to get at the truth.*' She laughed again. '*Now I'm part-retired, I find I miss out on the gossip otherwise.*'

'But if that's the case then it's curious—'

Kim cut across her. '*That he and Isla gave her a part in* Lindens? *Isn't it just? There's something odd going on. You think it's related to the deaths?*'

Eve visualised the woman's sparky eyes. 'I honestly don't know, but I warmed to Dot.' She was as forthright as Kim.

'*Me too,*' the woman replied, '*but who knows what people are capable of when they're pushed to the limits?*'

Eve shook her head as she rang off. Dot's motive had strengthened again. She might have stayed with Quinn and Beaumont through lack of options, rather than the desire for revenge, but finding Rufus was systematically destroying her reputation must have left her both angry and desperate.

# CHAPTER TWENTY-FOUR

Watcher's Wood emphasised the horror of recent events by its very peacefulness. Eve walked through glades filled with the scent of grass and honeysuckle, entwined with the trees. To her left, red campion had turned the woodland floor into a sea of pink. The carpet was alive with buzzing bees and butterflies moving from bloom to bloom. It was unthinkable that two people had been robbed of their lives in this special place.

As Eve approached the accommodation trailers, she heard voices: people discussing the death and when filming might resume. Someone asking about food for that night. A weird mixture of the domestic and the shocking, which had become the actors' and crew's normality.

Kip Clayton was talking to Drew as she reached the clearing at the centre of the camp.

'... gives me the creeps. I thought he was after Saskia, but I'd swear he was watching Dot's trailer when I went for a walk last night.' Kip flexed his shoulders.

Drew shook his head. 'Thanks. I'll take it up with the site owners and let the police know too. I don't know what the hell he's playing at.'

Eve stopped in her tracks. They must be talking about Rick Sutton. The theories she'd been constructing about him wobbled. Peeping at Dot as well as Saskia didn't fit. And if Eve was wrong about his obsessive interest in the younger actress, where did it leave his motive for killing his supposed rival Rufus, and Isla, who he might have pegged as Saskia's enemy? Yet his behaviour was no less creepy. She needed to press forward with her enquiries into him.

As Kip went back to his trailer, Drew turned to Eve.

'Dot asked to see me again.'

'She mentioned it.' He indicated a trailer with a door at either end. 'She's in the suite on the right.'

When Dot opened up, her eyes were screwed up against the sun and underlined with shadow. Eve guessed she hadn't slept much. Was it guilt, causing her turmoil? But Eve wasn't worried about entering her accommodation. There were plenty of people milling round the clearing outside her trailer thanks to the fact that filming was on hold. Talking to her there was as good as meeting her in the centre of Saxford.

'Coffee?' Dot closed the door behind them and raised an eyebrow. 'I'll be drinking from the same batch.'

Eve allowed herself a smile. 'Put like that, yes please. Just black. Not that I imagine you'd doctor the milk.' She wanted Dot to feel she was on her side. She'd learn more that way.

Dot grimaced as she prepared their drinks. 'It's my presumed guilt I wanted to talk to you about.' She leaned against the tiny worktop in her kitchen as Eve took one of the two upright chairs in the room. 'Toby suggested you might be able to help. I understand you're busy with Rufus's obituary but I know you've acted like an unofficial PI in the past. With good results.'

Eve's insides twisted. There would be so much riding on her work, and what if there was nothing she could do? Either because she failed or because Dot really was guilty? She might have decided to go along with Toby's suggestion to seem innocent, not because she had a clear conscience. Maybe she hoped Eve would be driven to find convincing circumstantial evidence against someone else if they became friends.

'There's been a lot of luck involved.' Eve didn't want to raise false expectations.

'It's clear DI Palmer thinks I'm guilty.' Dot bit her lip. 'I'm sorry. You might have found me out already. People are talking. The fact is, I had good reason to hate Isla.'

Eve nodded. 'I was so sorry to hear about your miscarriage.'

'It was hell, accepting this new part after her impatience over my grief. But it's nice to eat. And it was Rufus who made me unemployable. I should have admitted I had no other work and that was why I stayed on. Even before we wrapped up filming *The Pedestal* he'd started to taunt me. And I'm afraid I'm highly goad-able. The moment I started to give as good as I got I heard rumours were spreading that I was impossible to work with. And then, when I refused to half starve myself and beat up my body to act the part, the rumours accelerated. I couldn't take direction, I was only interested in myself… You name it.'

'And Palmer knows all that?' Eve asked as Dot poured their coffees.

She shook her head. 'Not about the work situation, as far as I know. But he's got witnesses who say how much aggro there was between me and Rufus. And how cruel Isla was. That's quite enough for him. He doesn't see anyone else's motive for killing both of them.'

Dot seemed most likely to Eve too, but again she tried to meet her halfway. 'Rick Sutton's an odd one, and Isla visited his chalet shortly before she died. And Kip hated Rufus, as well as being scratchy with Isla.'

'But neither of them have such convincing motives as me.'

Eve couldn't come up with a counterargument.

Dot sipped her coffee. 'So I understand if you think I'm guilty too, but I'm not. I really did go for a walk after I'd bundled Kip into his trailer. It sounds feeble, I know.'

'Where did you go?'

'I went back along the beach, then cut along some country lanes. Here.' She got up from her chair and reached a bit of A4 paper from a small square table. 'A copy of my statement to the police.

At least the journey was fresh in my mind. You can borrow it if you like, though I can't see it helping.'

'Thanks.' Eve put the statement on her knees, taking a sip of her coffee now that Dot was a little way down hers. Not that she was really worried. Dot had no reason to want her out of the way. Not at the moment.

Glancing down at the details Dot had given the police, she realised she must have been in much the same neck of the woods as Rufus's PA and the costume supervisor, as they walked back towards Watcher's Wood.

'You didn't see Margot Hale or Brooke Shaw on your travels?'

'Nothing as helpful as that.'

'And you still don't have a definite hunch about who's guilty?'

She shook her head with every appearance of despair. 'No one seems more likely than me.'

But was that innocence talking, or a clever double bluff? Eve couldn't be sure.

When she emerged from the trailer, having promised Dot she'd do what she could, she bumped into Margot Hale.

'I'm so sorry about Isla,' Eve said, holding her hand up to shield her eyes from the sun. It was the first time she'd spoken to Margot face to face since the producer's death.

'It's all so unreal.' The PA was as smart as ever in a stone-coloured shift dress and pearls, her face perfectly made up, but there were worry lines around her eyes. 'I wondered, would you like to see inside Rufus's trailer, now the police have finished with it?'

Eve leaped at the offer. You could tell so much by seeing some-one's home environment, even if it was only a temporary one, and she hadn't had the opportunity to take it in when she'd warned him about the flowers.

Inside, Rufus's past glories as a director were reflected back at her: press cuttings stuck to a magnetic board that was integral to his accommodation.

Margot followed her gaze. 'He needed constant reminders of his worth,' she said.

Yet self-doubt hadn't made him any kinder to the people he worked with, at least in Dot's case.

'Did you enjoy working for him?'

'I loved it.' Margot's eyes were damp as she touched the back of a chair where Rufus must have sat so recently. It was almost like a caress. Eve wondered what she'd thought of his affair with Saskia. When Eve asked for her fondest memory of Rufus, it was the relaxed drinks after long days that she mentioned. 'He was good company.' She drew a tissue (plain white, Eve noted, no pattern) out of her pocket and wiped away a tear.

Back in the clearing, Brooke Shaw had just come out of another trailer. Her gaze was on Margot's face as Eve and the PA emerged from Rufus's former accommodation, her brow furrowed.

Once Margot had left, Brooke wandered over. 'How's it going?' She was as glamorous as ever in a figure-hugging sleeveless black dress, with smoky make-up on her eyes.

'I've got lots of useful material for my article.'

'That's good.' Brooke smiled. Eve wondered if she knew about her contributions to past police investigations, just like Dot. After Drew had suggested Isla might ask for Eve's help, they were probably all aware. There was something knowing in Brooke's eyes.

'How's everyone bearing up?'

The woman shook her head. 'Not well. No one knows who to trust and there's nothing to distract us. If we could just get on with something it would help, but there's no decision about the production and we don't have permission to go ahead from the insurers anyway.'

Eve felt for her. She got twitchy if she wasn't occupied, even at the best of times.

The heat was intense and Brooke drew a tissue from her pocket and wiped her forehead. For a moment, Eve just stood there, staring.

Brooke caught her look. 'Something wrong?'

'Not at all. But what a beautiful tissue.' The peacock design was familiar. It matched the tissue she'd seen in Kip's bin, the day after Saskia and Rufus's affair was revealed. And the other contents hinted strongly that Kip had spent the night with whoever owned it. The tissue was like a tackier, more intimate version of Cinderella's missing slipper.

Brooke gave a deliberately ashamed smile. 'They're lovely, aren't they? I have to confess, they were Isla's. She'd left a packet in a box of kit that was hanging around and I'd run out, so I helped myself.' She put her head on one side. 'I suppose it seems a bit grim, pinching a dead woman's belongings, but she ordered them specially from Paris, if you can believe it. It seemed stupid to let them go to waste.'

# CHAPTER TWENTY-FIVE

That evening, Eve sat with Viv in the Cross Keys. Outside, the sun was getting lower in the sky and the tealight between them looked comforting, flickering in its holder. The pub was one of Eve's favourite places in the village: she loved the plentiful supply of battered books and games, and the glow of the picture lights showing off the sea-themed works of art. She'd even managed to get used to Jo the cook's forceful nature. Well, pretty much.

She appeared next to them now, plonked their meals in front of them and stood back, her arms folded.

'Smells like heaven,' Eve said immediately. It was good to get your appreciation in early with Jo, but her compliment was heartfelt; it really did. She'd chosen smoked salmon risotto. Viv was about to do battle with a breaded skate, which Eve knew would be complicated.

Jo beamed, then frowned for a moment. 'I hope you're not going to sully the experience by talking about the murders.'

'As if we would,' Viv said, putting her Sauvignon Blanc to her lips.

Jo shook her head and retreated. Over by the window, Eve could see Gus, cowering next to the pub schnauzer, Hetty, who sat to attention. They both relaxed when the cook disappeared to the kitchen again.

'So, don't be put off by her,' Viv said. 'Tell me everything.'

Eve provided all the latest updates. She'd already called Robin too, to fill him in.

By the time Eve finished, Viv was getting to grips with her meal. Eve had been enjoying mouthfuls of risotto as Viv digested each snippet of news. The mix of flavours was divine.

Viv sat back in her chair. 'I can't believe Isla would do that.'

'Hang on. I might be able to give you more evidence in a minute.' Drew Fawcett had entered the pub. Perhaps he was joining Margot and Brooke. Eve had noticed them sipping gin and tonics in a far corner, sitting opposite each other.

Eve stood and caught the assistant director at the bar, glancing over her shoulder before speaking. 'Sorry to pounce on you, but did Isla ever explain how she got Kip's mind off Saskia and Rufus?' At least he'd already know she was looking into the murder as well as researching Rufus's obituary.

He cocked his head and frowned. 'No, but she seemed confident she'd done the trick. She told me he ought to shut up now and then laughed.'

Toby had appeared. He was smiling at them both but Eve could see the question mark in his eyes as his gaze met hers. He was probably wondering if Dot had spoken to her yet. They'd both be relying on her.

Drew ordered a beer. 'Can I get you anything?'

'Thanks, but I've got wine back at my table.'

Drew nodded as she turned to leave him. 'Wait a moment, though. It's coming back to me. When Isla assured me she'd fixed the situation, she raised her eyes to heaven and said, "Let no one say my job's not varied."' He shrugged. 'To be honest, he seemed crosser than ever afterwards, but what can you do?' He turned again to pay for his drink.

After he left the bar, Eve paused as Toby waited close to where she stood, buffing a pint glass with a tea towel.

'Dot's asked me to help her,' Eve said, to a nod in response. 'I've got a plan. I doubt it'll help, to be honest, but I'll let you know if I find anything useful.'

He looked down at his hands and shook his head. 'It's crazy. It's not my business. It's not as though anything would happen between us these days. We live in different worlds, but you know – fond memories.'

Eve reached to pat his shoulder. 'It's only natural to want the best for a friend.'

She returned to her and Viv's table and took a seat. 'I think I'm right. What Drew just said backs it up.' She relayed his words.

'Blimey.' Viv ate another mouthful of skate. 'Well I suppose I can see it, though it seems so extreme, Isla seducing Kip to rob him of the moral high ground. But it's true, if he slept with her, he couldn't very well complain about Saskia going off with Rufus. Or mope as though he was really devastated.'

Eve nodded. 'And Isla was a cool customer. I suppose she might even have been missing sex too, after giving Rufus the boot. She wasn't the romantic type, or the sort to appreciate someone to share her concerns, but maybe she thrived on the physical side.'

'Where does that leave Kip?'

'With a big motive for both victims. Isla made a fool of him. And she didn't take his feelings seriously. I remember her in the garden here. She asked if he was still sulking and then laughed. The look he shot her was full of hatred. And now I understand why.

'And maybe she'd started to realise just how angry he was. The day I interviewed her she was arguing her case, I'd guess: telling him she'd "done him a favour". By trying to make him snap out of it, presumably.' Only Kip hadn't seen it that way, and Eve wasn't surprised. He might have imagined she was genuinely interested. Or been overtaken by the moment in his misery, perhaps.

'Okay,' Viv said, spearing a Parmentier potato. 'So Kip's right up there. With who else? Dot?'

Eve sighed. 'She had more than enough reason to kill them both. She might have asked for my help simply to look innocent. And Rick Sutton's still on my radar too, though the latest information on him is odd.'

Viv sipped her wine. 'Because Kip caught him watching Dot as well as Saskia?'

Eve nodded. 'That makes him sound more like your standard creep. If he was obsessed with Saskia I could imagine him killing Rufus as his rival, but it doesn't quite work if he's interested in Dot too. Though it doesn't make him safe. I overheard Drew say he'd let the police know the latest.'

'That's a comfort. So, what's your hunch?'

Eve closed her eyes for a second. 'I honestly can't choose. Kip's got a horrible temper, but I'd say Dot's containing plenty of rage too. And she seems more practical and controlled.' And the worse she'd been treated, the more likely she was to be guilty.

'It sounds like Dot's slightly more likely,' Viv said, lowering her voice.

'Perhaps.' She was right. Deep down, Eve did think that. 'Rick Sutton's still a question mark. His link to all the key players down in London has to be significant.'

'So, what's your plan?'

'I'm going to try to retrace Dot's footsteps on the walk she supposedly took, the night Rufus died. Maybe something will come to mind, though I can't imagine what. I'd love to rule her out.' But the prospect seemed highly unlikely.

Viv pulled a sympathetic expression. 'Toby's really fond of her, isn't he?'

Eve nodded. 'I'll dig deeper with Rick Sutton too. I want to know what he really gets up to at Watcher's Wood. Maybe I can follow him if I sneak onto the site. And I think I'll have to take a similar approach to Kip Clayton. Find a way to get a look at what he's up to without being seen. But again, it'll be a fishing expedition.'

Viv frowned like a mother whose child had just announced its intention to go and play in the road.

'Don't worry. I'll be careful. There will be loads of people milling around. And it'll have to wait in any case. I'll need plenty of time, and I'm due to interview Rufus's brother tomorrow afternoon, after my shift at Monty's. I'm going to get up early though, to retrace Dot's steps.'

'And the back lanes of Saxford will be deserted. Want me to come with you?'

'Thanks, but I'll have Gus. He's fiercer than he looks.'

'You could take your favourite horticulturalist,' Viv added, with a hopeful look.

'I'll bear it in mind.'

# CHAPTER TWENTY-SIX

Early the following morning, Eve stood on the beach, close to a path that led to the Watcher's Wood site. Gus dashed to the path's entrance and glanced over his shoulder at her, poised, waiting for the word go.

'Not this time, buddy.' She bet he was thinking of Margot Hale. The woman had treated him like royalty and Eve was starting to think she'd slipped him some doggie treats too. She wasn't saying Gus was ruled by his stomach, but he really did seem very keen to go back and visit.

'We've got a mission, and it involves walking away from the *Lindens* camp, not towards it.'

Gus had his head on one side, and was expressing his disappointment very eloquently with his eyes.

Eve reached in her bag for the copy of Dot Hampshire's statement to the police. It included what she could remember of her alleged walk after she'd dropped a drunk Kip Clayton back at his trailer, the night Rufus died. Now Eve was ready to start her reenactment it felt hopeless. What could she find that would possibly help? But she was out of options. Without anything else to go on it had to be worth a try.

It was another glorious day, contrasting her mood. As Eve urged Gus up the pebble-strewn sand, the sun lit the crests of the waves and the sea sparkled. She'd come early, before the heat built up, and the onshore breeze was refreshing. Gus dashed ahead now, having accepted the direction she'd chosen. His ears were flung back, legs trotting enthusiastically.

Eve glanced at her photocopy. Dot remembered walking north up the beach in the direction of Saxford, before turning inland through a gap in the trees, just beyond the Watcher's Wood site.

She glanced up to match the words with reality, the cries of the gulls ringing in her ears. Had she gone immediately left? Or walked a little further? There were lots of gaps in the trees.

She checked the map on her phone and found all the paths ended up at the same lane. She'd have to guess. She called Gus and then stepped up the beach, over a bar of denser shingle where yellow horned-poppies and blue-purple viper's bugloss danced in the breeze.

Gus followed, sniffing about in the dunes, his tail wagging.

As they headed off through the woods, Eve kept an eye out for wildlife. It was a common spot for adders, though she'd managed to damp down her paranoia about them. Apparently their bites were rarely fatal. All the same, she tended to feel anxious for Gus. His inbuilt desire to hunt things was a worry.

As they walked, Eve glanced to left and right at the dense trees. She wasn't surprised Dot had made her way without being seen, though from their account, Margot Hale and Brooke Shaw must have been nearby when she returned. Maybe she could spot something Dot should also have spotted. Something unusual that would give veracity to her story if Eve could get her to recall it on her own.

But whatever it was, it wouldn't prove she'd travelled the route at a particular time. If she'd invented her walk she'd probably checked out the details at some stage. She'd know it well enough to give a description that tied in with reality.

Eve emerged from the woods with the fluting song of a blackcap warbler in her ears. She'd come to a country lane and at this point, Dot said she'd turned right, away from Watcher's Wood.

The route was idyllic in daylight but it would have been lonelier in the evening. But of course, Dot wouldn't have worried. The first of the murders hadn't happened and the lane was in the heart of the peaceful Suffolk countryside. All the same, according to the timeline Eve had noted, dusk would have advanced and night fallen while she was out. She was supposed to have left Kip Clayton at his trailer at eight forty-five, and Greg said her outward journey would have taken at least twenty-five minutes.

'Then again, she was walking off her feelings,' Eve said to Gus. 'Assuming she'd only discovered Rufus was having an affair with Saskia the day before, she was probably still riled about it.' It would have been galling to feel his passions might have governed his casting decisions. Especially when she knew he was busy muddying her name in the acting world as Saskia enjoyed a boost.

According to Dot's statement, she'd walked 'some way' along the lane but then turned off left at a stile with a public right of way, running along some fields.

Eve continued until she came to a route that matched Dot's description. Once again, Eve's confidence in her story wavered. She would have reached this point as the light was failing. Would she really have hared off across country? Eve would have stuck to the lanes. But Dot had had fire in her belly that night. It could have given her confidence, out there in the fields. Or led her to kill, back at Watcher's Wood.

'Let's check it out anyway, Gus.' To their left, a field of golden wheat was almost ready for harvest.

It wasn't a right of way that Eve had walked before. It took them through a second field, round the back of a barn, which Dot mentioned in her description, and then at a right angle so they were heading towards Saxford again. In the near distance she could see Simon's stables and the back of another house on the same lane.

She sighed. Dot said she'd turned back before the path went through to the field after that. Her description had been good. So good it made Eve wonder whether Palmer was right, and she'd revised it before her interview. And retracing her steps had told Eve nothing.

It was only when she reached home again, and Gus was looking at her somewhat wearily, that a sudden realisation came. Goose-bumps rushed over her arms and the hairs on her scalp lifted.

'Oh my goodness, Gus. I missed something obvious. I need to talk to Dot Hampshire again.'

She was due to work an admin shift at Monty's that morning, but maybe the actress would come to her so she could slot in the chat before she began.

Eve dialled her number.

# CHAPTER TWENTY-SEVEN

'Tell me!' Viv was in top pleading mode. She was partway through baking a multi-layered occasion cake with blueberries and chocolate, a commission for a fortieth birthday. 'If you explain then I shan't mind you taking time out to talk to Dot during the admin session you promised to work.' A look of triumph lit her eyes.

'It won't be "during".' Eve smiled sweetly. 'Do you read the schedules at all? She'll be gone before I'm due to start.'

Viv sighed and turned back to her cocoa powder. 'I don't know why I ever let you come in and organise me. I'm always feeling outflanked.'

'I'll give you the low-down just as soon as she's left. I want to see if I get a result first.'

'Fine, fine.'

Eve had booked Sam, his girlfriend Kirsty – who was an old hand at Monty's – and Angie to serve front of house that day, so they were well covered. It was just as well. The teashop was chaotic. A large group of parents had come in with some boisterous toddlers. It might be hard for Dot to hear herself think, but at least privacy was assured. No one would be able to eavesdrop, what with the background noise.

But as Eve waited for the actress her feeling of excitement morphed into anxiety. She'd gone scampering along a path like Gus after wildlife but it might all go nowhere. Meanwhile, Dot was probably doing battle with the press, driving slowly past the group that still lingered outside Watcher's Wood. It would be a while before any of the cast or crew could stroll off again for a casual walk. Eve logged on to her computer, ready for work later, thinking of the effort Dot was making to reach her. She really hoped she wouldn't have a wasted journey.

At last, Sam poked his head round the office door to let her know Dot had arrived. 'Three people have already asked for her autograph and Kirsty was trying to deflect a woman who was making awkward comments about the murders.' He pulled an apologetic face.

'Heck.' Eve leaped up from her seat. 'My fault. I should never have asked her to meet me here.' Things had been easier for Margot and Brooke in the pub. They weren't public faces. Or the number-one suspect.

Kirsty had already shown Dot to a table and was taking her order, her back to the other customers. The actress toyed with the shocking-pink ribbon decorating the jam jar in front of her. The fresh cornflowers inside quivered in the faint breeze from the open door of the teashop.

Eve decided to join Dot in the Darjeeling, scones and jam she'd ordered. It was classic fare but Viv's cooking made them special and the jam was something else.

'So sorry for dragging you out,' she said. 'I thought it would be easier to talk here.' And faster. Eve had been impatient, asking Dot to come to Monty's because she didn't want to wait.

'A change is as good as a rest!' The woman glanced at the parents and toddlers.

'I should have thought.'

She shook her head. 'Don't worry. It's always a consideration for me but other people often don't realise. And they're only interested because of the murder. I'll be yesterday's news soon, with a washed-up career and a cloud of suspicion hanging over me. If the police don't charge me, that is.' Then she sat up straighter and pulled a

sucking-lemons face. 'Hell. Slap me if I talk like that again. If all
that comes to pass *and* I wallow in self-pity it'll be the final straw.
So, what can I do for you?'

Eve smiled, but again, nerves caught at her stomach. Maybe the
scone order had been a mistake. 'This morning, I walked the route
you took the night Rufus died.'

Her shoulders sagged. 'How accurate did it seem?'

'Perfectly.' Eve didn't admit that had made her suspicious. Dot
came across as a clear-sighted, organised person. Quick. It was
possible she'd just retained the details. Despite the intervening
stress.

'I was hoping you could cast your mind back,' Eve went on, 'and
relive each step of the way.' She wanted her back in the moment,
with the feel of the warm evening air on her cheeks and the sound
of nature settling for the night in her ears. 'Can you remember
enough now to talk me through it?'

Dot looked at her doubtfully. 'I don't see how it will help.'

'I get that. But can you humour me, just for a minute?'

Kirsty had arrived with their scones and tea. 'Thank you!' The
girl grinned and retreated, with half an eye on the parents and
toddlers. The volume of their talk was rising again. A second later
she scooped up an escaped child walking unsteadily towards the
crafts area and returned it to its father.

'Okay.' Dot had closed her eyes, rather than applying herself to
her food. It was just as well Viv couldn't see. 'So, I walked down
the shady path towards the beach. My stomach was screwed-up
and the drink at the pub had made me feel worse. I just wanted to
get the hell out for a while. I couldn't stop thinking about Rufus
and how unprofessional he was being. And how I was paying the
price for his mercurial nature.'

Eve nodded, though Dot still had her eyes shut. 'Thanks. Can
you remember how it all looked? How it sounded?'

'Well…' The actress paused for a moment. 'The sun was behind me but still filtering through the trees. The woods were a bit cooler than our campsite. It was a relief. And I could hear the sea, lapping on the shore, then pulling back again.'

'Great. And what about after that?'

Dot described walking along the beach. Getting a pebble in her sandal, the sand still being warm when she bent to remove it. The sky turning orange and purple as the light faded. And then Eve got her to retell her progress through the woods and along the lane. Dot remembered seeing an owl in the distance as she'd climbed over the stile, and feeling stray bits of the cereal crop scratch her feet so that she wished she'd changed into her trainers before heading out.

And then, in her mind's eye, she reached the point beyond the barn and Eve held her breath. 'What could you hear then?' *Please remember.* Eve found herself crossing her fingers under the table and prayed they weren't interrupted by anyone. The noise from the parent and toddler tables was intense.

'I…' Dot opened her eyes and frowned. 'I'd totally forgotten. But I heard music. Drifting on the breeze.'

Relief flooded over Eve, and swiftly afterwards a feeling of euphoria that was no doubt premature. She took a deep breath.

'I can't think why I didn't remember that.' Dot's brow was still furrowed.

'You probably didn't think it was relevant. Was there anyone close by? Could you tell where it came from?'

She bit her lip. 'No, there was no one near me that I could see. I had the impression the music was being played loudly, but some way off. It made me think of hearing a festival going on in the distance.' She shook her head. 'I can even remember the tune now the memory's a conscious one again. "London Calling" by The Clash. There were bits I could identify but then the wind changed, and it got fainter.'

'Dot, I think you should go and see the police again. Tell them you remembered that detail and add it to your statement.'

'Can't you tell me what this is all about?'

Eve took a sip of her tea at last. 'Better if I don't. They're more likely to believe you if you don't know why it might be significant. There's no guarantee, but it might just help.' Eve didn't want to raise false hope. 'And please don't mention you've spoken to me. Just say you were replaying the scene mentally, in case you'd missed anything.'

'Okay, thanks.' She looked mystified, but then she took a bite of her scone and smiled. Hope combined with Viv's excellent cooking perhaps. 'These are fantastic. Oh, incidentally, have you heard the latest news from our end?'

Eve shook her head.

'It's not public yet but I expect it'll leak out soon. Drew's found a new producer who can complete *Last of the Lindens*. Stefan Meyer, no less.'

Eve tried to look intelligent, though the name was only vaguely familiar. Dot laughed.

'He's really good, so the TV company are happy and to be honest, so am I.'

'And what about a director?'

Dot swallowed another mouthful of her scone. 'Drew's going to do it. He and Stefan have worked together before. So as soon as the insurers give us leave we can resume filming. Stefan has some contact who can fill in on the assistant director role.'

*Wow. That will get Palmer's antennae quivering.*

There was no suspicion in Dot's tone, but Eve suddenly wondered if she'd got Drew all wrong. Her mouth felt dry and she drained her cup of tea.

As soon as Dot had left, Eve thanked Kirsty, Sam and Angie for keeping everyone at bay, then went through to the kitchen.

'Right.' Viv had just put her cake into the oven and slung the oven gloves over the back of a chair. 'Tell!'

'Don't you want me to get started on the admin first?' Viv stuck out her tongue. 'All right then. When I retraced Dot's steps this morning, I ended up in sight of Simon's stables.'

'Hold the front page!'

'But what was happening at Simon's place, the night Rufus was killed?'

Viv put a hand to her forehead. 'Polly's party?'

'Exactly. And when Dot trawled through her memories again today she remembered she'd heard music. She even recalled the song. So suddenly her alibi's looking more believable – to me at least. But I can't remember when they played "London Calling".'

Viv's face clouded. 'Nor me, and without the timing, I suppose it won't put her in the clear.'

'That's right. I need to call Simon. But you mustn't tell him what I've just said. If the police interview him they can't know I've been interfering. Palmer will think I've been asking him and Dot leading questions. I know you regard Simon as one of the team, but in this case it's essential we keep quiet.' Eve didn't break eye contact until Viv responded.

She did so with a salute. 'Scout's honour.'

'But that's not the only thing.' Eve explained about Drew's promotion and Viv's mouth formed an 'O'.

'You think he could have killed Rufus hoping to get the director role, and then Isla too, when she didn't pick him?'

Eve frowned. 'It's certainly something to think about.'

# CHAPTER TWENTY-EIGHT

Back at Elizabeth's Cottage, Eve let Gus out into the garden and called Simon. She just had time before heading off to talk to Rufus's brother, Jasper Beaumont.

Viv's brother sounded bemused when she asked if he knew which song was played when. '*What have you got up your sleeve? Viv said you were working hard on the mystery of Rufus's murder.*'

'I can't go into detail. If the police end up interviewing you it'll be best if you sound natural.'

'*Got you.*' He didn't push. He was much more restrained than Viv. '*But in answer to your question, this is Polly we're talking about. She had a playlist. Put it on at eight on the dot, even though no one arrived until ten past. So if our deeply unloved detective inspector wants to know when a particular song was played, we'll be able to oblige.*'

'That's amazing. Thank you!'

'*Do you want to know the answer, too?*'

Eve fought with her emotions. She was desperate to. Had she managed to prove Dot's innocence? Should she shift her entire focus to Drew, Kip and Rick Sutton? But she pushed the desire down. 'It's all right. I'll wait to hear once Palmer's checked with you.' If Simon knew which song was relevant in advance, he might sound too prepared when Palmer called. 'Don't say I was in touch about this, will you?'

'*My lips are sealed.*'

'Thanks, Simon. You're a gem!'

Before she set off, she messaged Robin too.

*If Greg mentions music the night Rufus died, could you happen to mention Polly's party in passing?*

His answer came back moments later.

*Cryptic. Will do, but I'll demand more info in due course. See you tonight!*

With thoughts of a late supper and catch-up at Robin's cottage circling pleasantly in her mind, she called Gus back inside, locked up and bent to give him a cuddle.

'I won't be very long.' Jasper Beaumont, Rufus's elder brother, was meeting her at his family's country home. As Kip Clayton had said, it was close by: only just north of Blyworth.

An hour later, Eve was driving onto the Beaumonts' country estate. There were no press lurking at *their* gates – maybe because they knew there'd be no point. Security around their land looked comprehensive and Eve couldn't see the house from the road. Their privacy was assured.

She approached from the east via a sweeping driveway lined with lime trees, passing outbuildings, including some stables. Beyond, there were tantalising glimpses of the mellow red-brick house.

She parked her Clubman on the driveway to the right of the main building. The place was enormous. Sixteenth century, Eve guessed, with mullioned windows. It was impressive, but rather forbidding to her eyes.

The front door opened as she approached. Eve half expected a maid or butler to appear, but she recognised Rufus's elder brother from the films she'd seen him in. This was a far cry from the informal meeting she'd once had with Kim Carmichael in her

London townhouse. It would be harder, too, as Jasper had been such a close relative, but Eve was more than curious to see what he had to say. Information on Rufus's childhood might reveal a lot. Understanding him completely had to be key to working out who'd killed him.

Jasper's hair was a little redder than his brother's, but if anything he looked younger, despite being the elder sibling. His dark trousers and black shirt, open at the neck, looked both stylish and sombre.

He leaned forward as he shook her hand.

'Thanks so much for seeing me.'

'You're welcome.'

They walked through an impressive wood-panelled hall with a wide staircase and Jasper showed her into a vast living room. He motioned her to a beautiful French-polished table at one side of it. Even resting her wire-bound notepad on its surface made her nervous.

'I'm only recently back from filming in Paris,' he said. 'I'd promised myself a few days in Suffolk.' He shuddered. 'I heard about Rufus on my way up here from the airport.'

'I'm so sorry for your loss. And especially in these circumstances. It's such a shocking thing to happen.'

He leaned forward, his head in his hands, elbows on the table. She could see his reflection in it. 'Even more awful for my parents. I'm sorry they're not here to talk to you but they're just not up to it. And my sister's stuck filming in the States. She'll be back as soon as she can.'

'Of course. I totally understand.'

His gaze met hers. 'I feel I should start by correcting some false-hoods. I suppose you've heard the gossip about Rufus's love life?'

'Yes. I was an extra on the set of *Lindens* when the affair with Saskia came out.'

'I had no idea about that until I read it in the papers. And he planned to leave Cassie, I gather. I always thought the marriage might come apart. It can't have been easy for her, living with someone who was constantly looking for a mythical better life. But he wasn't a true womaniser. Far from it, despite the speculation in the press. They always focus on his love life because of Emily, his childhood sweetheart who died in a drunken stupor.'

'Were he and Emily together a long time?'

Jasper closed his eyes for a moment. 'Let's see, from when they were fifteen until near the end of their third year at Ryland. She acted too.' He shook his head. 'She came here once, years later, to ask if any of us knew why he'd broken up with her. I assume he'd had his head turned by Dora, the actress he worked with on that film just after he left drama school. I guessed he might have already met her at the auditions. I didn't admit as much to Emily though. She and Rufus were just kids for most of their time together. You don't expect that kind of puppy love to last.' He sighed. 'And I couldn't tell her that either. Especially not when I could see she was so lost. But you get the picture.'

Jasper shook his head. 'I could never have imagined Rufus being killed of course, but I always feared for him.'

Eve waited for him to form words to express what was on his mind.

'He made great television, but that was never enough. He wanted to make it in acting. So much so, that when he was young I used to think he was on a path to self-destruction. He'd go to any lengths to up his game. And the rest of us all felt terrible. This constant dragging guilt that we happened to have the talent he lacked in that department.'

The look on his face robbed his words of arrogance or schadenfreude. He really had felt uncomfortable about the situation, she could see.

'It got to the point where he was going to extremes, not just before he played his roles, but even before auditions.'

'I know he was keen on method acting,' Eve said.

Jasper nodded. 'He got his actors to do it and before that, he practised what he preached. But to a damaging degree. He went for a part in a war film and starved himself for days beforehand, then made a dangerous jump off a bridge to feel the sort of mortal terror a soldier might endure, crossing a battlefield. Almost killed himself.'

Suddenly he pulled himself up straighter and Eve guessed his thoughts.

'I don't have to include anything specific. Or to make it clear which bit of information came from which person. I hope to give *Icon*'s readers a true portrait of your brother but not to cause pain.' She guessed guilt and sorrow had made him speak more freely than he'd meant.

'Thanks. And I understand you'll want to tell the truth, but maybe leave out that detail.'

She nodded.

'I know there was gossip about my mother getting him his first job as a director.' He shrugged, his face pinched. 'It's at least partly true, but I'd be grateful if you didn't quote me on that either. It's what most people think anyway. Mum introduced Rufus to a producer contact of hers. He decided to give him a go independently, but he was a close family friend. Rufus felt it: the favour. He called any support we gave him "the curse of the Beaumonts", but some people would have killed for that chance.'

He stopped suddenly, as though he realised what he'd said, and Eve thought of Drew Fawcett. She could understand how hard it must have been for Rufus, but it would be galling for other, less fortunate colleagues to hear him moaning.

Jasper took a deep breath. 'Mum was protecting him. Acting had become an obsession. He'd started to drink, and to make irrational decisions. She helped launch his career in directing to steer him away from all that.'

And what mother would do different? Eve would help her twins without a single doubt if she thought they were in harm's way.

'Rufus always maintained he could have got there without her, and he was certainly good enough. But there's more to career progression than talent. Everyone in the business knows that. Connections and luck play a part.'

'You must have felt frustrated that he couldn't just be grateful.' She said the words gently; she could hear the hint of resentment in his tone.

He looked sheepish. 'A little. He had all the means to be happy but he couldn't accept life as it was. It seemed such a waste. The critics were commending his amazing work but all he could think of was the nasty whispers about how he'd got his first job. It made Mum's life harder. She started to question her actions, but she was desperate at the time.'

Eve nodded. 'He never suggested working on a project together?' It might have made Rufus feel he had the upper hand, if he and Isla had recruited Jasper. And Jasper did television work as well as film.

But the actor shook his head. 'My sister broached the idea once, but Rufus talked across her as though she hadn't spoken. The suggestion was no good if it came from us. It just looked patronising.'

A short while later, Eve was back in her car, exiting the Beaumont's grand grounds, past neatly clipped topiary to either side of the main gate. The gates opened automatically as she approached.

Maybe Rufus couldn't stand working with anyone who was better at acting than him. Couldn't tolerate the comparisons his critics might make.

And then suddenly she was sure that was why he'd always nurtured new talent. He could only endure upcoming actors in his midst. Seeing their success validated him, but the moment the rave reviews came in he'd distance himself. And now she bet it had been as simple as that with Cecilia Dunwoody: not some disagreement between them, or an affair gone wrong, but simply that she'd outshone him so completely. Eve imagined it had still hurt from afar, watching her go on to win her Oscar. Now, it seemed to Eve that he'd refined his plan when it came to Dot; gone one step further by ensuring no one else would hire her. She guessed it was Isla who'd pushed to keep Dot on for *Lindens*. However harsh and unfeeling she'd been, Eve believed she'd genuinely admired Dot's talent. But despite Dot being in a lesser part, Rufus hadn't been able to hide his feelings towards her, or stop himself finding fault and pulling her down. All to bolster himself up.

Had his plan to marry Saskia been driven by the same desire? All that romantic talk of having babies. It seemed early to start that type of discussion, but maybe Rufus had brought it up. It would have kept Saskia where he wanted: back on the ranch, not showing him up.

She shuddered as she made it to the road back towards home. If she was right, she wondered if he'd inwardly acknowledged what he was doing. Or had he buried it? Come up with excuses for the way he'd behaved? Eve guessed the latter. Either way, it was as Kip had said; he'd damaged people he got close to.

Deep in her gut, she wondered if this facet of his character might provide a key to the murders. It was extreme. He'd been belittled and patronised since his schooldays. His success as a director had made no difference to the gossip about him. People still only believed he'd achieved what he had thanks to family influence. There'd been a desperation about him: a need to strive to succeed and pull himself above the rest by any means possible. And he'd worked overtime to ignore or bury anything that brought him face to face with what he saw as his failure. Even filming in the same county as his family home had been hard to bear.

At some stage, Eve could believe this had caused him to cross a line that had caused the murderer to cross one too, far more terrible.

And perhaps Isla, in accommodating him for so long, had met the same fate for the same reason.

Eve's mind was still on Rufus's psyche when she drove over the Old Toll Road, crossing the River Sax, and pulled up in her usual spot by the village green. She was just in time to see a patrol car drive past. She recognised Robin's friend Greg Boles at the wheel.

And behind him, in the shadows, next to a second officer, was Drew Fawcett.

# CHAPTER TWENTY-NINE

By eight that evening, Eve and Gus were on their way to Robin's. He'd texted to say he could offer her an update on Drew Fawcett as well as dinner.

There were clouds amassing in the sky and a storm was forecast, but it was still warm as she walked past the cottage gardens on Love Lane. The scent of lavender wafted on the breeze. A tiny thunder fly landed on her bare shoulder and she blew it off. She was wearing her emerald-green shift dress, but she had her raincoat stuffed into a tote bag, just in case.

She was planning to cut through Blind Eye Wood again and was just passing the Cross Keys when Moira appeared on the other side of the road and came to meet her.

Her eyes said 'politely concerned' and Eve wondered what she'd done.

'Eve, dear.' She stopped, instead of launching straight in with her worries, issued in a tactful tone. They usually related to Gus: that she was walking him too often or not enough. And were Angie and Sam really responsible enough to look after him in her absence? It was irritating but Eve was equal to it. She could do tact, and she knew Gus was well looked after; that was what counted.

'Yes? Is everything all right?' Eve resisted the urge to look at her watch. She was itching to get to Robin's.

'The last thing I ever want is to interfere, you know that. But I'm just a little worried. I've noticed… I mean, there's your walks. And then later…'

*Oh dear.* Moira must have spotted she didn't always come home after the regulation time. She'd probably already invented reasons for it. Hopefully alone and not in collaboration with the other village gossips. Thank goodness the wine Eve had brought to share was underneath her raincoat.

'It's just… Well, that is to say… Do be careful, won't you?'

Eve smiled. 'I'll certainly do that. The woods can be quite lonely at this hour, but Gus and I are always cautious. We'll keep to the main paths. It's kind of you but there's no need to worry.'

Moira blinked quickly. 'Oh well, yes, of course. That's all right then.'

She bit her lip and frowned as Eve hurried on her way. Thank goodness she was too prudish to spell out her real concerns.

'Heck, Gus,' Eve said, once they'd walked down Heath Lane and disappeared amongst the trees. 'She probably thinks I'm having an affair with a married man or something. I only hope she's not already speculating publicly.'

Fifteen minutes later, she was sitting at Robin's kitchen table, the curtains drawn against the oncoming night. Gus was tensed against her toes as Robin dished up pasta with chorizo and tomato sauce.

The source of his tension was the weather. It had finally broken just after she'd walked through the door. She could see violently flickering lightning beyond the curtains and hear the crack of thunder seconds later. Each instance was marked by Gus pushing up against her feet a little harder. She glanced under the table to utter some words of comfort and stroke his head.

The temperature had dropped a little but it was still humid.

Robin slid into the chair opposite Eve and poured them each a glass of the Rioja she'd brought.

She raised her glass to his. 'This smells amazing. Thank you.'

'My pleasure.'

She'd invited him over to Elizabeth's Cottage, but slipping into his place undetected was that bit easier. Or so she'd thought. She'd already told him about her run-in with Moira. Varying the venue for their meetups might be in order.

'So, what news of Drew?'

Robin relaxed in his chair. 'He's back at Watcher's Wood, but Palmer's not happy, according to Greg. It's clear he's benefited substantially from Rufus and Isla's deaths.'

Eve nodded. 'I thought the same too. The outcome's pretty convenient. Almost as though he had Stefan Meyer lined up to take over. I wonder why he wasn't busy.' She'd looked the man up after she'd got home from visiting Jasper Beaumont. There was nothing to hint at what he'd been working on these last several months.

'It could just be luck, but Palmer's suggested Meyer might be short of work for some reason. He's an old contact of Drew's, apparently.'

Eve sipped her wine. 'I noticed they'd worked together before, a while back, with Drew as a runner. I can see why Palmer and Co might think it's a stitch-up. But the more I think about it, the more it doesn't make sense. I get that he could have doubled back from the manor in time to kill Isla, but why come up with that story in the first place unless it was true? It's an entirely breakable alibi, so as an invention, it's not any use to him.

'And the idea of committing a double murder simply to get a promotion doesn't wash. Even if you leave aside the horror of it, it would be too big a risk with too little reward. Drew's got loads of good experience with a top producer–director partnership. I appreciate getting the next step up the ladder must be competitive, but I'd imagine he'd be in pole position to find an opening.' She shook her head. 'I just don't see it. And then there's the objections I came up with before: he wants the case solved. He's shown that more than once. And his and Isla's relationship was cordial – profes-

sional. I never saw her treat him like a protégé. She had no reason
to cover for him the night Rufus died.'

'Well, you might be right. They had to let him go. Not enough
evidence. He was just "helping them with their enquiries".'

'And did he? Help, I mean?'

Robin laughed. 'Not at all. Greg says Palmer's livid. They did
everything they could to rattle him but nothing worked. I made
a note.' He grabbed a pad from the top of a nearby dresser and
glanced at it. 'He said he understood why they were suspicious
about his alibi but, like you, he asked why Isla would lie for him.
And he pointed out that she regularly kept him up working half
the night. Then he said they'd just have to wait until they got at the
truth, and that if he'd wanted a promotion he'd have gone about
it in the standard way.'

Eve found it hard not to laugh when she imagined Palmer's
reaction, though the situation was all too serious.

Robin bent to fuss Gus as another crack of thunder made
him jump. 'For what it's worth, Greg agrees with you.' His voice
became less muffled as he reappeared from under the table. 'The
overpowering desire for promotion doesn't make sense to him either.
As he said, *Lindens* is only the second project Drew's worked on
with Quinn and Beaumont, and he's not even completed that. A
double murder to move forward would seem a bit impatient. But—'

Eve held up a hand. 'I know, I shouldn't discount him completely.
I won't, I promise.'

Robin grinned. 'What about the other suspects? Does Kip strike
you as a calculating and careful planner with a long-term desire to
kill for emotional reasons?'

Eve frowned. 'I doubt careful planning would come naturally.
I'd say he's more of an off-the-cuff type. But I think hurt ego and
fury would go a long way towards focusing his mind. People can
achieve a lot when the stakes are high, and I think Kip's thin-

skinned, just like Rufus was. He's been nursing a grudge since Rufus convinced Saskia to leave him. It could have been that that led him to plan the first murder. Maybe he was all set up to do it and the revelation about their affair gave him the final push into action. And whoever's guilty might have moved far more quickly for Isla. They just had to re-use the same plan.' She sighed. 'But I think even someone driven to kill at short notice could be guilty, if they had the sedatives to hand.'

Robin nodded. 'It's possible. Without enough evidence to requisition anyone's medical records, that line of enquiry's gone nowhere so far. And what about Rick Sutton?'

Eve pictured the jittery custodian. 'It's even harder to see him as a successful planner, but I could imagine him being reckless enough. And he could have nursed resentment for as long as Kip. He was already keeping tabs on Saskia down in London, but his new interest in Dot muddies the waters. I need to know more.'

Robin nodded. 'Oh, congratulations, by the way!'

Eve raised an eyebrow.

'"London Calling" was playing between nine fifteen and nine eighteen. Unless Dot Hampshire flew or had a copy of Polly's playlist to work from, she's in the clear.'

Eve's chest felt as though it was fizzing with champagne bubbles. 'That's amazing.' It brought new possibilities too. 'I might go and see Dot tomorrow.'

He raised an eyebrow.

'I need some time just hanging around quietly, observing Kip and Rick Sutton. I might pretend to leave after talking with her. That way, if anyone spots me later I can claim I had reason to come back. I'll say I left something in her trailer by accident. Now I know she's innocent, I can ask her to cover for me.' Normally she'd avoid spying on a Sunday, when people might be off site, but for the *Lindens* production every day was a holiday now. And as for

Rick, Eve couldn't imagine him leaving Watcher's Wood unless he had to. He was too involved with the cast.

Robin grinned and shook his head. 'You know what I'm going to say, don't you?'

Eve nodded. 'I'll be careful. But the place will be crawling with actors and crew. Unless they're all in it together I ought to be safe enough.'

# CHAPTER THIRTY

The following day, Eve sat in Dot Hampshire's trailer, unable to quell her feeling of euphoria at one small victory. The folder on her laptop with details about the case now had an updated timeline for the night Rufus died. The relevant section read:

**8.45 p.m.:** Dot and Kip arrive back at Watcher's Wood (According to Dot. Long walk, and Kip was drunk. A brisk walker could have done it in fifty minutes, but sounds plausible.) Dot sees Drew and Isla in Isla's trailer

**8.45 p.m.:** Rufus signs into internet banking in his trailer

**8.48 p.m.:** or thereabouts. Dot leaves for her long walk after bundling Kip into his trailer.

**8.50 p.m.:** Rufus cancels direct debit to Cassie

**8.53 p.m.:** Rufus reaches the vestry. (Earliest possible time. And he was drunk. Might have been slower.)

**9.15 – 9.18 p.m.:** 'London Calling' playing at the stables. Heard by Dot as she stood in the field visited by Eve

**9.20 p.m.:** Brooke and Margot pass house beyond the stables on their way back from the pub. (Seen by occupants. More than ten minutes' walk away from Watcher's Wood. Couldn't have arrived back before Rufus was killed.)

**9.30 p.m.:** Rufus's phone alarm goes off. (Police guess he was dead by this time and his murderer gone from the vestry.)

**9.40 p.m.:** earliest time Dot could have arrived back at Watcher's Wood (25 minutes' walk from where she heard 'London Calling')

Dot hadn't stopped smiling since Eve had arrived. 'I'll still have to repair the damage Rufus has done to my reputation, but not being suspected of murder is a major step forward. Thank you.'

'It's the first time I've been grateful for a party of Polly's. I don't fit in.'

Dot laughed. 'And of course I'll cover for you. It's the least I can do. Why don't you really leave something here? It will look more convincing if you do get caught.'

Eve had had the same thought and produced the tote bag she had with her, with a spare notepad and pen inside. 'Thanks. I'll make my way back to the main exit, then, and creep back in soon after that. I managed to climb over a wall once – I could do that again. Though if anyone drives along the lane they'll spot me.'

'You might be better off making for the crumbling bit of wall right round the back, beyond Rick Sutton's chalet.' She shook her head. 'Very easy to climb over, and a lot less overlooked.'

Eve smiled. 'Noted.'

As she exited the trailer, she spotted Brooke Shaw the costume supervisor, talking to a man she didn't recognise. Brooke raised her hand when she saw Eve and sauntered over. She was perfectly turned-out again, in a black halter neck. She looked like a model.

'How's the obituary coming along?'

'Fine, thanks. If there's anything you'd like to add, favourite memories, anecdotes or insights, please let me know.' Eve handed over a business card and remembered Brooke's words, back before Rufus was murdered. She'd said he and Kip both had vile tempers. She must have a story to tell.

Brooke's eyes were half closed against the sun as she took Eve's contact details. 'I can't think what I'd say, but I'll keep it in mind.'

Maybe she had memories she'd rather bury. Or perhaps they weren't personal recollections. Robin said Rufus had yelled at Margot Hale when she tried to tempt him out to the pub, the night he died. And Margot would have likely told Brooke as well as the police. They spent a lot of time together.

Eve had kept moving towards the exit as she talked with the costume supervisor. She wanted to give a clear impression of her intent. They were out beyond the trailers when she saw Saskia a little way to their right, talking on her mobile. Eve guessed she'd moved beyond the main camp for some privacy. She had her hand up as though to hide her face, but Eve could see she was crying. Her voice was thick with tears too.

'No, no. But I wish I'd been there. I'll come home now.' A pause. 'No. I've already spoken to the police. They don't need me. You can't think I'd stay away at a time like this.'

She moved out of their sight now, with a quick determined step. She must have seen them.

Brooke carried on walking with Eve. 'Sounds like her dad's died. She's been nipping back to Norfolk to see him ever since filming stopped, but I didn't imagine the end would come so quickly.'

Poor Saskia. Another massive loss, hard on the heels of Rufus. 'So it was expected?'

Brooke nodded. 'She heard he was ill the day you and all the extras came on set.'

The bad news the mouse-haired actress had referred to in the Cross Keys was real, then. Yet Isla had dismissed her emotion as affected reaction to her intense performance. Poor woman. And the grapes and flowers she'd bought at Moira's store made sense now too. No wonder she hadn't wanted to come to the pub, the night of the murder. Rufus would have stayed behind to comfort her.

Only he hadn't, Eve reflected. He'd drunk himself stupid instead, after Isla told him she wanted to end their partnership. It was as Jasper had said: he couldn't just value what he had, and look after what was under his nose. They could have shared their woes, given each other comfort.

After Eve had made her official exit from Watcher's Wood, she walked back up the lane in the direction of Saxford. She checked over her shoulder regularly but the place was silent except for birdsong and bees buzzing around the wildflowers.

A short while later she turned right into the trees which bordered the site and skirted the edge of a woodland ride. The sound of crickets filled the air, but again, there was no sign of another human. She swallowed. If anyone was watching her, they'd find her utterly alone. Her mind turned to Robin and the promise she'd made him, and to the shadowy figure she'd seen crouched in her garden.

She walked on quickly. She'd chosen a leaf-green jumpsuit for a reason and swapped the open ride for the woodland canopy now. It would be less easy to see if someone followed her, but she'd be better disguised too.

In the far distance she could see Rick Sutton's chalet. A little further and she'd be at the site's perimeter. Hopefully she'd find the tumbledown wall Dot had mentioned.

Five minutes later, she'd discovered it – or a place that would do just as well – and clambered through. She was well beyond the main thoroughfares of the site, but people were probably stir-crazy by now. There was no knowing who might come wandering in her direction. And of course, Rick Sutton was responsible for the whole place, though she didn't imagine he spent much time patrolling it.

Eve decided to set up camp near his chalet. His creepy behaviour made her want to pursue him. Even if he was innocent of murder, he might be a danger to Saskia and Dot and it might get overlooked with everything else going on.

She found a hawthorn thicket between other larger trees and edged her way round so she could approach it from behind. A bead of blood appeared on her arm as she slipped into her hiding place, but it was worth it. She could see the door to Rick's chalet from her vantage point. Unfortunately, she could also hear Rick's voice, singing along to the radio. She needed him to go out so she could follow him. What did he really get up to all day? He certainly hadn't been answering letters or phone calls, from what she'd seen previously.

But after waiting in the thicket for over an hour, Rick hadn't appeared. He'd stopped singing but she knew he was still in there. She spent another ten minutes deciding whether to cut her losses. She might be missing something elsewhere. It was just on lunchtime. If that was a communal affair, that might mean Kip Clayton would emerge from his trailer. It could be a prime time to listen in if she could make it to the main camp without being seen.

Reluctantly, Eve extricated herself from the thicket again and crept back, further into the woods. She went from tree to tree, checking all directions each time she moved, until she was level with the trailers. She could see the back of Drew and Kip's accommodation from where she was. And between the location vehicles she could just glimpse people pottering to and fro. Someone had a folding table out and was sitting at it. As she'd hoped, it looked as though lunch provided a time for the team to socialise.

Eve moved beyond the camp as quickly as she could. If she approached the trailers from the south side, she'd have cover for longer. When she reached the edge of the woods there, the trailer that had belonged to Isla Quinn was only a couple of metres away. Eve wondered if it had been cleared out, ready for Stefan Meyer.

If she managed to listen in to Kip's idle chat he might give something away. His colleagues must be suspicious, especially now the police had cleared Dot and let Drew go. With any luck the latest developments would trigger new discussions about the case. And she'd promised Robin she wouldn't discount Drew either.

*Now or never.*

She moved swiftly across the grass to the relative safety of the cover of Isla's trailer, but her heart was hammering. *Hello!* she rehearsed mentally. *Me again.* (Face palm.) *I left my notebook and bag at Dot's place.*

It might work, but no one must see her loitering. That would look odd, whatever she said.

She crouched low and crept round the side of the trailer, peeking to get a view. The result took her breath away.

She was virtually on top of Kip Clayton and Drew Fawcett. They were sitting between two cars at a white folding table. They'd been screened from view as she worked her way through the woods, below the level of the car roofs.

'Knock it off,' Drew was saying, nodding at the flask Kip had just swigged from.

'You'd want a drink, if you were me. I won't feel calm until we're in the clear.'

'I'm the one who got hauled in by the police yesterday.' Drew had an orange juice next to him.

The camera operator shrugged and picked up his flask again. 'I've only had a nip. No one would think twice if it was a lunchtime beer. And it's Sunday.'

'So long as you come back to work with a steady hand and a clear head, once we're able to carry on.'

'I'm touched by your concern.' Eve could hear the edge to Kip's voice. 'Not surprised the police suspect you.'

'Thanks.' Drew sounded totally calm. 'The idea that I'd kill two people for a job is crazy. And I admired Isla.'

'Like hell.' Kip seemed to have forgotten he was only taking a nip of his drink. He upended it as Drew ate a sandwich. 'No one liked her. She was a ruthless—'

'I didn't say liked. I said admired. She was ruthless, but excellent at her job.'

Kip's fists were clenched. 'She was on Rufus's side over Saskia.'

'So you've got reason to hate them both yourself.'

'Which is why I'm stressed and why I'm drinking.' Suddenly he laughed. 'Funnily enough, I slept with Rufus's girlfriend too, so we were quits. I only wish he'd known before he died.'

Drew frowned. 'What, you and Saskia got it together again? After she took up with him?'

Kip shook his head. 'No. She hasn't given me the time of day. It was Emily, the one who died. We were on the same production around nine months before she fell down the stairs and broke her neck.'

Drew stilled. Maybe he was as disgusted as Eve was. Kip clearly saw women as weapons in his armoury: useful for point scoring. The callous way he referred to Emily's death horrified Eve. And Isla had been right – Kip couldn't have been that bothered about Saskia if he'd welcomed her to his bed so readily.

After a moment, Drew said: 'She was drunk, if I remember rightly? A lesson to us all. And she wasn't with Rufus when she slept with you. Was it anything more than a one-night stand?'

Kip gave a snort of irritation, got up and took his flask with him.

# CHAPTER THIRTY-ONE

Eve thought Drew Fawcett would finish his sandwich but his outward calm left him the instant Kip Clayton's back was turned. He snatched up his plate with its half-eaten contents and Eve's heart hammered worse than it had before. What if he came her way, rather than risk running into the camera operator again?

But at that moment she heard Margot's voice calling Drew's name and he turned towards the main clearing of the campsite.

There was no time to lose. She took her chance to slip back into the trees again. She wondered how Margot felt about Drew taking over from Rufus. The memory of her touching the things in Rufus's trailer came back to her. She'd been tender. She must have been fond of him, despite his temper. Eve was sure she'd have lost patience if she'd been his PA.

As she walked through the trees, she reflected on what she'd learned during her eavesdropping session. Kip's link with Rufus's old girlfriend was interesting. It looked like Drew had guessed correctly and it had been a one-night stand or Kip would have contradicted him. And according to Jasper, Emily had still been hooked on Rufus, despite the passing years. Maybe she'd used Kip to blot out her feelings. She might even have been drunk at the time. Kip might have slept with Isla for the same reason, but she still didn't like his attitude.

When Eve got back to the thicket where she'd hidden before, she noticed Rick Sutton's chalet door was shut and the radio was no longer playing. *Heck.* She must have missed him leave, and now he could be anywhere. What she'd learned from Drew and Kip had been intriguing, but not hugely useful on the face of it. She should have stuck with her stakeout here.

Of course, Rick could have retreated into his living quarters at the rear of the chalet. He must have some time off and Sunday was a likely day, even if he had to keep a watching brief. There were several windows open. Rather than staying there for hours or going straight home, she decided on a different approach. She could knock on his door and engage him in conversation if he answered. He'd been obsessively interested in the *Lindens* team. Or some of them at least. It might not seem too odd if she asked to interview him about Rufus, then steered the conversation to her needs. She walked up to his door and knocked.

No reply. She tried the door, found it unlocked and went inside, leaving it open behind her. She wasn't as well protected as she'd thought in this deserted part of the site. Before she went any further, she checked her phone coverage and keyed in three nines. She'd dial if she needed to. Her palms felt sweaty as she knocked on the door to Rick Sutton's living quarters.

No reply again.

'Rick?' she called out as she tried the door, but as before, the entrance to his private space was locked. Maybe he only cared about his own belongings. Or perhaps he had something to hide.

As she crossed his office again she noticed the magazine she'd seen before, with Saskia on the front. It was underneath piles of other papers; she'd only recognised it because of her prior knowledge. The place was a mess.

A half-drunk cup of coffee sat on his desk, and there was an empty packet of caffeine tablets in his bin. No wonder he seemed nervy. Yet his work didn't look pressured. She couldn't imagine him burning the midnight oil.

At that moment, she caught sight of his notepad. It had an odd diagram on it. She was just about to open her camera, dismissing the 999 she'd entered on her phone, when she caught movement out of the window.

Rick Sutton was coming back.

She saw him through the trees in the distance. Where had he been? It wasn't a natural route to anywhere else on the site. More the kind she'd taken earlier, to keep her presence secret.

Her legs felt like jelly and her movements seemed slow. It was like being in a nightmare, where she needed speed but her body wouldn't react. She didn't want to talk to Rick now, she wanted time to think about what she'd found, and it would look odd if he discovered her there.

At last she came to a decision and dashed outside. If he saw her she'd just have to brazen it out. Say she'd come looking for him. But he was staring down at his phone, laughing about something.

She hid herself on the windowless side of his office, waited until he'd gone inside, then made for the woods again and the bit of broken wall.

She was well away by the time her pulse returned to something like normal. Through her fug of panic, she tried to remember the details of the diagram, doodled on his notepad. If only she'd managed to get a photo.

# CHAPTER THIRTY-TWO

At a quarter to six that evening, Eve answered a knock on the door of Elizabeth's Cottage to find Toby on the step.

'Hello! Come in.'

He was beaming, but he shook his head. 'Jo would have my guts for garters if I did. I'm due on the bar in a moment. But I wanted to thank you.'

She raised an eyebrow.

'About Dot. It's such a relief.' His face was glowing. 'I mean, not that I thought she was guilty, even for a minute, but I was worried for her. You never know what the police are up to behind the scenes and I wouldn't rely on Palmer to get the right person. So to have what amounts to an alibi…'

'I just jogged her memory.'

'You made the connection.'

She smiled, but inside it was hard to quell her happiness too. 'I'm just glad a possible solution came to mind.'

As she closed the door and watched Toby heading up Haunted Lane from the window, she spoke to Gus. 'So Dot contacted Toby to let him know her news. There's definitely a bond between them.' It made her feel all mushy inside.

The warm glow remained, but Eve switched tack quickly, back to the matter in hand. After supper, she sat in the dining room, the leaded casement windows open, hoping the gradually cooling air might help her think. Gus had pottered in and was looking up at her quizzically. They'd already walked to the beach and back but nothing had clicked.

'Here,' Eve said, 'take a look at this.' She held her notepad close to his nose and the dachshund looked startled. 'It's what I can remember from the doodle on Rick Sutton's notepad.'

He'd written the names of several key players in the murder investigation in a circle. She was sure Saskia had been down there, and Dot too. And Kip. And she thought Isla and Rufus as well. And there'd been arrows. Dot, Kip, Saskia, Rufus, Isla. She was pretty sure they'd been in that order. And there'd been some question marks, but she couldn't remember their position in relation to the names.

'No idea?' she said to Gus, removing the pad from his line of sight. *Nor me.* She'd sent Robin a photo of what she could remember and asked him for his thoughts. She looked again at his responses now.

*Two of them are dead.*

True enough.

*Three involved in love triangle.*

Also true.

*All worked ultimately for Isla, except for Isla herself... Am I helping?!*

Eve wasn't getting it either. Were they all connected in some additional way she'd yet to uncover?

She decided to let the problem sit in her subconscious for a while and switched topic, turning to her laptop to google Rufus's teenage sweetheart Emily. Kip's revelation that he'd slept with her (if it was true) was the other thing that had intrigued her that day. It seemed like quite a coincidence that they'd met. But when she looked, she found she was wrong. It was a smaller world than she'd thought. According to the Internet Movie Database, Kip and Emily Longfellow had worked on the same production, and it had been produced by Stefan Meyer, who'd employed Drew as a runner on his next project. Emily hadn't been on the cast list for that one, but Dot had had a walk-on part. They were like aircraft narrowly missing each other's flight paths, only Emily and Kip had happened to land at the same airport.

She looked at Emily's photograph on the site. She wasn't unlike Saskia, physically. Maybe Kip had a type. Her bio said she'd acted as an ambassador at her and Rufus's drama school, going out to clubs and schools around the country to promote the establishment and giving welcome talks to new students. She must have been confident back then. It was sad. Why had she failed to get over Rufus? Her life seemed to mirror his. She'd had talent, and she could have found someone else, but she'd never managed to move on. For her it had been Rufus, for him, acclaim as an actor. She might have slept with Kip but Eve guessed it hadn't meant anything.

Her mind drifted back to the doodle on Rick Sutton's pad. If only she had a photo. She wrote the names down again, in a larger circle this time, and tried to see the links.

The list put a whole new spin on things. She'd spent so long assuming he was obsessed with Saskia, and then later, that he was fixating on Dot as well. But whatever the truth, it seemed it was never about that.

Eve saw his movements in London in a new light too. She'd put his path crossing with Kip and Rufus down to his obsession with Saskia and his need to keep tabs on his rivals. But now she guessed it was more complicated: that he was watching them all for their own sake, maybe.

Wanting to understand the dynamics before he took up his post at Watcher's Wood?

She jotted down every link she could think of between the people he'd noted. Kip and Saskia had been lovers. Rufus had taken over with Saskia. Dot hated Rufus and Isla, and probably resented Saskia. But she had no significant relationship with Kip that Eve knew of. Though of course they'd left the pub together, the night Rufus was killed, and Dot had bundled Kip into his trailer.

Had she gone in with him for a moment? Eve had returned Dot's copy of her police statement, but not before photographing it. She checked it now. Yes, she had, apparently, though not for long. She said he was ranting and she couldn't wait to get out of there.

And then there were Rufus and Isla, who'd also had an affair.

Suddenly she stood up and Gus jumped sideways, startled by her unexpected movement.

'Gus, I've been focused on the wrong thing! Whatever Rick's up to, whether he's a gossip hound or a stalker, the result is the same. He's been keeping a heck of a close eye on a tight-knit circle of people, two of whom are victims, and one of whom is likely a murderer. If he's not the killer himself he's indulging in a very dangerous hobby. I need to talk to him.'

An hour later, she was standing with Robin close to the tumble-down wall Dot had told her about. He was dressed all in black: a long-sleeved T-shirt and jeans. She tried not to think how good he looked. It was unprofessional and hardly the point. She knew he was intending to fade into the shadows and it should work well. It was completely dark now and the trees provided good cover. He was there in case Eve ran into trouble. She still didn't know what she was dealing with.

'I'll be right outside,' Robin said. 'If I hear you so much as raise your voice I'll be in there.'

'Thank you.'

She took a deep breath and walked towards the custodian's chalet for the second time that day. She could see a light on in his office. He must be at his desk for once, though Sunday evening was an odd time to catch up on work.

She knocked on the door but there was no reply. It was starting to feel like a pattern. Maybe he was somewhere on the site, peering at Saskia again, and the light was a decoy. She knocked once more.

'Rick?' And then she tried the door.

A moment later she was staggering backwards, her breath gone, gooseflesh rising all over her body, legs weak.

Robin was at her side in seconds. He peered through the door and saw what Eve had seen.

Rick Sutton was lying on the floor looking peaceful, a cushion to one side of his body. But all around him the room was in chaos. Drawers pulled out, books torn off the shelves, carpet pulled up. The door to his living quarters had been kicked in.

This time the killer had wanted something.

Robin held her close. 'I can't leave you to deal with this alone.'

Eve wished she could agree but he had to go. 'How will you explain it if Palmer finds you here? If you cross his radar too many times he'll start looking into your background. And who knows what sort of contacts he has?' Robin was still in potential danger from corrupt coppers and their criminal associates. 'I don't suppose he's bent himself. I suspect he'd run a mile from organised crime, if he was fit enough. But word would get out. Go now, and I'll call the police.'

He paused with a long look at her, but at last he nodded. 'I'm not leaving Watcher's Wood until they're here though. I'll stay out of sight until you're surrounded by coppers.'

She managed a shaky laugh. 'Thanks.'

# CHAPTER THIRTY-THREE

'What the hell were you doing at Watcher's Wood? How did you come to find his body?'

It was the first time Eve had seen Palmer lose it. He was normally snide or bored, and always dismissive. She'd got under his skin. She mustn't let him get under hers.

She was sitting in the costume trailer, which Margot Hale had invited them to use. Greg Boles had managed to get her a cup of tea from somewhere. She bet the DI hadn't sanctioned that.

'I've been interviewing all Rufus Beaumont's contacts, as you know. Earlier on today I came to look for Rick Sutton in case he had anything to add to the material for the obituary.'

'An interesting tale, considering Sutton hardly knew Beaumont.'

'I had Rick down as a big admirer. He had showbiz magazines in his office and I spoke with him when we were extras. He knew all about Rufus's passion for method acting. I thought it would be interesting to get a fan's view.' She didn't feel guilty about lying. She'd been trying to solve a murder. It wasn't something she could admit to Palmer but it was hardly immoral.

The detective inspector looked at her, his arms folded. 'And how does this story relate to your appearance here this evening?'

He'd emphasised 'story'. Eve took a deep breath and explained how she'd gone to Rick's office earlier in the day and found him absent. 'But I saw an odd diagram on a pad on his desk.' It made her sound nosy, but it was best to stick to something like the truth. 'It was the names of Rufus, Isla and several of their on-set contacts, with arrows between them and question marks.'

'Remind me not to leave my office unlocked when you're in the vicinity.'

'It's hard not to notice something with familiar content. Like recognising words in a wordsearch.'

Palmer said nothing. Greg was there too, blushing and concentrating on his shoes. Eve wasn't sure if he was embarrassed for her or Palmer.

'Anyway, I couldn't get the doodle out of my head. It seemed like such an odd thing to jot down. But the more I thought about it, the more… gossipy it seemed. It was as though he'd been speculating about who was having affairs with whom. Some of the names didn't fit.' Eve didn't want Palmer to know she'd held out on him about Isla and Rufus's relationship. 'But Rick might have imagined some of the liaisons. If he'd seen Dot Hampshire go into Kip Clayton's trailer, for instance. She helped him home when he'd had too much to drink, the night Rufus died.'

'So you think he was gossip hungry?' Palmer made a face as though he had a small fly stuck in his mouth. He clearly thought she was waffling, but she needed to explain her thinking.

'To an unhealthy degree. I put it together with the way he'd been peering at Saskia Thomas through her trailer window, under cover of darkness.'

'And your conclusion led you to come and visit him tonight?'

Eve nodded. 'I suddenly realised what a threat he might be to the killer if they knew the extent of his spying.' She shook her head. 'Rick hasn't been subtle. He seemed very… young to me. Not just in years but in the way he tackled life. So I came to warn him.'

Greg looked interested now, whereas Palmer looked red and sweaty. 'You didn't think of calling us?'

'It didn't seem like a police matter.' And she'd wanted to reach him quickly, not wait for the official wheels to grind into motion.

'It was an unfortunate decision. As it is, what evidence Mr Sutton had will have gone and we're no further forward.'

'I never seriously imagined Rick would have acquired anything that proved the murderer's guilt.' Eve still had no idea what had been taken.

'Clearly,' Palmer replied. 'You can go now. I want no more interference and if you do "happen to stumble" on any other clues, I want to know about it.'

He got up and stormed out of the trailer, knocking a feather boa from a hanger as he went so that it caught round his ankle and he had to kick it away.

Eve looked at Greg Boles. 'If I'd come to you, like he said, and told my story, do you think he'd have dashed straight over to interview Rick?'

Greg gave her a solid look. 'Perhaps not.' He blushed. 'He tends to call you fanciful.'

Eve sighed. His confirmation didn't make her feel any better. 'Thanks.' She got up and reached for her car keys. She couldn't wait to be back home at Elizabeth's Cottage with Gus.

# CHAPTER THIRTY-FOUR

Eve called Robin as soon as she reached home. She knew he'd be wondering how Palmer had taken her presence, but other than reassuring him, they had no news to exchange. Greg was sure to fill Robin in as soon as he was able; they'd meet for an update then.

At last, Eve sank into bed, but the image of Rick Sutton's face haunted her. What had he acquired that might convict a killer? And why hadn't he handed it over to the police? Eve all but discounted the idea of Sutton blackmailing the guilty party. Gut instinct told her he'd have been too nervous to try anything like that. The horrible possibility lurked in her head that Rick had had no idea he'd stumbled on the truth, but the killer had taken his life anyway, as an insurance policy. They were ruthless and reckless. Either they'd sneaked into his chalet and spiked a drink he'd left unattended on his desk – not impossible, given Rick's carelessness – or they'd walked in calmly and got him to accept one they'd brought.

She lay there, staring at the bedroom ceiling, its beams arching over her head. The timing was quite a coincidence. Could the killer have known she'd hung around at Watcher's Wood after seeing Dot? Had they seen her enter Rick's chalet, and noticed her reaction? The look of confusion on her face as she'd dashed out to avoid the custodian?

Could they have gone in themselves, later, to try to see what Eve had seen, guessing it might be related to the case?

She might have been responsible for focusing the murderer's attention on Rick. If only she'd thought to warn him sooner.

'Blimey,' Viv said as Eve entered Monty's the following day, 'you look awful.'

'Gee, thanks.' Eve had hoped she'd look more human by now.

'Sorry. Concern made me go all honest.' She rushed up and virtually pulled Eve through to Monty's crafts area. They were meant to be changing the display that morning before Eve got down to some admin and Viv some baking.

'I heard about Rick Sutton's death,' Viv continued in an undertone. The area was off the back of the main teashop and currently unoccupied, so they could talk freely if they kept their voices low.

Eve shook her head. For a moment she found it hard to speak. She swallowed. 'I found his body.'

Viv pulled her into a hug, narrowly avoiding knocking a crackle-glazed jug to the floor. 'I didn't know. The police team must have kept it quiet. I saw Moira earlier and she didn't say a word.'

Margot Hale must have been discreet too. As for Palmer, he always assumed Eve wanted attention; he'd be glad to deny her. She breathed a sigh of relief. She'd been dreading the thought of everyone bearing down on her, asking questions. 'That's good to know.'

She pulled a trolley out from under a table and they began to stack it up with existing items from the beechwood stands. Viv would be in charge of arranging the new display, but Eve wanted to cross-check the stock with her sales records.

Her friend moved a porcelain vase decorated with reeds and glanced sideways at Eve as she reached in the vague direction of the trolley. 'So, what happened?'

Eve swung the trolley so that it was underneath where the vase would land, causing the ceramics on it to rattle.

'Careful.' Viv smiled and patted Eve's arm as Eve gritted her teeth. 'You're all over the place. Very unusual.' There was an ill-disguised note of satisfaction in her voice. 'We can stop work for a moment while you fill me in if you like.'

'It's no problem.'

Viv frowned. 'If you're sure you can manage.'

'Certain.'

From Viv's expression she could tell the word had come out more harshly than she'd meant. But a second later Viv was listening with rapt attention as Eve updated her on the previous day's events.

'I can't believe you hung around Watcher's Wood like a private detective.'

'I couldn't think how else to get more information.' And she'd felt so pleased at what she'd picked up, but her efforts might have led to Rick Sutton's death.

A short while later, some beautiful espresso cups and saucers with an iridescent sea-green finish were raised up and surrounded by other items in blues, greens and purples.

'Come on,' Viv said. 'You need to sit down for a cup of tea before the admin. It's no use arguing. You look run-down. You need cake.'

Viv was convinced her baking cured everything. Kirsty and Tammy were busy and she fetched them a pot of Assam and some chocolate raspberry cupcakes herself.

They'd only just sat down when Moira bustled in through the open teashop door, clutching a newspaper.

'Oh dear me, Eve,' she said breathlessly as she reached their table and pulled out a third chair, 'you *do* look tired.'

Eve's teeth re-gritted themselves.

Moira put her head on one side. 'I do worry... I mean, I can see you've been out for some late walks recently and—'

'What can we do for you, Moira?' Viv asked with a bright smile.

'Oh, well, yes, of course. Thank you for reminding me. It's this!'

She spread the newspaper she'd brought with her in front of them, nudging their cakes to one side. She had it turned to the arts pages. 'It was Babs Lewis who alerted me. Only I know Drew Fawcett was under suspicion, so I thought it might be relevant. And with the latest death, I didn't want to wait. So shocking.'

Eve read the headline.

## New Partnership to Film Modern-day Bleak House

Veteran producer Stefan Meyer is to work with new director Drew Fawcett on a contemporary adaptation of Charles Dickens' novel *Bleak House*. The production will continue Meyer and Fawcett's partnership, just established due to the tragic murders of Isla Quinn and Rufus Beaumont.

'I can leave the paper with you if you like,' Moira said, her cheeks pink, eyes shining. 'I'd stay to chat longer, only I've left Paul minding the shop.'

'Don't you worry,' Viv said. 'We quite understand.' Moira's husband wasn't a people person.

'Thank you, Moira.' Eve tried to look as lively as possible as she faced the storekeeper. 'This is really useful.'

The woman beamed. 'Only too happy to help, Eve. You know me. I thought I should put my mind to the case. Babs Lewis was determined to look for clues too, only she's lost interest now Dot's been discounted.'

She dashed off again.

Eve scanned the text. 'I guess this explains why Stefan Meyer was free to take over on *Last of the Lindens*.' She tapped the paper. 'This was the secret project he'd been working on. It sounds as though a lot of the planning's been done now and they're looking to start work later this year. I suppose he'll divide his time between rounding off *Lindens* and preparing for *Bleak House*.'

'Makes sense.'

Eve polished off some more of her chocolate and raspberry cake and read on. Viv was right. The food was making her feel better. As her friend craned forward, Eve pointed to the most relevant part of the article.

*Meyer approached Fawcett early this year and the deal was sealed then, though kept under wraps. 'I admire Drew's dedication and creativity enormously. He stood out from the moment he came to volunteer on my team. He wanted to make the move into television and I employed him as a runner on my next project. After that he spread his wings, gained more experience and then took up the assistant director role with Quinn and Beaumont. Now I'm delighted to welcome him back and take our partnership to the next level.'*

'So Drew's known about this job for ages.' Eve took a large drink of her tea. 'I guess he didn't want to break the publicity embargo. He probably didn't trust people at the station not to gossip and I suppose he figured another couple of days wouldn't hurt, but Palmer will be livid he didn't come clean. Bang goes his motive. He'd got no need to kill for self-advancement. I never did buy it anyway, to be honest.'

And suddenly, the angry words she'd heard Isla throw in his direction came back to her. All that business about disloyalty. Drew had come up with a story to explain that: told the police he'd been criticising the way Isla was handling Kip Clayton. But now, Eve wondered if that had been an excuse. Wasn't it more likely that Drew had just broken the news that he wouldn't be working for her any more? He'd have wanted to tell her in confidence before the official announcement.

'Where does this leave the investigation?' Viv asked.

Eve frowned. A lot depended on the updates she expected from Robin. He'd texted to say Greg had promised them something interesting, but not until the following day. They were booked to have lunch then. Eve was on tenterhooks, but she couldn't tell Viv any of that. 'I'm wondering what Rick's death tells us. We know Saskia saw him peering in at her window at nine forty-five the night Rufus died. That was only fifteen minutes after his time-of-death window. And who knows how long he'd been hanging around, or where else he'd been? He might have come perilously close to seeing the killer leave the church.' She shook her head. 'And it's the same thing with Isla. His habit of prowling about under cover means he could have seen something crucial then too.'

Viv nodded. 'I hope the police work out what the killer was searching for inside his chalet.'

'Me too. Other than waiting for more details to go public, I'm due at Watcher's Wood again tomorrow morning.' The site was off limits until then. The forensics people would be scouring the place, and Eve imagined the police would be working their way through the cast and crew again, desperate for new leads. '*Icon*'s sending photographers to get some key shots for Rufus's obituary. Maybe I can find out more then. I need to know Kip Clayton's whereabouts when the latest murder took place. He's my top suspect now.' But Eve had no idea how she'd unearth that information.

After her stint at Monty's, Eve worked in the dining room at Elizabeth's Cottage, paring down the information she had for Rufus's obituary. She wanted to plan the article's structure, ready to complete a first draft, but it was almost impossible to concentrate.

What did Greg have for her and Robin? Whatever it was, it had to be something complex. Something he couldn't pass on in the normal way. She couldn't wait for tomorrow lunchtime.

# CHAPTER THIRTY-FIVE

Dot was the first person Eve saw at Watcher's Wood the following day.

She shook her head and handed Eve the tote bag she'd left in her trailer. 'I can't believe there's been another death, but I'm even more grateful to you for putting me in the clear. I owe you a drink, and that's an understatement.'

Eve smiled. 'Not at all, but it sounds like a nice idea.'

Nearby, she could see Kip Clayton through his open trailer door. She walked past slowly, raising a hand to wave at him. It gave her a moment to look inside his quarters. She could see a ready meal container and a plate and cutlery on the side, next to his small sink. They must be left over from the night before: the day after Rick Sutton's death. And he was slouched in his chair too. So he was relaxed enough to eat and rest, but that didn't tell her anything. Maybe he enjoyed comfort food and was currently lethargic from tension.

A short while later she was looking after *Icon*'s photographers, but even that was depressing.

'So he actually died inside the church?' one of them said, as Eve tried to interest them in the isolated tranquillity of the woods and parkland. She bet the captions would all relate to the murder, not the well-chosen location. And of course Rufus hadn't been in favour of Watcher's Wood anyway.

'Could we look inside the vestry?' The photographer was already making for the church door.

Eve was dead against having pictures of the scene of Rufus's death appearing alongside her article. They'd be there for all the wrong reasons. 'I'm afraid it's out of bounds.' She crossed her fingers behind her back.

'Still?'

She lowered her voice. 'The local police are a bit slow.'

In fact, they'd already vacated the site again after completing their work on the chalet and grounds the previous day.

The photographer looked dejected. 'I guess that's us finished then.'

'Would you like to see the manor house, where some of the filming took place?'

'You're all right.'

*Hmm.* Eve tried to look less prim and grumpy than she felt.

As they walked off, lugging their equipment, the church door opened and Saskia appeared. Her face was tear-stained, but on seeing Eve she tugged a tissue from her pocket and wiped away her streaked mascara.

'Are you all right?' Eve rushed forward, but she could see Saskia couldn't talk. She nodded, but as she left the churchyard another gulp escaped her.

Eve looked at the ranks of tombstones and thought of all that Saskia had lost within days. Not just Rufus and a future she'd been sure she wanted, but her father too. She turned to leave as well, but up ahead she could see Saskia disappearing through the trees, her head down. She looked crushed.

It only took Eve a moment to decide to go after her.

She watched her retreating form, just out of reach, moving through a clearing edged with poppies. It made her think of the flower Rufus had given Saskia, just after she'd acted the scene inside All Souls Church. She'd looked so drained. But of course, she'd only just seen her family for the first time in six months. That would have been emotional, unbearably so given her father's news.

Eve could have dashed ahead and caught Saskia up, but something made her slow her pace instead.

A poppy for remembrance. It was almost as though Rufus could see his future, but of course that made no sense. If there was any symbolism involved, Eve guessed Rufus had been thinking of Saskia's father. The inescapable march of his illness and what was to come.

The distance between her and Saskia was increasing now and Eve upped her pace a little.

The family must have kept the news from her during her six-month exile: the result of Rufus's insistence on method acting. Saskia had missed the few months her father had left. The family had made a huge sacrifice, keeping her in the dark so she could follow her director's advice.

How had it left Saskia feeling about Rufus?

Eve thought of Moira. The storekeeper said Saskia had resisted Rufus when he went to kiss her. What if her feelings towards him *had* changed? What if anger built up inside her, making her see him in a new light?

She'd looked broken when Eve had interviewed her at Monty's, but she was on her way out of town, with grapes and flowers, bought from Moira's store. Maybe she'd been nipping back to see her family. Dimly, Eve remembered Rick and Brooke mentioning they were quite close by, in Norfolk. Her emotion could have been down to guilt, and grief at the news about her father, rather than sorrow at Rufus's death.

Up ahead, Saskia's pace had slowed. Her hair was falling forward over her face, her hands running through it in her anguish.

Eve's mouth felt dry. She could be guilty.

Eve had overheard her telling her mother she was coming straight home after she got the news of her father's death on Sunday. That ought to mean she was off-site that night, when Rick was killed. But she could easily have driven back to Watcher's Wood. Eve imagined the scene at Saskia's family home: her mother on sleeping pills perhaps, supplied by her doctor to help her rest. What if she'd gone to bed early and Saskia – feeling she had an alibi of sorts – had driven south with murder on her mind? She knew Rick had been watching her and if she was guilty she must know he could have seen something crucial. Eve guessed Rick would have spoken up if it had been anything obvious, but Saskia could have worried about something more subtle. A penny that was likely to drop, sooner or later.

And what about Isla? The producer could have guessed the truth. She knew all about Rufus's methods. Maybe when she found Saskia's 'bad news' was real, something had clicked. Eve had thought initially that Isla would have gone to the police if she'd guessed the killer's identity, but now she wasn't so sure. At least, not in the case of Saskia. Although she'd been short-tempered with the young actress, she'd been protective of her interests too. She remembered how Isla had advised her not to broadcast her relationship with Rufus because it might affect her career. And how she'd explained her tough-love attitude towards Saskia: *I wouldn't bother criticising her if I didn't think she was worth it. She's got a marvellous career ahead of her, but she needs to grow up.*

Isla had been an analytical, unemotional person, seeing things in black and white without the nuances that might affect others. What if she'd sympathised with Saskia about Rufus? Felt he was using her, putting her career on the line, and that his method-acting demands had gone over the top? Maybe she'd even felt Saskia was a kindred spirit. After all, she and Rufus had been lovers, yet he'd let her down professionally: protected his own ego rather than doing what was best for the Quinn–Beaumont partnership.

Eve paused. She could easily catch Saskia up, but she was in a deserted part of the wood. She glanced around, but over to her right, from somewhere through the trees, she could hear voices. And if she could hear them, she could call out and be heard too. And it wasn't as though Saskia knew Eve had followed her or the suspicions running through her head. She wouldn't be prepared.

Eve jogged forward. 'Saskia.' She spoke softly. 'I'm so sorry to disturb when you're upset.'

The woman raised her tear-stained face to Eve, her expression all sorrow and confusion.

'I saw you as you answered your mobile on Sunday,' Eve explained. 'And then Brooke told me the background. I'm so sorry about your father.' She walked a little nearer and put a hand on the woman's arm. 'Can't you go home for a few days? Take some time?'

Saskia nodded. 'I went as soon as I got the news – the police gave me permission – but Drew's called a meeting for later today with Stefan Meyer. He said I didn't have to attend, but I wanted to. One of my mother's neighbours is sitting with her until I get back.'

The fact that she'd nipped over for the meeting showed how easy the journey was.

'It must have been awful, to be kept away from your father because of your part.'

Saskia's head was in her hands. 'I feel so guilty. I went into it with my eyes open. I was shocked when Rufus asked me to cut myself off, but I could have said no.'

Eve shook her head. 'It was your big chance. And you had no way of knowing what would happen.'

'I wish they'd told me. But they didn't realise how quickly the disease would progress and my father was a stalwart. He was insistent.' Her look was utterly bleak. 'He didn't even want to tell me when we were reunited, the day we filmed the funeral scene. But I knew immediately there was something wrong. He was so thin.'

Eve hesitated, searching for the best approach. 'Did Isla think you'd killed Rufus because he kept you apart from your family?'

Saskia's eyes opened wide. 'How did you know?'

'It just fits with a couple of things I heard.' She remembered Kip Clayton saying Isla hadn't wanted Eve involved when Drew Fawcett suggested it. Eve had wondered at the time if she was protecting someone, but she hadn't taken the idea seriously enough.

'It was odd.' The actress shook her head slowly. 'Isla was impatient with me most of the time. I didn't think she liked me, but it turns out I'd won her over without realising. And she minded about talent. About people with promise getting their chance. She took me into her trailer, late in the afternoon, the day I spoke to you in the teashop, and told me she understood what I'd done and why. She said I should put it behind me. I was young and Rufus had treated me badly. It was time to move on and once the police gave up I must live my life as though none of this had ever happened.'

Eve waited, her breath held. Saskia was still round-eyed. She turned to Eve.

'I could hardly speak. I told her I hadn't killed him! I loved him. He couldn't have known my father would get ill, any more than I could. And it was up to me to put my foot down if I objected, but I didn't.'

'What did Isla say?'

Saskia's chest was rising and falling quickly, as though she was back in the moment. 'She brushed my words aside. Said she could understand I didn't want to admit it, even to her. It took ages before she'd believe me. At last, she snapped out of it. It was like watching someone wake up.'

Eve breathed more easily. She was in no doubt, watching Saskia, that she was telling the truth. But what had happened after that? Once Isla realised she was wrong she must have looked elsewhere for the killer. Was that why she'd died the following day?

But if she'd guessed the truth, how the heck had the murderer managed to drug her drink? Rick Sutton was different – he'd been careless and distracted – but Isla was way more savvy. And they'd all known the method Rufus's murderer had used.

Eve couldn't figure it out. Isla had been sitting at a picnic table. She was sure she'd never have left her drink unattended, nor accepted one from someone she suspected.

'Can I get anyone for you?' Eve asked Saskia. 'I hate to see you so upset and coping with it on your own.'

But the actress shook her head. 'I'll just take a moment. Walk around a bit. I've got time to work up to the meeting – it's not until mid-afternoon. And then I'll head back to my mum.'

'Okay. Take care out here, won't you?'

Saskia shivered and nodded.

# CHAPTER THIRTY-SIX

That lunchtime, Eve and Robin were sitting under a parasol in the garden of the Swan at Wessingham. They'd taken a secluded table, giving them a good view of other patrons as they came and went. They could slip away if anyone from Saxford appeared, but in reality it was unlikely; not many people ventured beyond the Cross Keys, what with Jo Falconer's excellent cooking and the easy walk involved. For a second, Eve imagined what it would be like to stride in there with Robin at her side. To be able to relax with no secrets involved. She pushed the thought away.

Robin had a cool beer at his elbow but Eve had opted for Coke in lieu of a decent night's sleep. Her mind was too busy to switch off at the moment. Gus had pottered over to the paved area just outside the pub's conservatory to sample the water for dogs.

'What news from Greg? Do any of the key players have alibis for Rick's murder?'

Robin shook his head. 'Not rock-solid ones. Apparently Saskia Thomas had nipped back home to Norfolk.'

'I overheard her get the news about her dad dying.' Eve's insides contorted at the thought of the woman's upset. 'But even if her mum can't vouch for her, I don't think she's the one.' She filled Robin in on her talk with Saskia and the conclusions she'd drawn.

'Interesting.' He sipped his drink. 'Let's leave her to one side then. For the others, Drew Fawcett was on the phone to Stefan Meyer around the crucial time, but it's not quite precise enough. Though Palmer's not really interested in him any more, what with the revelations about his new partnership with Meyer.' He shook his head. 'I gather the atmosphere's been a bit tense down at the station. Palmer's still livid with Fawcett for holding out on him. And then Kip Clayton says he was in his trailer, apparently. The only one who's definitely out of it is Dot Hampshire, thanks to you.'

Eve smiled. 'Glad I got something right. And the method of killing was the same as before, I guess?'

Robin nodded. 'They're in no doubt we're dealing with one killer. They reckon Rick died between eight – when he was last seen on the site by a couple of the crew – and nine thirty.'

Eve closed her eyes. They'd only missed him by an hour.

'I know.' Robin put a hand on hers. 'I'm sorry.' He sighed. 'They've worked out what the killer was looking for in his chalet, by the way.'

Eve's eyes widened.

'Photographs.'

'Wow. I can imagine him wanting keepsakes; he seemed the sort. It's so creepy.' She shivered, despite the warm day, imagining Saskia in her trailer and Rick outside, a long lens trained on her.

Robin nodded. 'It doesn't make it any better, but it seems he had a professional purpose. A friend of his had made a mint selling photos to the papers. Apparently Rick wanted a piece of the action. When he heard about the TV crew coming to Watcher's Wood, he applied for the custodian job, then bragged to the friend about how clever he'd been. He was in a bit of debt. Drove a fancy sports car and the repayments were sky high.'

Eve let the news sink in as she sipped her Coke. Even the smell seemed to knit her senses together. It all made sense now. Rick must have been doing his background research down in London, wondering what scandals he might pick up on. 'A get-rich-quick scheme. But he didn't have the right skills and it would have been a miserable way to make money.' She frowned as her drink did its work. It triggered a memory. 'The empty packet of caffeine tablets I saw in his bin makes sense now. Moonlighting must have been wearing him out.' But then a fresh thought struck. 'Hang on a minute, though. If the killer took the photos with them, how did the police work all this out?'

Robin grinned. 'They made a mistake at last. The team found a single SD card, dropped in the grass outside the chalet.'

'And there were photos on the card?' Eve held her breath.

'Don't get your hopes up,' Robin said, as Gus pottered back to their table and settled himself in the shade between their feet. 'I'm not sure they tell us anything. And I'm afraid it's pretty creepy, like you said.' He unlocked his phone and handed it to her. 'The contents are all there. No one at the station can see anything significant so Greg decided to break all the rules and sneak a copy of the files to me too, in case you or I can spot anything they've missed. He couldn't get access to them immediately – hence the delay – but he's keen to hear back from us. He knows you've been interacting with the suspects.' He sipped his beer. 'I've been through the lot around ten times now and nothing's slotting into place, but I don't know most of the people involved.'

'Most?'

'I'm afraid there are a couple of you. Looks like we've found the intruder who visited your garden.'

Eve tilted the phone screen so the reflections on it were reduced. Robin had scrolled so that the ones of her came up first. She was lit by the lamps in her dining room, just next to her open window. The second photo showed the shock on her face. He must have taken it as she realised there was someone out there. She found herself shaking.

'Why take any of me?'

'Maybe he'd found out your reputation by that stage. Perhaps he wanted some pictures in case you solved the case.' He gave her a sympathetic look and held her hand for a moment. 'Those were the last to be taken in that batch.'

Eve scrolled back to the beginning and tried to view them calmly, despite the crawling feeling she got from seeing her own photo. It was a pretty random selection and Rick's inexperience showed. There was one of Saskia applying suntan lotion outside her trailer. There was no one else in shot. Several more were equally unenlightening. One featured Kip Clayton with a drink in his hand. From the position of the sun she guessed it had been early in the day, but she doubted the papers would have been interested in that. There was one of Rufus and Drew Fawcett. Rufus was scratching his backside (awkward) and the image didn't even show Drew's face. He was tugging off a jumper and had rucked up his T-shirt so all you could see was chest, a leather beaded necklace, crumpled clothes and a tuft of messed up hair. The quality of the photographs made Rick's death all the more pitiful. Eve doubted he'd produced anything saleable.

Then there was one of Dot talking to Kip. They were standing close together and she had her hand on his shoulder. Maybe she'd been sympathising over something, though it had been before the news of Rufus's affair with his ex-girlfriend broke.

She scrolled on to see a photo featuring Saskia and Rufus. They were gazing into each other's eyes, but again, it was nothing a newspaper would take seriously – not sufficient to raise a scandal. It would have been enough to make Rick Sutton keep digging though. Eve guessed glimpses like that had tantalised him. He must have felt sure they were having an affair, and that sooner or later he'd catch them out.

Behind them, caught in the shot, were Margot Hale, looking on, and Brooke Shaw, looking at Margot, concern in her eyes. It seemed Margot had picked up on the spark between the pair, though that image had been taken before their affair went public.

Of course, the gossip was all over the papers now, but the press had used standard publicity shots of Rufus and Saskia to illustrate their stories. If Rick had tried to sell them any of his work, it seemed his attempts had fallen flat.

'Interesting,' she said at last, handing back Robin's phone. 'Apologies to Greg, but nothing leaps out at me.'

Robin swigged his beer and nodded. 'I'll forward them to you in case you want a second look. But don't worry if nothing comes of it. Greg's already your number-one fan after the Dot Hampshire breakthrough.'

Eve blushed. The comment took her back to her talk with the actress, and then to the evening of Simon's party as she'd danced in his grounds, wishing Robin had been there but knowing he couldn't be. Images of the vicar and Viv flying round the dance floor came to mind, and Simon's somewhat gushy speech about his fiancée.

And then suddenly, in the baking hot pub garden, Eve went cold all over. 'Oh no.'

Robin put a hand on her goosebump-covered arm. 'What is it?'

'There's something I've overlooked. I'm just wondering if Simon did too.' She hoped to goodness he'd been more clear-sighted than her.

Robin looked puzzled. 'Do you want to call him?'

She nodded, mechanically taking her phone from her bag.

'Hi, Simon.'

'*Eve! I've been meaning to call you. Has Moira been acting oddly around you lately? She took me to one side in the store yesterday and said: "You and Eve will be careful, won't you?" She must think I've been helping you with your sleuthing.*'

*Heck.* The uncomfortable tension gripping Eve developed to include a queasy feeling in her stomach. So Moira had got Simon down as her mystery lover. And she thought Eve would go behind Polly's back! She bit back her irritation. Thank goodness Simon hadn't guessed what the storekeeper was on about. 'I suppose she must do. I might have mentioned asking you for advice now and again. I'll talk to her, let her know I'm not dragging you into harm's way.'

He laughed. '*I'd rather you didn't get into harm's way either. Anyway, what can I do for you?*'

'A quick question on the evidence you gave to the police about the night of Rufus Beaumont's death.' Eve's insides curled with embarrassment as she spoke.

'*Sure.*' Simon sounded as jolly and upbeat as ever. '*What do you need to know?*'

'The police worked out where Dot would be based on Polly starting her playlist at eight?'

'*That's right.*'

'It's just come back to me: the music went quiet when you made your speech. I didn't notice if you'd turned it down or actually paused it.'

Eve could hardly bear to look at Robin's expression. Agonised realisation just about summed it up.

'*Oh hell.*'

'I was afraid you'd say that. I can't think why it never occurred to me before now.'

'*It's my responsibility. I ought to have remembered.*'

'Can you recall how long you talked for?'

'*Damn. I think I went on for quite a bit, didn't I? Viv told me off afterwards for being mushy.*' The was a long pause. '*I suppose I'd better call the police and let them know.*'

'Actually, Simon, do you think you could hold off, just until this evening? I'd like to tackle Dot face to face. She asked for my help and she thinks I've put her in the clear. Going to Palmer immediately without warning her feels wrong.' Eve couldn't help picturing Toby's face too. He'd been so happy when Dot was alibied.

'*Of course.*' Simon's tone was sympathetic. '*Just let me know when to go ahead.*'

'Absolutely.'

She hung up and put her forehead on the pub table. 'I have been a colossal idiot.'

'Maybe it won't matter.' Robin gave her hand a squeeze. 'Surely he can't have gone on for that long.'

'He'd had a few drinks by then.' The scene was spooling through her head. 'There was a whole series of amusing anecdotes about Polly.' She closed her eyes. 'Oh no. And then she took a turn as well, before handing back to him.'

'Ah. So you think Dot Hampshire's alibi is shot?'

'I'd guess so. Heck. The music could have been stopped for as long as twenty minutes.'

'Want a rum in that Coke?'

She managed a weak smile and picked herself up when she noticed a woman in a flowery dress eyeing her from a neighbouring table. 'That would be the final straw.'

Reluctantly, she took out her phone, accessed her files and adjusted her timeline for the night of Rufus's murder yet again.

'There.' She scrolled to the relevant bit of the evening and turned the screen to Robin. 'Take a look.'

**8.45 p.m.:** Dot and Kip arrive back at Watcher's Wood (According to Dot. Long walk, and Kip was drunk. A brisk walker could have done it in fifty minutes, but sounds plausible.) Dot sees Drew and Isla in Isla's trailer

**8:45 p.m.:** Rufus signs into internet banking in his trailer

**8.48 p.m.:** or thereabouts. Time Dot *ought* to have left for her long walk, if she'd only spent a few minutes bundling Kip into his trailer as she claims (BUT see 9.10 p.m. entry)

**8:50 p.m.:** Rufus cancels direct debit to Cassie

**8.53 p.m.:** Rufus reaches the vestry. (Earliest possible time. And he was drunk. Might have been slower.)

*9.10 p.m. approx.: the real time Dot must have left Watcher's Wood, in order to hear 'London Calling' playing at around 9.35 p.m.*

'With this timetable she had just over fifteen minutes in which to kill Rufus.'

'Not long.'

'But enough, when he was so drunk already. I guess the sedative would have worked quickly.'

'I'm sorry,' Robin said. 'Finding that alibi was such a triumph.'

'It was a massive mistake on my part.' Robin gave her a sympathetic look and Eve's heart sank further. 'Dot knew I was hanging around on site on Sunday. If she's guilty she might have followed me to monitor my progress. Maybe she saw me sneak into Rick's chalet and managed to do the same later, to investigate.'

The more Eve thought about the implications the worse she felt. All her conflicted feelings about Dot came rushing back. She liked her, but it wasn't hard to imagine her rage and hurt being enough to make her do something terrible. Rufus and Isla had kicked her in the teeth, metaphorically, and she might not have felt much sympathy for Rick Sutton. According to Kip, he'd been seen creeping round her trailer as well as Saskia's. Plus she was sharp, determined and clever.

'What are your plans? You asked Simon not to tell the police?' He raised an eyebrow.

'Dot said she owed me a drink earlier. They've got some meeting with the new producer this afternoon, but I could take her up on her offer after that. Get her over to the Cross Keys. Tell her what I've realised. I'll be completely safe with the Falconers and sundry villagers on hand.' Once again, she thought of Toby and her heart twisted. He'd be so disappointed. 'I promise I'll ask Simon to call Palmer if she can't explain herself.'

'Bear in mind, she might be a good liar. She'll know there's a discrepancy; she'll have been waiting for someone to notice it. There's been plenty of time to get her story straight.'

'True.' Time that Eve had given her. She felt like hiding under the table.

'Fancy dinner tonight so you can fill me in?'

She put her head in her hands again and told him what Simon had said about Moira's questions.

'Ah.' His mouth was twitching.

'Not funny! Half the village is probably speculating. I'll have to work out how to tackle her. But to avoid setting her antennae going again, how about supper round at mine? Could you sneak along the estuary path?'

'I could indeed.' He took her hand. 'Joking apart, I'm sorry the cloak and dagger stuff is causing you problems.'

'It's Moira who's doing that.'

'And please watch your back.'

Eve raised an eyebrow. 'Don't worry. My word is my bond. Your meal will be forthcoming.'

'*Not* my primary concern!' Robin gave her a playful flip on the nose, but Gus looked solemn. Eve wondered if she'd tempted fate.

# CHAPTER THIRTY-SEVEN

Dot was still cheerful when Eve called her, which made her feel even worse. She was more than happy to join Eve for an early evening drink at the Cross Keys. Eve wished Toby wouldn't be looking on, but there was no other pub in walking distance and asking her to drive to Blyworth or Wessingham seemed too weird and would feel too isolated.

Thoughts of confronting her with the discrepancy played on Eve's mind, but she put her anxiety on hold. She knew what she had to ask. Her plan was in place, now she needed to take a deep breath and get on with her work.

She spent the remainder of the afternoon working on Rufus's obituary, using the plan she'd created the day before. Once she'd managed a rough draft, she looked again at the facts she'd gathered. Ordering them to convey the director's life story had pulled them into a new pattern. It was complete in terms of his history, but the bits she'd weeded out might be crucial to the case.

She made up her mind to add all the seemingly disparate facts back in and reorder everything, in case the process revealed a pattern.

She began to work her way through her notes, thinking of the different ways she could arrange her findings. By date, certainly – and perhaps by location. Then by Rufus's personal relationships versus his professional ones. But she didn't get beyond the planning stage. It was time to go and meet Dot at the pub.

Eve was already sitting at a table when the actress appeared in the doorway of the Cross Keys and waved at Toby. His face lit up and nerves and shame at her mistake clutched at Eve's stomach. A moment later, Dot had caught her eye too. She looked buoyant. Was that because two of her enemies were dead? But even if she was innocent she might be relieved that the man who'd tried to destroy her career was no more. She could be horrified by his death, and feel shock at Isla's murder, yet still have hated them both.

But alternatively, Dot could be guilty, Eve thought, as she got up to meet the woman at the bar, and asked what she'd like to drink.

'No way!' Dot said. 'This is my treat.'

It was agonising to accept the glass of Pinot Grigio, and to see Toby's smiles.

After a moment, Eve and Dot were back at the table she'd chosen, tucked into a corner. Eve could see Brooke Shaw and Margot Hale sitting across the room but they were well out of earshot; she only hoped they wouldn't read too much into her and Dot's expressions. The pair almost looked like mirror images of each other, sitting either side of their small table. Margot could be a vision of Brooke in thirty years' time.

'Dot, I'm sorry.' Eve met the actress's eye as she sipped her wine. 'You must have been prepared for this. I mean, I guess you realise there's a discrepancy with the time you heard music across the fields.' Even if Dot was innocent, she must have been doing something in the spare minutes, either before she'd left the site or en route. She'd know there was a gap in her account of the evening.

The actress went absolutely still, her glass halfway to her lips. After a moment she put it down, slowly.

'The couple hosting the party the night Rufus died turned their music off for around twenty minutes while they made speeches and proposed a toast. They'd forgotten all about it, but it means there's extra time to account for in your movements.'

There was hurt and anger in Dot's eyes, but she might be acting. 'You think I killed Rufus?'

'I think it's odd you didn't tell me everything. You're hurt that I don't trust you, but you didn't trust me. You asked for my help, then sent me off with partial information.'

Dot put her elbows on the table, her head in her hands. It was a while before she spoke. 'You're right. And I'm sorry. Have you told the police?'

'Not yet. I thought you might like to explain.'

Dot groaned. Toby's anxious eyes were on them as he served a customer a pint of Adnams.

'I knew there must be some mistake over the playlist. I've been waiting for the axe to fall.' Her eyes met Eve's. 'I was embarrassed. And what I'm about to tell you gives me even more of a motive. I'm sure the police will think so. The fact is, even though Kip was being foul at the pub, I didn't reject his offer of a drink when we got back to Watcher's Wood.'

'What happened?'

'We talked on our walk home. It's a fair distance, and we each poured out our woes, essentially saying how much we both hated Rufus. And Isla as well, as a matter of fact. He'd sobered up a bit by the time we reached his trailer, and he invited me in for a nightcap.' Her eyes pleaded with Eve for understanding. 'He's not my usual type, but I was down and we both felt reckless. That's really going to help my case, isn't it?'

Palmer would love it, that was for sure. He might decide they'd been in it together, Dot to administer the sedative, say, and Kip to finish the job. And they could have been.

'Kip cracked open a bottle of whisky and, we… well, we… Anyway, you can imagine. Only we must have been silhouetted against the curtains of his trailer. They're pretty thin in the more basic accommodation. Things were about to get X-rated when we heard Rufus's voice from outside. "Making a night of it, Dolly? Glad someone's picking up Saskia's leftovers."'

Eve tried to imagine her feelings at hearing his words. His comment must have left her raging. No wonder she'd left the episode out of her evidence.

'What I should have done was ignored Rufus. But I couldn't get his words out of my ahead. Kip and I carried on kissing but the mood was broken. I suddenly realised how much I'd regret sleeping with him. He was livid when I decided to leave. He tried to talk me out of it, at which point I said some hateful things and then, finally, I left. That was why I was in such an appalling rage afterwards, and why I marched off into the middle of nowhere, even though it was getting dark. Kip and I are barely on speaking terms now. My fault. As if life at Watcher's Wood wasn't complicated enough.'

Eve thought of Kip telling her how cruel Isla had been about Dot's break-up and miscarriage. He'd highlighted her motive. Perhaps that had been his revenge on her for walking out on him.

'I can see why you didn't tell, but I wish I'd known.'

Dot nodded. 'I'm sorry.'

'It makes Kip's motive look as strong as yours. Stronger, maybe, if he blamed Rufus for you walking out on him.'

If this latest version of events was true, it explained the missing minutes from Dot's account. She'd be in the clear again, though Kip wouldn't.

But it was a big if. Eve's instinct was to believe her, but as Robin said, she'd had time to prepare a story. And this one made Kip look guilty. If she was the murderer, that would be a handy side effect. And if Kip denied her tale she'd be able to accuse him of lying to save face. He was just the sort who would.

'Did Kip drink much whisky while you were with him?'

'He poured a tumblerful and knocked it back. He's been a heavy drinker for as long as I've known him.'

So he'd topped up his alcohol levels back at the trailer. Could Eve really imagine him leaving his accommodation when Dot did and traipsing across to the church without anyone noticing? He was a bulky man and the drink would have made him clumsy.

And even if he'd managed that, he'd have to have been dextrous and organised enough to drug Rufus. Dot had seemed a lot more controlled that evening, and more capable overall.

Eve wasn't sure of her innocence. Unless she could find proof that Kip or a third party was guilty, she'd have to ask Simon to tell the police. It wasn't the thought of the shame that felt worst now, it was what lay in store for Dot if she was innocent and Eve made the wrong call. And for Toby, if she happened to be guilty.

Dot got up to go. 'Could you have one more go at trying to identify the real culprit before you report me? Please?'

Eve nodded. 'I'll go through everything I have.'

As the actress turned to leave the pub, Eve glimpsed Brooke and Margot watching her.

The pair alibied each other of course, and they'd been seen by a third party, which bore out their version of events. It was no use looking in their direction for the answer to her troubles. Instead, Eve took out her notepad and began to examine all her evidence again. She still had just over an hour before Robin was due at her place. Reviewing the problem in a new setting might help her think.

# CHAPTER THIRTY-EIGHT

Eve tore out a page from her notebook and made a chronological list of all the details she'd gathered, not just those she'd wanted to include in Rufus's obituary. She went back and forth to the pages where she'd recorded events. Gradually, disparate facts meshed together.

The unfavourable comparisons tutors had made between Rufus and his siblings at school.

Rumours that his place at the Ryland School of Drama had been swung by his parents.

Rufus's break-up with his childhood sweetheart, Emily, while he was still at Ryland.

Emily's role as an ambassador at the drama school.

Her inability to get over Rufus, never understanding why he'd left.

Rufus's fragile ego and desperation to make it big.

His early film success – with a role offered while he was still in drama school – as supporting actor in *Shadows in the Trees*, where he'd played a man who'd broken up with the love of his life.

His dedication to method acting, which his mother had seen as a threat to his physical and mental health.

She'd reached an ad hoc note on Kip and added it onto the list: him working as a camera operator on a Stefan Meyer production where Emily had been one of the cast.

Her list was far from complete, but as she looked at it, a tiny shiver ran down her spine.

Rufus had split with his girlfriend, Emily. She'd finally died after falling down stairs, drunk. The implication in the media was that she'd gone off the rails after their break-up.

Her reaction to the end of the relationship had been extreme and long-lived. What might have accentuated that effect? Being left when she had no idea why? When she'd thought their relationship was thriving? Of course, lots of people had experienced that situation, but sooner or later they normally figured out what had gone wrong. They realised there'd been signs the relationship was cooling off. But Emily hadn't. She'd been poleaxed.

And now, Eve thought she might have seen why. Rufus had left Emily in his final year at drama school, around the time he'd landed his one film part: acting a broken-hearted lover.

What boyfriend would leave the girl he loved dearly, plunging her into a state of utter confusion?

A boyfriend who was desperate to give his best performance ever. One who loved Emily, but who couldn't be happy with what he had. One who was prepared to sacrifice his relationship to feel the pain he needed for his role. After all, it might be his big break. A chance to prove his worth to his family.

Eve closed her eyes. She had no proof, but suddenly she was sure that was what Rufus had done: abandoned Emily as part of his method acting. And he *had* got excellent reviews in *Shadows in the Trees*, in return for his sacrifice. He'd left Emily desperate, knowing something wasn't right; that their relationship hadn't come to a natural end. But it had worked out all right for him. And to dull the self-inflicted pain he'd had a passionate affair on the film set: the one with the married actress which had featured in the article Eve had read. After that he'd simply moved on, and ultimately married Cassie. It had been different for him: not the huge, emotional question mark it had been for Emily.

And Kip claimed he'd slept with her. Was there any chance he'd been in love? Enough to kill Rufus later for the way he'd made her suffer?

Eve pulled up the article she'd read on Emily Longfellow when she'd first started to research Rufus. It felt like months ago already, yet it had been less than two weeks earlier. Of course, it was Stefan Meyer who'd been quoted. She'd forgotten that.

She looked again at the slender woman with eyes that were both haunting and haunted. She took in her elegant bearing and the leather beaded cord around her neck.

And then, suddenly, something resonated.

Eve navigated to her photos, where she'd saved copies of the images from the SD card that Rick Sutton's killer had failed to remove.

Within moments, she got up to leave the pub, not bothering to finish her wine. If Toby said goodbye, she didn't notice.

Outside, she turned right towards Haunted Lane and home, her mind working furiously. A car's engine revving made her look over her shoulder. It was just some speed-freak, leaving the pub at the same time as her. But beyond it, she saw Brooke and Margot again.

They must have left the Cross Keys immediately after she had.

# CHAPTER THIRTY-NINE

Back at Elizabeth's Cottage, Eve closed the door behind her and bent to greet Gus. As she walked through to the kitchen, she was working on autopilot.

In the photograph Rick Sutton had taken of Rufus and Drew Fawcett, Drew had been tugging a jumper over his head, revealing a leather beaded necklace. It matched the one Emily had been wearing in the newspaper photograph.

Eve told herself it must be coincidence. For all she knew they were mass produced. But as she had the thought, her mind focused on the assistant director.

What other connections might he have had with Emily?

She hadn't got as far as adding his information to her timeline in the pub, but she focused on it now.

He'd attended the Ryland School of Drama, just like Rufus and Emily had. He'd been in his first year, Emily and Rufus in their third, but he'd said everyone knew Rufus. He'd have seen him around, picked out his famous Beaumont features in the college bar, at parties and balls. Seen Emily on his arm, before their break-up. Yet he hadn't mentioned her when she'd asked him who Rufus mixed with during his drama-school days.

Wasn't that a bit odd, now she came to think of it? Emily had been an ambassador for the school, visiting drama groups up and down the country, welcoming new students. And she was very beautiful. She would have made an impression on the teenage Drew.

Eve opened the back door to let Gus into the garden. As he pottered down to its far reaches, her mind was still on the case.

It had been Kip who'd worked on the same show as Emily, under Stefan Meyer. Drew hadn't come on board until the production after that. But then another memory touched the edge of Eve's consciousness.

She went to fetch the newspaper Moira had given her, announcing Drew and Stefan's new partnership.

Her mouth went dry. Drew had been on set when Kip met Emily. Meyer talked about him volunteering on the production before the one where he'd employed him. It wasn't until now that she'd married up the order of events. Drew and Emily's paths had crossed a second time.

Robin would arrive soon. She could run it all past him, see what he thought.

Eve's mind ran on. Could it be *Drew* who'd fallen for Emily? Maybe even as long ago as at drama school? And then asked her out when they met years later? Kip said he'd slept with her and Eve assumed it had been around then. She remembered how furious Drew looked just after Kip told him. But it was Drew who had her necklace – if Eve was right and it was the same one. Whatever had happened with Kip, that implied it was Drew and Emily who'd become close – developed an emotional connection.

Could Drew have found out why Rufus had left Emily? He and Rufus had been working together, after all. The director might have let something slip. And then maybe Drew had killed him for his selfishness. Destroying him because he'd destroyed Emily.

Eve frowned, her heart hammering. It couldn't be true; she must have got it wrong. Drew had Isla's alibi. Why would she have covered for him? He was just one person on site, but if she hadn't been with him, she'd have known he could be guilty, however unlikely it seemed. But at that moment a fresh realisation rushed over Eve.

The producer had been convinced Saskia was guilty. So certain, that Saskia said it had taken ages to persuade her otherwise. Eve hadn't known that when she'd decided Drew's alibi was probably solid. And of course, Isla had wanted to avoid calling the police just to save trouble. Fibbing to free herself from lengthy interviews was in character. She probably thought it was harmless: a way to give herself more time to manage the fallout from Rufus's death.

Desperately, she looked for other arguments against Drew's involvement, but as she examined them they fell apart.

Yes, he'd encouraged Isla to call in the police after Rufus was killed, but Eve was sure they'd have attended anyway, after a sudden death. An icy shiver played down her spine. It was exactly the same when he'd suggested Isla should ask for Eve's help. If he knew her history, he'd have realised that was bowing to the inevitable as well. But it was an excellent way to look innocent. And if Isla had agreed, he'd have been able to monitor Eve's progress too. Even his account of his movements the night Isla died looked suspicious now. Eve had thought his sketchy alibi – the time the alarm was disabled then reset at the manor house – was too badly arranged to be a ploy. In her mind that meant it was probably the truth. But he could have thought of that. Been careful not to make his preparation look too solid.

There was a knock at the door and Eve rushed to open up. She couldn't wait to get Robin's opinion.

But it was Drew Fawcett who stood on her doorstep.

# CHAPTER FORTY

The breath went out of Eve as he pushed his way into the house, taking advantage of her shock.

He was wearing a black donkey jacket, despite the warm evening. As he slammed the door shut behind him he pulled a knife from under it.

His determined dark eyes were on her. 'I just bumped into Brooke and Margot. They were certain you'd had some kind of revelation about the case back in the pub. I couldn't risk leaving you to your own devices. I guessed you might work it out sooner or later. It was one of the reasons I kept hanging around the village.'

Eve's whole body felt weak. Robin ought to arrive imminently, but she'd lost track of time. Was he due in a minute, or in ten? She couldn't let Drew see her glance shift to the clock on the wall. He might guess her thoughts.

Her mind turned to Gus. He must have found something interesting in the bushes down the garden. If he came back in now, he'd go berserk. Her eyes were on Drew's knife, her mind on what he might do with it: how quickly it could reap devastating consequences.

Drew walked nearer to her. She could hardly breathe.

'You're expecting someone,' he said. 'You were totally unguarded as you opened the door.' He glanced quickly towards the lane-side window in Eve's sitting room, then nodded at her, his knife pointed at her stomach. 'Bolt the door and close the curtains.'

She had no option but to do as he said. He kept close to her, tracking her every move.

'If there's a knock, you're not to make a sound. If you do, I'll have to kill you and your visitor. Switch your mobile off and put it on the coffee table. Show me.'

Eve made her movements as slow as possible but still there was no knock at the door. And even when Robin came, could she risk calling out? At least he didn't have a key. He couldn't walk into an ambush.

'Dot told me about this place,' Drew said. 'She used to visit when she came at Christmas as a child. We'll hide where the young boy did in the 1700s until your visitor gives up and goes away.'

A cold chill crept over her. She'd only climbed into the space where the boy Isaac had hidden once. She'd never pulled the trapdoor down after her. Even standing where he'd cowered had left her claustrophobic and panicky. Drew would have her well and truly cornered. No chance of lunging at a window to make her presence known. No option to run for it.

The point of Drew's knife touched the thin cotton of her top. 'Lock up first. We can't leave the back door wide open.'

He must have felt the draught.

Suddenly he paused. 'Wait. Where's your dog?'

'I left him with Viv Montague – from the teashop. It's easier if he's not around when my, er, visitor shows up. He gets jealous.' The lie sounded feeble to Eve's ears. Thank goodness it was a warm evening and she might have had the back door open anyway.

She'd intended to play for time but now she was anxious to reach the door and lock it quietly. She had to avoid alerting Gus and setting him barking. She hastened towards the kitchen, Drew's knife to her back, her breath juddering. What if Gus pottered up the lawn, just as they got to the back door?

As she reached it, she stood to one side and made every effort to avoid sudden moves. He must still be in his favourite place, down at the bottom of the garden, half into a hedge, or behind a bush, in the shadows.

With her heart hammering, she turned the key carefully in the lock, making little sound, despite her shaking hands. No barking. *Please keep quiet, Gus. Please be safe.*

'Now,' Drew said. 'Take me to the hiding place. I'll deal with you after your visitor's left.'

As Eve led the way through to her dining room, she glimpsed the clock on the sitting room wall. A feeling of utter hopelessness filled her chest. Robin wasn't due for thirteen minutes. There was no way she could stall Drew for that long. She opened the door to the cupboard under the stairs. It housed a number of items but none of them blocked the trapdoor. She kept it clear for the twice-yearly open-house sessions when she gave visitors her guided tour.

'Pull up the trapdoor and get inside. I'm coming in after you.'

Eve dropped down into the dark, dusty space. It was a little under four feet deep and less than six feet square.

'Move as far away from the trapdoor as you can and sit down.'

Eve did as he asked but all the time she was thinking: visualising the space when it was lit, what it had looked like when she'd last been down there. How she always left it for future visitors.

There was a creak and the light levels lowered. Drew must have pulled the under-stairs cupboard door shut. In a second he was down in the hiding space with her, his eyes just visible in the near-darkness.

'My friend doesn't have a key to the house,' Eve said, as he reached to pull the trapdoor shut.

'Forgive me if I don't take your word for it.' Drew brought the door down and the darkness was complete. 'One sound and that's it. I don't want to use the knife but I will if you make me. You'll be dead before anyone hears you up above.'

And a moment later, she heard him draw the rusty bolt across.

# CHAPTER FORTY-ONE

Within a second, Drew's phone lit the small space with a pale glow.

'Brooke and Margot said you looked like you'd seen a ghost,' Drew said. 'They were excited that you might have finally solved the case. They've been scared.' His eyes met hers. 'So, you worked it out.' It was a statement, not a question.

'I realised you had the necklace Emily Longfellow was wearing in an old publicity shot.'

'How the hell did you know that?'

'You dropped one of Rick Sutton's SD cards in the grass outside his chalet. It contained an image of you pulling off a jumper that revealed it.'

'He was a lousy photographer. When I worried he might have taken something incriminating that's the last thing I thought of.' He looked at Eve meditatively. 'So you knew I'd taken Emily's necklace.'

'Taken?' She spoke automatically, but as the implication of the word settled in her head fresh waves of heat and chill washed over her.

'Ah.' Drew's eyes met hers. 'You didn't realise I'd killed her.'

'But she fell…'

He shook his head. 'She was pushed. I loved her. I never wanted to harm her, but it was so frustrating. It was all Rufus's fault.' He swore. 'He left her for no good reason. It was no wonder she couldn't get over him. There was no closure, no sense that their relationship had run its course. He ruined her forever. By the time I found her again, she was obsessed. I knew I could make her happy, but she still wasn't over him. One night I went back to her place for a drink. I thought we were making progress, but at the top of the stairs, outside her bedroom door, she pulled back. She couldn't sleep with me when she still loved Rufus.'

'But she slept with Kip.'

The moment Eve said it she knew she'd made a mistake. He lunged at her and the knife grazed her arm as she flung herself back against the wall, shaking. She felt sick, her mouth dry. She could see he was fighting with himself: dying to finish the job, yet dimly aware that killing her there wasn't part of the plan.

At last he regained control.

'If she did, it meant nothing. It was we who had a connection. But she couldn't forget Rufus so she could be with me. We'd both had a lot to drink and I lost it. I was so furious, but it was fury with him, not with her. I don't drink much these days.'

His thinking was so warped. 'You knew he'd left her as part of his method acting?'

Drew looked surprised. 'You worked that out? No. At the time, I just knew he'd developed an unhealthy hold over her. I took the job with him to try to understand it. What happened with Emily is always on my mind. It haunts my dreams.'

It was as though he expected sympathy. Eve felt sick to the stomach.

'It was only when I heard Rufus boasting about the sacrifice *he'd* made in giving up Emily that I got it. That was when I decided he had to die. He destroyed her life and mine. And now yours too. I need to work out how to deal with you.'

It gave Eve a tiny flicker of hope. He was acting on the spur of the moment after bumping into Margot and Brooke. He took out a flask from his jacket pocket, placed his knife on his lap and unscrewed the lid.

The drugged drink. It had to be. Eve wondered if she could lunge forward and grab the knife but she'd never manage it. He'd be on her in half a second.

She watched as Drew put the flask to his lips, took a swig then put it back in his pocket again. A second later he took it out once more and looked at Eve.

'I'm sure you must be feeling tense. Would you like some?'

Eve stared at the flask and then back at Drew. It looked like the same one, but… 'You've got two?'

He nodded. 'A matching set, his and hers. I was able to manage it more artfully when I picked off my previous victims. I'd had more chance to prepare, when I asked Rufus to come to the vestry for a private chat about Kip. He found me in there, already swigging from a flask. He had no idea I'd switched them when I offered him some. As for Isla,' he laughed, 'I played the same trick on her. I knew she'd demand a glass, but each flask has a little silver cup that fits on top. I lured her out by saying I was suspicious of Kip. It fitted with her current thinking. She'd just realised Saskia was innocent.'

'But she didn't suspect you…' Eve's voice shook.

'No, but she would have, in time. We weren't really together when Rufus was killed. It was cavalier of her to ask me to vouch for her, but she was worried the police might think she was guilty. She and Rufus had just had one hell of a row, and they had a past. She didn't want the speculation and publicity, and I was the one person who seemed to have no reason to murder Rufus. It was fortunate for me that Kip and Dot both had such excellent motives. She was sure one of them had to be guilty once she'd decided Saskia wasn't responsible. But I knew I'd have to silence her eventually. It was too much of a risk to leave her alive. And then there was stupid Rick Sutton. Initially, I thought he was your average creep, but when I spotted him peering through *my* window, I realised my mistake. I put him down as a particularly useless private detective when I went to have it out with him. He didn't think twice about accepting my offer of a drink either. As with the others, I managed to get him to think we were sharing the same flask. I guess he thought a nip of spirits would ease the tension. It certainly did from my point of view. I dosed him up and eventually he slumped to the floor. I dialled Stefan Meyer while he was drifting out of consciousness. The conversation gave me an alibi of sorts. And you know the rest.'

He'd been so bold. So ruthless. Eve's skin crawled as the scene played in her mind's eye.

He reached into his jacket pocket with one hand, the knife still pointed at Eve, and drew out first one flask and then the other.

'Go on. Take your pick. I kept both topped up, just in case. You know I drank from one of them. Are you feeling lucky?'

'You can't kill your way out of trouble every time.'

Drew looked solemn. 'I've been thinking, and I won't have to. After I've smothered you I'm going to fake Kip Clayton's suicide. He'll get the blame. I'm not taking any risks. I'm ready to start afresh now.'

He pushed the flasks towards her. 'Drink up.'

# CHAPTER FORTY-TWO

At that moment, came barking. Not loud, but perfectly audible. Gus must have got bored. He'd be outside the back door.

'You lied about your dog.'

Eve swallowed. Drew looked close to the edge. She didn't know what might push him over it.

A second later, she heard a faint knocking from up above too. Robin. As the volume of the muffled knocking increased, so did Gus's barking, but then her dachshund went quiet. Eve guessed he'd dashed round the side of the house and found Robin. He'd be leaping all over him.

Drew put his phone light out and they were plunged into darkness again. Eve held her breath.

She heard the house phone ring. She guessed it was Robin, calling to double-check she wasn't home. He'd probably tried her mobile too, which was switched off. He'd know there was something wrong. The closed curtains would look odd as well.

Eve felt a cold sweat pour over her. If she waited until Robin broke in, Drew might act in a panic. Kill her perhaps, out of desperation, then spring out at Robin. Robin was good in a fight, but if Drew took him unawares, armed with a knife, she couldn't be sure what would happen.

When she'd dropped down into the hiding place, she'd formulated the beginnings of a plan. It was chancy in the extreme, but there were no safe options. She couldn't have risked it when

Drew had his phone lit. He'd have reacted too quickly. Even now, she had to get the timing exactly right. Everything had to run like clockwork. She held her breath.

In the pitch darkness, she clasped the torch she always left in the hiding place for visitors: strong, solid, metal. In a second, she brought it down in front of her, knocking its base on the floor, tilted in Drew's direction. She was banking on him turning instinctively towards the noise in the darkness. In the same instant she switched the beam on.

It worked. She'd caught him head-on, the blinding light shining straight into his eyes. As he reeled in surprise, she swung the torch up at him with every ounce of strength she had.

It all happened in an instant. His yelp of pain. The sound of his knife landing on the stone floor. The knowledge that he'd managed to dive sideways, so the torch only caught the edge of his jaw. The torch flying out of her grasp. Darkness descending again as it hit the floor.

Eve lunged in the direction of the knife. It was all from memory. She was flailing in the dark as Drew kicked out at her. His shoe hit her shin as she touched metal, grabbing instinctively, the sharp blade cutting into her hand. She cried out and in a second Drew had his phone torch back on, his eyes on the knife she'd just dropped.

Eve picked up one of the flasks and slammed it down onto Drew's hand as he reached out. In another second she'd grabbed the knife and flung it behind her. In the same instant, they heard a crash from up above.

Drew went still. The trapdoor rattled as someone tried to lift it.

He grabbed the torch and raised himself into a crouch, ready to fight back if the bolt gave way.

Eve shouted a warning, and in that split second as she heard the wood splinter around the bolt, she went for Drew's knees. She pulled at them with her full force, her legs braced against the walls of the hiding place.

As he buckled, the trapdoor flew up and in moments Robin was leaning into the space, grabbing Drew by the shoulders and hauling him out, to a crescendo of furious barking from Gus.

# CHAPTER FORTY-THREE

The following day, Eve was sitting opposite Viv at Monty's, trying to field her questions. There were three things that made it awkward: Viv knowing about her secret relationship with Robin, but not about his connection with the police; Eve's hatred of lying to Viv; and the possibility Robin's safety might be compromised if she gave away too much.

'So Robin was there?' Viv's eyes were sparkling as she ate a summer fruits tart.

'We were due to meet.'

'And he saved you? I love it!'

'Excuse me, I saved myself. Well, pretty much. I think tonking Drew with a torch and a hip flask counts.'

Viv patted her hand. 'Sip some of your tea. You're overwrought.'

Eve lowered her voice. 'I haven't told anyone else Robin was present. Greg Boles turned up after an anonymous nosy neighbour called about Gus barking, and Robin made himself scarce.' That was the story she, Robin and Greg had agreed to tell. People might ask what a detective sergeant was doing answering such a call, but Greg would say he was passing. And Drew might mention a second man – one who'd hauled him out of Isaac's hiding place – but who would believe him? Robin had briefed Greg and he was going to say he'd played Robin's part. It wouldn't harm anyone. Thankfully the security camera hadn't caught him so there was no other proof he'd been there. It was as Eve had thought: Gus had dashed round the side of the house in response to Robin's knocking. By the time

Robin had called her mobile and landline, he'd known something was wrong. He'd been about to go and check round the back when he'd heard a shout – presumably when she'd hit Drew with the torch – so he'd forced one of her front windows without further ado.

'I understand.' Her friend nodded. 'It would be all over the village if people knew you were entertaining Robin at your place in the evening, which is, I must say, positively scandalous.'

Eve groaned. 'Please don't tell.'

'Scout's honour. Though if your relationship's staying secret you might need to do something about Moira. I've got a nasty feeling she thinks you're carrying on with Simon.'

Eve took a larger gulp of her tea for strength. 'I know. She's decided I'm heading for the stables each time I walk through the woods. Goodness knows what she imagines Polly's doing while I'm there.' Her eyes met Viv's. 'I wish you hadn't said how good Simon and I looked on the dance floor at the party. I'm sure Moira heard you.'

Viv bit her lip. 'Sorry. She did look interested. I thought it was funny at the time.'

'Hmm. Well, if you have any bright ideas to save me, please feel free to say.'

She nodded earnestly. 'I'll give it my attention.'


Eve and Gus walked down to the beach, then tracked back across the dunes and heath and into Blind Eye Wood before making their way to Robin's cottage that evening. If she had to make the route any more elaborate, she'd need to set off hours in advance.

'No Moira on your tail?' Robin drew her into a kiss just inside his back door. Gus was running excitedly round their legs.

Eve bent down to fuss him after Robin had let her go. 'I think we gave her the slip.'

She grinned up at him and, after a second, he crouched down too and pulled her into another hug. She raised an eyebrow.

'I just want to make sure you're really there and solid. I can't take too many more close calls like that.'

'Thank goodness for you and Gus.'

Robin laughed. 'Well, Gus, anyway. I knew there was something up the moment he met me in the front garden.' He patted the dachshund. Gus looked eager though a little confused. 'But you were managing well on your own. Nice work with the torch.'

'Thanks.' She hadn't had time to explain everything the night before. 'Greg told you what I said at my interview?'

'That's right.'

'I would still have been dead if it weren't for you.' Despite her protestations to Viv, she honestly believed that. Drew was bigger than her, and he'd been between her and the trapdoor.

But Robin shook his head. 'You had the upper hand. Using the knife would have been horrific but you'd have managed it if there'd been no other option.'

Would she? Eve hoped she'd never have to find out.

His eyes met hers. 'All the same, please don't make a habit of one-to-one combat. My nerves can't take the strain.'

They both stood up.

'Does Greg know how Drew got hold of the sedatives?'

Robin nodded. 'He was prescribed them in the aftermath of Emily Longfellow's death. He told his GP he was getting over a bad break-up with a girlfriend.'

She shivered. 'And he saved them to use on Rufus?'

'He claims he just stopped taking them; they dulled his senses. But he admits he took the job working on *The Pedestal* to get close to him.'

Eve nodded. 'He told me that. And how he finally found out Rufus had left Emily to help his acting.' It had been an appallingly selfish act, but Rufus would never have foreseen the consequences.

The trouble was, Eve doubted he'd even tried to imagine what he'd put her through. He was too bound up in his own feelings. 'Drew blames Rufus entirely for Emily's death.'

'And Greg says he thinks he saved Saskia Thomas by committing murder,' Robin replied. 'His statement says she seemed spellbound by Rufus's words. He saw her as another young woman falling for his overblown lies.'

Eve closed her eyes for a moment. His thinking was so messed up. Rufus had let his selfish desire for success rule his actions to the detriment of everyone else, but Drew was a monster. He'd killed through jealousy and frustration, and behaved as though a relationship with Emily was his God-given right. Before he'd robbed her of her future, she'd been treated appallingly by both men. And by Kip as well, probably.

'What about the wolfsbane? Has Drew admitted to delivering it?'

Robin nodded. 'He said Dot once gave it as an answer to a pub quiz question, when they were both working on the production of *The Pedestal*. He admits that put the idea in his head, but not that he was trying to frame Dot.'

Eve frowned. 'But he managed to engineer getting her and Kip back from the Cross Keys, so they were handily on site at the time of the murder, ready to fulfil the roles of prime suspects. He engineered a lot. I wish I'd seen things more clearly from the beginning. Putting my information into chronological order was the key: seeing the times when Drew and Emily's paths overlapped.'

'Come here.' Robin drew her to him. 'At least Dot's got a happy ending.' A moment later, he poured her a glass of Shiraz and put a board of olive bread and a plate of cheeses on the table. 'But I know it's been horrific. Food and time. That's what you need.'

She found his warm embrace and Gus's head against her leg didn't go amiss either.

*

In the days that followed, Eve heard from Dot Hampshire, who was able to update her on developments at Watcher's Wood. Filming was still paused due to staffing, but Stefan Meyer had made contact with the director Arielle Jones. They'd each found themselves without partners for their next projects and Arielle had decided she'd have time to work on the remainder of *Lindens* after all. If they got on well, Dot thought other ventures might follow, including the Dickens adaptation. Both Meyer and Jones had been full of warm words for Dot's performance in *The Pedestal*. And apparently Kim Carmichael had been putting it about that Rufus's complaint about her attitude had been driven by his personal problems, not her behaviour.

Good old Kim. People knew she told it like it was.

Eve had seen Dot with Toby in the Cross Keys too, laughing, their heads inches apart across the bar and at a table for two when he'd had a night off. Their closeness was the new topic of gossip in the local amateur dramatics and flower clubs.

Eve had had tea and cakes with Saskia at Monty's too. She was still grieving over her father and Rufus, but she was much calmer than when Eve had seen her last. Eve had the impression that was about more than just coming to terms with what had happened. There'd been a new sadness in her eyes as she'd spoken about Rufus. After shaking her head slowly she'd told Eve: 'It wouldn't have worked. I hope I'd have realised that in time if he'd lived, though I'd have hated hurting him. I think I was high on excitement. I mistook it for love.'

She was planning to take a break as soon as filming was finished to spend some time with her mother, but she'd already had offers of work after that. Eve was sure she'd go from strength to strength. She'd bear her scars though – and probably channel them into her acting, just as Rufus had, but with a clearer head. As for Kip Clayton, apparently he'd approached her in hope of a reconciliation, but Saskia had seen him chatting Brooke up on the sly. Eve had the impression she'd found rebuffing him a satisfying experience, and wished she'd been a fly on the wall.

The tale about Brooke had reminded Eve to ask Dot about her and Margot. They spent a lot of time together, and in the pub Eve had noticed they looked alike too. 'It's a well-kept secret,' Dot had said at last. 'I only found out by accident. Brooke's Margot's daughter. Margot recommended her for the costume supervisor job without letting on. You can see how it would look if word got out. Brooke wasn't born Brooke Shaw. She changed her name by deed poll, if you can believe it. Thought it made her sound more Hollywood.'

Everyone had been fooling someone.

Eve shook her head. She needed to snap out of it and go to the village store for a bottle of wine. Robin was due at her place that evening for a rerun of the meal they'd planned the night Drew interrupted proceedings. She was looking forward to it for more reasons than one. She wanted to overwrite what had happened when Drew burst through her door. To make the house feel safe and secure again: a place for happy thoughts.

As for going to the store, it was the perfect opportunity to tackle Moira, but she still couldn't work out what excuse to give for hanging around in the woods.

As she walked through the door, Moira's face lit up. 'Ah, Eve. Viv's been telling me about your owl project.'

'Ah.' Eve rallied her mental resources. 'Erm, good.'

The storekeeper was smiling eagerly. 'And I was ever so relieved… I mean, pleased. I'd love to see the photographs when you've got time. It must be challenging to take them after dark and in the woods.'

Eve nodded mechanically. 'It is.'

'I was surprised you took Gus with you.'

What had Viv done? 'It's safer to have him there, but I've trained him to keep quiet, of course.' *Like heck. He'd bark his head off.*

'Oh, of course.' Moira smiled again. 'And it all makes sense. After all, I know how keen you are on nature. To think that I… But never mind about that now. What can I reach for you?'

'A bottle of Malbec please.' Moira would think she'd got a drink problem next. She'd have to invent a wine-tasting hobby involving her neighbours. The whole thing could get thoroughly out of hand.

After she'd paid and left the store, Eve unhooked Gus's leash from the fixings outside and saw Viv appear in the doorway of Monty's. Eve marched towards her and Viv bit her lip.

'You haven't just been to Moira's?'

'Uh-huh.'

'Did she mention owls?'

Eve counted to ten. 'Perplexingly, she did.'

Viv clutched at her hair. 'Sorry! I was just about to call you to explain when I dropped a tray of cakes and it went right out of my head. Was it… okay?'

She looked so anxious that Eve relented. 'I think I muddled through. She wants to see photographs though.'

Viv smiled. 'No problem. Sam really did do an owl project in Blind Eye Wood for school. I can give you his.' She looked apologetic. 'I'm afraid they'll make you look a bit rubbish, though. He did it when he was thirteen and he only got a C.' But then she brightened. 'But hey, you can tell Moira you need lots more practice. Your excuse for being in the woods will be ongoing.' She glanced at Eve anxiously. 'Am I forgiven?'

'On balance, yes. Weirdly, she seemed to buy your story, in spite of everything.'

'Oh thank goodness. You're so alarming when you're annoyed.'

Eve smiled as she turned back towards Haunted Lane and home. It was nice to have the upper hand from time to time.

*

### Rufus Oswald Beaumont – actor and television director

Rufus Beaumont, the celebrated actor turned television director, has died in Suffolk at the age of thirty-nine. A man has been arrested for his murder.

Beaumont had a background many in his profession would envy: born into the famous acting dynasty, the press and rivals perceived him as having a head start, but that wasn't his view. As the youngest of three siblings, he felt forever in his family's shadow.

No critic doubted Beaumont's talent as a director, yet there was constant speculation that his family might have helped him land his first job. He saw their influence as a poisoned chalice. It meant he would never be judged on his talent alone.

Meanwhile, his early attempts to launch an acting career failed. His only film appearance, as Marcus Rudd in *Shadows in the Trees*, met with critical acclaim, but he took method acting to shocking extremes to portray the required emotion and never managed to produce the same heartfelt performance again.

His brilliance as a director was offset by an intensely defensive personality which made him push away or sabotage the stars he created, harming them as much as his own career.

The constant striving for something out of his reach meant he was forever restless and unable to enjoy what he had. However, his ability to spot raw talent gave many actors their big break and won significant acclaim, as well as captivating his viewers.

Eve looked down at Gus. 'I wonder how his life would have panned out if he'd lived. If Saskia would really have pulled out of the marriage. And if he'd have found another producer to team up with. It's so sad, and such a waste.' She knew she was talking about his life, as well as his death.

Gus cocked his head, an impatient look in his eye.

'Are you telling me I should put a sock in it, and we should seize the day? Get down to the beach and stop moping?'

Gus had sprung up at the word 'beach'.

'You're quite right, and may I say, you're good for the soul. C'mon then. Let's go!'

# A LETTER FROM CLARE

Thank you so much for reading *Mystery at the Church*. I do hope you had as much fun puzzling over the clues as I had creating them! If you'd like to keep up to date with all of my latest releases, you can sign up at the following link. Your email address will never be shared, and you can unsubscribe at any time.

*www.bookouture.com/clare-chase*

The idea for *Mystery at the Church* evolved as I walked up Scafell Pike on a family holiday, during a brief period between lockdowns in 2020. One of my (adult) children suggested a film set might be a hotbed of intrigue, and the idea took hold!

If you have time, I'd love it if you were able to write a review of *Mystery at the Church*. Feedback is really valuable, and it also makes a huge difference in helping new readers discover my books for the first time. Alternatively, if you'd like to contact me personally, you can reach me via my website, Facebook page, Twitter or Instagram. It's always great to hear from readers.

Again, thank you so much for deciding to spend some time reading *Mystery at the Church*. I'm looking forward to sharing my next book with you very soon.

With all best wishes,
Clare x

ClareChaseAuthor

@ClareChase_

www.clarechase.com

clarechaseauthor

# ACKNOWLEDGEMENTS

Much love and thanks as ever to Charlie, George and Ros for the cheerleading and feedback! Love and thanks also to Mum and Dad, Phil and Jenny, David and Pat, Warty, Andrea, Jen, the Westfield gang, Margaret, Shelly, Mark, my Andrewes relations and a whole bunch of family and friends.

And as always, heartfelt gratitude to my fantastic editor Ruth Tross for her perceptive and inspiring input. It makes a vast difference. I'm also indebted to Noelle Holten for her tireless promo work and to Alex Holmes, Fraser Crichton and Liz Hatherell for their expert input. Sending thanks too to Tash Webber for her amazing cover designs, as well as to Peta Nightingale, Kim Nash and everyone involved in editing, book production and sales at Bookouture. It's a privilege to be published and promoted by such a skilled and friendly team.

Thanks also to the wonderful Bookouture authors and other writers for their friendship and support. And a huge thank you to the hard-working and generous book bloggers and reviewers who take the time to pass on their thoughts about my work. I know it's a massive job. I really do appreciate it.

And finally, but importantly, thanks to you, the reader, for buying or borrowing this book!

Made in the USA
Las Vegas, NV
13 June 2022